Warlord

Warlord

Robert Mercer-Nairne

a novel

GRITPOUL, INC. • WASHINGTON

First Edition 2007

ISBN-13: 978-0-9748141-3-1
ISBN-10: 0-9748141-3-X
Library of Congress Control Number: 2006936123

Published in the United States of America by Gritpoul, Inc.,
10900 NE 8th, 900, Bellevue, WA 98004-4448
www.gritpoul.com

Interior Design and Typesetting: Publishing Professionals, Port Richey, FL
Cover Design: Larry Rostant
Author Photograph: Christine Muscat-Azzopardi

Printed in Canada by Friesens Corporation

10 9 8 7 6 5 4 3 2 1

The paper used in this publication meets the minimum requirements of the American National Standard for Information Sciences—Permanence of Paper for Printed Library Materials, ANSI Z39.48-1984.

Anna Stepanovna Politkovskaya
30th August 1958—7th October 2006

Author's Note

Chenchia is an imaginary country on Russia's southern border, in which civil war is rife. As the young migrate to the capital, Zoldek, the traditional ways in Chenchia's three regions, Vorsky, Sharosky and Urus, each run by a warlord, are breaking down. Inside Zoldek, Democrats and Faith Radicals fight it out with each other and with the Russian soldiers stationed there. In writing this story, I had Chechnya and its tragic history in mind, but only as a metaphor for the many traditional societies that have been, and continue to be, swept aside by that demon god we call progress. Although some events in the narrative parallel historical events, the story is mythological and resemblances to actual persons living or dead are coincidental.

CHAPTER 1

*A*lu Dudayev, perching like an eagle on a rocky outcrop, looked down the valley at the approaching party. Small wisps rising from the desolate earth like spirits from the dead were all that announced its progress. So many dead. His was a land of the dead. But wasn't every land more full of its dead than its living? He was not fearful of death, only of humiliation.

He had lived longer than most of his countrymen, longer, certainly, than he had expected. His wish was to die in this land. This land of rock and mountain. This land of his ancestors. Even his gnarled face, creased and sharp-edged, had taken on its appearance. Only his dark eyes hinted at the possibility of life—moisture in a parched wasteland—and they were growing dim. It would not be long before Aslan took his place.

To have a son—and a fine son, that was a blessing. So many had lost their sons in the struggle, a struggle that seemed to stretch back to the beginning of time; a struggle that defined their lives; a struggle that was as noble as their barren land of a million souls was not. A million souls of whom half lived in their country's worn-out capital, torn between conflicting desires. Accommodate the Russian Federation, some urged. Give us Western democracy, pleaded others. Expel all infidels, demanded the Faith Radicals. Only outside the capital did a spirit of true freedom flourish.

Zoldek, Chenchia's capital, lay to the west, surrounded by small farms, on the nation's only flat land. Stretching from the Zoldek plateau all the way to the east, joining the country's two halves, was the narrow Mhemet Valley. North of this valley were the Vorsky mountains. The Vorsky region, covering almost 45% of Chenchia, gave its allegiance to Alu Dudayev. South of the valley, the country was split into two regions, Sharosky to the east and Urus. Both were mountainous and separated by the fast-flowing Klist that tumbled over cliffs and burrowed through gorges until it joined the Mhemet River in the valley below. Sharosky, the smaller of the two, was controlled by the hot-tempered Sergei Kadyrov. Urus had been ruled by the Bassayev family for generations.

Even with his weakening eyes Alu could see the source of their present troubles snaking along the valley floor. It was as if the green belly of his country had been cut open and its brown intestine laid bare. Day after day Federation oil flowed down it from somewhere in the east to somewhere in the west. Several times the pipe had been blown apart, but each time Federation soldiers had responded with indiscriminate reprisals. Men from one of the villages in the Mhemet Valley would be rounded up and shot. Rarely did Federation soldiers venture into the mountains. They knew the odds were stacked against them when they did. Bombs dropped from Federation planes fared little better so an accommodation, of sorts, had been reached. If the oil was left to flow, the valley villages would be left in peace. So what had changed?

A vulture circled overhead. Alu watched it until the bird flew into the sun. His father had been shot by Federation soldiers and his body left in the open to rot. But it had not rotted. By the time his men found it the vultures had stripped the carcass clean. They would never understand, these people from the north. They could come, cause trouble and go. But the people whose land this was would remain: in the rocks, in the sagebrush, in the wildlife, in the tumbling brooks. Alu shielded his eyes and looked again for the bird.

Before oil, the Federation had only bothered to station soldiers in the capital. A governor and his entourage had pretended to govern, entertaining those families in Zoldek willing to be entertained, but mostly entertaining one another. Until the oil, Chenchia had not been important to the Federation. Its Russian people had simply pushed into the west displacing the Turks from the south who had brought the Faith to Chenchia. None of Chenchia's conquerors had actually conquered the country. They had merely occupied Zoldek and periodically sent soldiers into the mountains to crush resistance. These disturbances occurred most often when a new governor arrived, anxious to assert his authority. After a period of activity in which the outsiders shed most of the blood, an uneasy balance would be restored.

But oil had upset this balance. Federation soldiers now patrolled the pipeline constantly and a highway was being built alongside it that would take away still more valuable land and slice the country in two. Over the centuries, the tribespeople from the mountains had come down into the valley for food and companionship. Increasingly, these days, they just came down to fight.

HE HAD MET Ran, his wife, at one of the great summer gatherings on the valley floor. The hill people would come with their goats, their semi-precious stones, their sons and their daughters, to bargain and trade. The valley people grew wheat and vegetables. Sometimes valley people married mountain people, but mostly they kept to themselves. Their ambition, now, was to find work in the capital. It was the capital with its cafes and shops, not Federation soldiers, that would destroy the old ways. That had become clear to Alu. In the capital, even the Faith was becoming radicalized by a violent minority or rejected by a youth that looked to the West for inspiration. Almighty God's great majesty was only cheapened by a doctrine of hatred and intolerance. And as for freedom and democracy, Alu did not know what these terms meant. Could any man be freer than he was in the mountains?

It had been Ran's idea to send Aslan to the West. "There is a world out there we do not know," she had said. "If our son is to lead his people, he must know that world." Alu had been afraid. Afraid of losing his son to something he did not understand. But he had agreed. When the boy had returned as a young man, Alu realized the two could never talk the same language again. The symmetry of experience between father and son, teacher and pupil, had been broken. Aslan understood things his father could not.

Ran had borne him five children. Three sons and two daughters. Two of his sons had been killed fighting Federation soldiers and his oldest daughter had died giving birth to their first grandchild. Only Aslan and Roaz remained. She was married to Malik Bassayev who was expected to take over Urus from his father, Akhmad. Every year the tribal leaders of the three regions met, to discuss common problems and resolve disputes. Alu admired Akhmad, but was unsure about his son-in-law. There were rumors Malik operated a black market with Federation soldiers. But it was Sergei Kadyrov, the fiery leader of the Sharosky region, who concerned him most. Whenever it was wisest to hold back, Sergei would lash out. Whenever steadfast action was needed, Sergei would be the first to lose interest.

A THERMAL WAS carrying the great bird ever higher. Alu watched its circular flight, each pass further away, as the invisible stairway it climbed was pulled towards the great winds that raced across the stratosphere like bolting stallions. The party was getting closer now, its ascent steeper. He could make out five figures on horseback. He thought he could tell which one was his son. The dust demons still rose around them, pulled up by heat rising from the baked earth, the same heat that was lifting the bird. Everything was connected. The people from the north had forgotten that and perhaps the people in the city had too.

He'd been twenty-one when he and Ran met, she, seventeen. She said she'd noticed him over many summers turning from boy to man. Before the great race, it was the custom for girls to hand ribbons to the young men about to compete. Ran had handed him hers. He could conjure up her bashful smile even now. Several other girls had handed him their ribbons, but it had been Ran's alone he'd worn for the race. Five miles. Thirty horses at full gallop, each small, powerful, and maneuverable, descended from the animals brought west by Genghis Khan.

Alu rocked back and forth on his bony haunches remembering. What a race that had been. The first mile along the flat. The horses bunched together, their riders jostling for position. You tried to stay in front to avoid the dirt and stones thrown up by the others. Gory, his main rival, had pushed him hard, forcing him onto soft ground. The cloying mud had slowed him, but instead of rejoining the pack he'd crossed onto firmer ground. By forcing him closer to the river, Gory's maneuver had ended up giving him an advantage. He reached the rushes behind the leaders, but his tighter angle brought him to the river crossing level.

It was there his friend, Terek, fell. His horse must have stumbled on a rock, forcing up a spray of sun-filled water droplets, and catapulting its rider through the air. As Terek arched over into the swirling Mhemet River his body had missed Gory's horse by a whisker, causing it to start and Gory to almost lose his balance. By the time they reached the other bank, Alu had taken the lead.

But the steep shale ascent on the far side had not gone well. His horse had struggled to get a good footing and three others pushed past him. When the ground leveled, the track narrowed making passing impossible. All the riders could do was race along the trail, nose to tail, trying to ignore the sharp drop which fell away into the gorge the river had doggedly chiseled away over many thousands of years.

The descent had been gradual and the way had opened up, giving each rider a chance to steal the lead, but all knew that a sharp drop lay ahead before the second river crossing. Arrive too fast and your horse would be forced to jump into the river—into oblivion most likely. Somehow you had to slow enough to slide down the bank and enter the water under a semblance of control. Alu had started to lean back, pulling at his mount's head, straining to judge distance and speed. The two riders who had passed him on the ascent were still just ahead. He recalled sensing a rider closing on them from behind.

The little bay that passed them was flying like the wind. It had been Sado from the Sharosky region, arms and legs flaying, a wild cry coming from his mouth. As the rest had pulled their animals up for the drop, they'd watched Sado fly into the air ahead of them. The little horse, wide-eyed, legs tucked beneath her, neck stretched forward as if straining for the other side, had seemed to float for several seconds before crashing into the water a third of the way across the river. The animal had submerged for a moment but as the other riders entered the water to make the crossing the horse surfaced and it looked as though Sado's mad display had secured him the lead.

In the confusion, Alu had forgotten about the bay and Sado. Reaching the far side amid the thrashing of water, melee of animals and force of the stream was all that had mattered to him. Only as his horse lunged up the opposite bank had he become aware of the sound coming from the river—a frantic, desperate whinnying. Later he learned that the bay must have broken all four legs on landing. Sado had tried to haul her to one side, but she had been swept downstream a mile or more before sticking between two boulders and drowning. He remembered thinking that meat from a dead horse was poor compensation for a live one, especially with that much heart. He'd never rated Sado after that.

For a mile and a half the race had then run through a thicket of birch with crisscross paths. Although the river edge had been clear it was strewn with large round pebbles. A few riders tried it, but had quickly reverted to the woodland. Horses had cut and crossed each other at a gallop as the trails wove in and out of the silver-stemmed trees.

Alu reached the first river ford for the second time ahead of the others and crossed it at a gallop from the opposite direction. It was far shallower than the other and was the one used most by the local villagers, so the river bed had been cleared of large stones. Three other horses were close to him. The final mile was through a grove of old walnut trees, well spread out and on flat ground. There was always the risk of hitting a hole in the earth, some small animal's burrow, but that couldn't be considered. Speed was all that mattered then. He could even remember the rich smell of his horse, lathered in sweat, as he urged the tiring beast on. Akhmad followed him across the line, with Gory third. He'd been allowed to dance with Ran that night. The following year they were married. She'd come with one hundred goats, twenty mares, countless colored blankets and a silver encrusted saddle Alu had used from that day forth. It had been the biggest wedding of their generation lasting seven days and nights. These were the memories that would have to sustain him now.

HE COULDN'T SEE the bird any more and the approaching party was lost in the fold of a hill. Even the dust spirits had become invisible. The old man sat pensively as the sun dropped towards the far mountain range.

THE DAY WAS falling away fast now. But at last he could make out voices. Just occasional snatches that seemed clear yet carried no meaning. He gauged that they would be another fifteen minutes and braced himself against the cooling air. The mountain tops across the valley stood out in saw-toothed clarity against the sliver of remaining light. He turned in time to see the crest of Abochevo blush pink at the sun's last touch.

FINALLY THE RIDERS came into view. At a canter, Aslan's horse broke away from the others and Alu walked forward to greet him. Would the woman his son was bringing help their cause? He couldn't see how. If the world knew what was being done to his people, would it change anything? He doubted it.

Aslan dismounted. Protected by unfolding darkness, the two men looked into each other's grief-stricken eyes and embraced.

CHAPTER **2**

$\mathcal{B}$athed in the stark light from Michael's camera, I started my report.

"Just over twenty-four hours ago, helicopters of the Russian Federation brought soldiers here to Argun, an isolated village high in the Vorsky mountains of Chenchia.

"This remote land of just over one million people has been fought over for centuries. In the 15th, the Turks from the south conquered the country and eventually converted its people to the Faith. But in the 19th, to the dismay of Faith Radicals, the Russian Federation in the north gained control.

"With increasing quantities of oil now passing through Chenchia from Federation refineries in the east, Federation President Nitup has been waging a fierce war against Chenchian freedom fighters. Anxious to show progress to his tiring people back home, and still unable to fully control the capital, Zoldek, after years of fighting, he has resorted to attacking unarmed women and children in a previously peaceful region and claiming it to be a great victory.

"According to eyewitness accounts, three Russian-built XK25T transport helicopters, each carrying around fifty soldiers, landed here yesterday at approximately 3:00 in the afternoon. The attack had been well planned, because most of the men were away from the village attending the regional football championships in the valley.

"These men have touched nothing, in spite of their grief and anger, so anxious are they that the world should see the hideous atrocity carried out in this place. Lights have been put up around the village so that I can show you what has been done. What you are about to see is horrific.

"The first house I will take you to is the home of Alu Dudayev, head of the Vorsky region and of this community, well, what is left of it. The soldiers approached the house with flame throwers. You can see that it is badly burned. Now, come inside. That charred body is Ran, aged 62, Alu Dudayev's wife of 44 years.

"I will take you to another home. What has happened here is utterly depraved. As you can see, this house has not been torched. The girls and women, rounded up in here from other houses, were repeatedly raped and then bayoneted. This brave little girl, Alisia, was hiding and saw it all. I will translate her words. What happened, Alisia?"

"The men, they went on and on. My mother pleaded with them to stop, but they went on. She knew I was hiding. She didn't want them to find me. I was so scared. The other mothers pleaded. The young girls just screamed until they stopped screaming because the men kept coming. Then the men stuck big knives into everyone and I cried. But I cried without sound because I knew the men would kill me if they discovered I was there."

"Thank you, Alisia. You have been very brave. Now go to your father.

"Next, I want to show you what these barbarians did to young boys. We have to go further down the street. Take a look at the burned houses as we go. Yesterday these were homes, like yours or mine. Not any more. . . .

"Here. Follow me inside this burned-out shell. Those five objects you can see hanging from the rafters by wire are the charred bodies of five boys. Their genitals have been removed.

"I am now going to feed you an image of the whole village. Even in this artificial light you will get some idea of the devastation. . . . It was Shakespeare's Julius Caesar who said that the evil men do lives after them. What more can I add? This is Orla Kildare from what is left of Argun village in Chenchia for DEMOS-TV."

"Did you get that, Steve? Steve, did you get that?" I shouted, knowing all too well the fickleness of the technological marvels that had transformed our business.

A crackling voice came back down the satellite link.

"God, Orla. That was awful."

"Of course it was goddamn awful, Steve. But did you get it?"

"Yeah, Orla. We got it."

"Well, you make sure Bernie puts it out. Every ghastly scrap of it."

The sudden silence that followed our broadcast felt like death itself.

"WHAT'S THAT sound?"

Even in the muted light of the paraffin lamp Michael looked ashy white, his camera equipment strewn around him like discarded baggage.

"The generators?" I suggested.

"No. The scraping sound."

"That'll be the men dealing with their dead."

Fully clothed against the cold we sat on the floor of a room with a clear view of the night sky through its ceiling, in what remained of Alu Dudayev's home. The smell of smoke and burned flesh permeated the air. A smoldering roof truss glowed red as the passing wind conjured up small blue flames from its charred end and carried off dancing sparks into the blackness.

I tried to imagine Aslan, as a little boy, playing with his brothers and sisters in this very room. Had his parents really been right to send him to my country, to America, light of the free world? What could *we* teach him about democracy? Hadn't I listened to him for hours, fascinated by stories about life in Vorsky, and thought that in spite of the hardship, his people had rich lives imbued with a sense of community we could only envy?

So, I had fallen in love with an attractive man from a strange land. Had that colored my judgment? Of course it had! But all students want to think about their country for themselves, don't they; to question what they are told about it; to question its assumptions about itself? Perhaps that was why I had gone on to become a journalist. Arrested development. Still asking the questions.

Was I still in love with him? I suppose I was, a little. He seemed harder now. Still fine looking. If anything, better looking. More assured. No longer the innocent, believing only good about America. I guess, on that score, we had both grown harder. I had wanted to visit him, but I wasn't sure whether it had been him or his situation that had persuaded me to accept his invitation. And now this.

The Chenchian struggle wasn't of much interest to the people in America and Bernie had needed persuading. Bottom line Bernie was about the politest thing we called him. Bernie Eisner was a ratings man. "I need audience, Orla, and frankly darling, I don't think anyone could give a damn about these Chenchians of yours," he had said. "So the Russians are screwing them half to death. Tell me something new. Someone's always screwing someone half to death in this great world of ours. Find me someone, other than his wife, who's screwing our president half to death and you've got a story." That was Bernie. But a massacre, a cold-blooded massacre and not another journalist within hundreds of miles.

"I think I'm going to throw up," announced Michael lurching towards the door, but not finding it. "Oh, Christ!"

"Here, drink some water," I suggested, and offered him my flask.

"I need fresh air," he groaned.

TWO, OR POSSIBLY three hours passed before anyone came to us. While we waited, Michael slowly recovered and cold replaced nausea as his main concern. We gathered together some of the burned wood that had recently formed part of the house and soon had a good fire going in the center of the room, which didn't seem so odd when we allowed ourselves to see things for what they were, rather than what they had been. I had no desire to eat, but Michael found an old packet of dried biscuits inside one of his camera bags, and nibbled tentatively until he was sure his sickness had passed, then devoured them all.

"Feeling better?" I asked.

"Yes," he answered and then seemed guilty about it. "Do you ever get used to this?"

"I don't know about *used to it*. But you stop being shocked. In Rwanda this sort of thing went on all the time."

"You were there?"

"For three months."

Michael seemed impressed, although there was little to be impressed about. My reports had been largely sidelined in favor of more important things, like the latest fashions from Rome or whether Prince Charles of England would marry his mistress.

"It must feel good to do something important," he asserted.

I didn't want to disabuse him. He looked as though he needed reassurance and after what we had just witnessed, who could blame him.

"But *you* are doing something important," I insisted.

Michael shrugged.

"I didn't really mean to be here," he confessed. "I follow the Hollywood crowd, mostly. But Cindy, she's my girlfriend, at least I think she is, said I should stop ogling mammary organs and do something important."

"You had a fight?" I speculated, laughing.

Michael tossed his head.

"You can say!"

"Can I ask what about?"

"She found my collection."

"Collection?"

"Stuff I'd sort of put by. Pictures and things."

"Pictures of what?"

"Stars, mostly. You know, when they aren't posing. Private stuff. My friend Ziegler and I sort of compete who can get the best stuff. Not for sale, or anything like that, it's just a bit of fun. He's a cameraman for the Celebrity News Channel."

"That's pretty sick, Michael!"

"Yeah, I guess. That's what Cindy said. So with your regular cameraman off I volunteered, just to show her I could do something important."

"If I find you have used one single image that you take while you're with me for your own private use, I'll see that you are fired and that no one else hires you. You got that? These people deserve respect and I don't want you taking any cheeky shots of me either!"

Michael grinned for the first time that evening.

"That's a pity. I rather fancied. . . ."

"Michael!"

"OK, OK, just kidding."

The fire was burning down now and spreading an aura of warmth around the room with its friendly half-light, shrinking existence to itself and leaving cold and invisible the desolate sadness that lay beyond its reach. I wondered if dark matter, that elusive material physicists knew must exist, but so far had not found, would turn out to be a depository of sorrow. All the anguish of the universe trapped in perpetual blindness on the dark side of the moon.

"How did you know what President Nitup would say?" Michael asked.

"About this being a great victory?"

"Yes. There haven't been any news reports out of the Russian Federation yet, have there?"

"So I jumped the gun on that one. Very unprofessional of me. But he's hardly likely to say that it was a great defeat."

"Power sucks," declared Michael.

"Except when talented cameramen use their skill for nefarious purposes," I chided, and then wished I hadn't.

But Michael was up to my carping.

"Or when respected journalists announce that something has happened before it has."

"Touché!" I conceded.

It was Aslan who came to tell us that everyone was moving to the next village and that we should get ready.

THE EXODUS FROM Argun was carried out in silence, except for the noise of the horses working their way along the narrow trail. Each man walked ahead of his animal, which he'd loaded with whatever possessions he'd been able to salvage. Michael and I rode at the rear of the column except for one Chenchian, whose task it was, no doubt, to keep an eye on us. No one had suggested that we relinquish our mounts for more treasured or useful belongings. More likely the latter. These were not sentimental people. Even our packhorse with all our effects seemed under-loaded by comparison to theirs. We were guests and this was their tragedy, not ours, is how they would have seen it.

There was a good moon, not full, but bright enough to light the way. The hot breath of the horses steamed up in bursts ahead of us and moonbeams bounced off pots and pans and any other shiny object able to send them on their way. Ahead of us, a line of men who had just buried what was left of their wives and children, and combed through the pathetic remnants of homes each one had probably built himself. Feelings of sadness, anger, sadness and anger, loss and fury, must have enveloped them all. A deep passion for revenge must surely have been boiling up inside every soul. It was small wonder that blood feuds could last for generations. Didn't they have every right to?

In our modern, civilized world we had given away the right to revenge. The state would mete out justice, not us. That was the contract. But what did this say? It said that human feelings were unreliable, that a rational response by the uninvolved was better than action by the aggrieved. Would anything happen to the soldiers who had discharged their frustrations into Argun? Probably not. Would anything happen to those who had given the orders? Probably not. So what was I doing here, other than feeding a media machine designed to nurture an addiction to stimulus, almost any stimulus, in order to sell products?

Could people tell the difference anymore between the imagined violence of the moviemakers and what had happened here only yesterday? Were people actually interested in reality, or was the sanitized reality of their own limited lives as much as they could handle? *Oh, not another report from Orla Kildare. Let's see what's on the other channel.* Had not most of us been turned into the human equivalent of battery hens, kept docile and productive on a diet of mildly satisfying pap, so that the decision-makers could orchestrate our lives? Who were these decision-makers? And did they have any idea what they were doing? These were the thoughts that occupied *my* mind.

"Why are we stopping?"

Michael's question was almost lost in the desolation. The Chenchian at the rear hurried past us on foot, leaving his horse behind.

"Somebody! Somebody!" he repeated in an excited voice.

"Are we there?" Michael asked. "Have we reached the next village?"

"I doubt it," I told him, turning around in the saddle. "Aslan said it was a good hour away. We've only been going ten minutes."

He looked disappointed. His rear end had not recovered from the ride up.

"Perhaps this is a rest period," he muttered without conviction.

I just hoped that Cindy was the sort of girl who would appreciate his penance.

It was hard to make out what was happening. All the Chenchian men seemed to have clustered together at the head of the line.

"Prayers?" Michael wondered.

"I don't think so. It looks to me as though they may have met some other travellers."

"Do you think this place looks any less desolate in the daylight?" he asked.

"More desolate, I suspect. Now the rocks and mountains have an almost mysterious appearance. In sunlight they probably just look barren."

"You have to wonder what the Russians want with this place," he said.

I had been wondering the same thing. If the village had been a base for freedom fighters, why go to such lengths to attack when they were not there and in such a provocative manner? But the sight of Aslan approaching, with what looked like four pygmies in tow, redirected my attention.

"A gift from God!" he shouted as he approached. "They were with their mothers collecting berries when the attack took place. They've been hiding ever since. I was hoping they could commandeer your mounts."

"Of course," I said almost glad to be sliding out of the saddle. "Their mothers?"

Alsan nodded towards the line.

"With their men. Can you imagine the joy? They thought they had just buried them."

I wondered about the others, whose wives and children had not walked out of the shadows. How many would harbor a hope? It would be impossible not to.

"These are Zargan and Doku," Aslan said lifting a girl of about ten onto my horse, and then placing her young brother into the saddle in front of her.

In the meantime, two boys of about seven and eight were staring up at Michael who was looking down at them.

"Off you get," I said. "Time to stretch your legs."

"Of course," he acknowledged, not having fully appreciated that his transport had just been sequestered. "I could do with a walk."

Aslan lifted the boys up and handed Michael the reins, although the animal would doubtless have followed the others anyway.

"How long to the next village?" Michael asked, trying to sound casual.

"An hour. Two at the most," Aslan told him.

I looked up at the children on my horse and Zargan gave me a wide smile. She had the prettiest face. Little Doku still looked terrified.

THE LIGHTS OF Ichke came into view shortly before midnight. We had been walking for nearly two hours. Doku sat on my horse, asleep, wedged between the arms of Zargan who held the pommel of the saddle with a fierce grip. I had found an old stick of gum in one pocket. She had wanted to cut it and give half to her brother, but after I pointed out that he did not seem interested, as his eyes were tight shut, she took it and chewed away contentedly for most of the journey.

As we approached, Ichke seemed so vulnerable. A hamlet, surrounded by danger. News about what had happened in Argun must have spread quickly. In my world dangers, as a rule, lurked within cities, not outside them. The trail dropped towards the houses and the horses seemed to move a little faster, even though this was not their home. As we came to the edge of the village I could see light pouring from one house half way down the main street: the only street. All of our men were abandoning their horses and making for this house. As I lifted the still sleeping Doku to the ground, his mother came to me and took him. Zargan appeared reluctant to leave at first and squeezed my neck as I placed her on the ground. But soon she was following Doku and the other survivor who had come to collect her two boys from Michael's horse.

"Alright?" I asked him.

"I wish I'd brought some decent boots."

We followed the rest. The door of the house was open, so we went in. The front room was full to bursting, with everyone staring at a small television set. The twelve o'clock Russian news was under way in all the anodyne certainty that was the hallmark of a government-controlled television station. The boys from Umsk had won the national team gymnastics championships and were a credit to the Federation. A new megastore, the biggest in the world naturally, had been opened in Moscow by the mayor's wife. Oil production had reached record levels, thanks to the untiring efforts of the men and women who worked in the oilfields. I had learned Russian while watching old news bulletins. They were always clear and almost always predictable. Learning Chenchian had been more fun, though. I'd been in love with my teacher.

Most people in the room did not seem to speak Russian, and one person was translating. Jeers greeted most of the self-congratulatory proclamations. Just when it looked as though what they were waiting for would not come, the newsreader informed the Russian world that brave Federation forces had attacked three terrorist bases deep inside Chenchia. A grainy picture of an obliterated something that could have been a terrorist base accompanied the announcement, followed by footage of President Nitup pinning medals onto the chests of smiling soldiers. The room fell silent. The sense of disgust was palpable.

THE FAMILIES OF Ichke made space. The now single men were absorbed. The two intact families from Argun were given rooms and we were given a whole house. I say 'we' but it was really Alu Dudayev and Aslan who were given the house and we were their guests. The woman whose home it was stayed to prepare a meal for us, a stew of goat meat and vegetables that must already have been in the pot when we arrived because it did not take long to appear. It was ladled into bowls and handed out with thick pieces of bread.

We sat in a semi-circle in front of a fire that had burned down to its embers. I wondered what the old man was thinking. He betrayed no hint of self-pity. He dipped the bread into the stew and took a bite. We did the same. I then realized how hungry I was. In silence we ate. First the bread. Then we extracted pieces of meat and vegetable with our fingers. Finally we lifted the bowl to our mouths and drank the juice. Even Michael restrained his impulse and followed Alu Dudayev's measured rhythm.

The woman collected our bowls and handed us cups into which she poured tea. Only then did Alu Dudayev speak.

"I am pleased to have met you, Orla Kildare. You meant much to my son when he was in America."

I felt embarrassed and must have looked it.

"I am pleased that you let him leave," he added with just the barest hint of a twinkle in his eyes. "His mother wanted him to go, but I did not. I was frightened of losing him. But she was right. Ran was often right. I hope my son is as fortunate in his choice when that time comes."

The woman placed the jug of tea on a tray between us and asked if there was anything else we needed. Aslan said no and I was surprised he did not thank her, but she clearly did not expect it. I had virtually lived with this man for three years and yet knew so little about the ways of his people.

"Orla," said the old man. "It has a nice sound to it. What does it mean?"

"Nothing of significance. My mother wanted a boy and had de- cided to call him Orlando."

Alu Dudayev laughed.

"And so you have been becoming a boy ever since!"

I shrugged.

"And Kildare. Does that mean anything?" he asked.

"It's a place," I told him, "where my great-grandfather came from."

"What sort of place?"

"A place that had to fight for its independence."

"Did this great-grandfather of yours fight?"

"He did, I'm told."

"Why did he leave?"

"To find work—and stay out of prison."

"Was it long, your country's struggle for independence?"

"Many hundreds of years," I told him. "Empires don't give in gracefully."

Alu Dudayev looked pensive.

"Tell me about Kildare. What was the place your great-grandfather came from like?"

"I believe his parents had a small farm in the Wicklow Mountains."

"Like the mountains here?"

"Oh, no. You would call them hills. They are mostly round and green."

"And the place where you come from, what is that like?"

"Very ordinary. It's just a small town."

"Does it have a name?"

"Sweetwater."

"Sweetwater," Alu Dudayev repeated. "And what does that mean?"

"Sweet-tasting water."

"Well that's a nice name," he said. "Is that where your parents live?"

"My mother. My father is dead."

"So you live with this mother who thinks you should be a boy?"

"I don't live with her. I just visit her."

"You should be married and have a home of your own, and children."

"Father!" Aslan protested.

"Look, he's asleep," Alu Dudayev said, pointing at Michael who was now curled up on the floor. "Will his pictures help us?"

"I honestly don't know," I answered. "Sometimes all you can do is shame your tormentors."

"Shame. There is so much shame. Some people are beyond shame."

It was the first and only time I saw the old man show any hint of bitterness. Soon he too had curled up and fallen asleep.

"Are you ready to sleep?" Aslan asked.

"Not quite."

"Walk?"

"Yes."

"Wrap up warm, then. It's cold."

His firm, considerate tone rekindled old feelings and for the second time that day, I wondered what I was doing there.

THE BULKY COATS we both wore did little to reduce the intimacy of our being together, properly together. It was the first time we had been alone since my arrival in Chenchia. Without thinking, I slipped my arm through his, and he—from the same force of habit—accepted it with a gentle squeeze.

I had been walking across the campus quadrangle for my first class, not entirely sure where I was going or what to expect, when this striking-looking man with a chiseled, copper-colored face, long black hair and the sort of brown eyes a girl could fall into, stopped me. "I look, please, for politics 101. You know, yes?" Of course I knew. It was where I was going. Only six months later did Aslan admit that he'd seen me in the registration building and found out that we were both down for the same course. That, at least, had been chance.

I suppose I had fallen for him then and there. "You look like a boy," he had said, as we walked to our first encounter with Professor

Strong, whose mission in life was to disabuse idealistic students of any notion that the political world was, ever had been, or ever could be, ideal, "you should grow your hair." I remember being angry with him for trying to tell me what to do, but three months later my hair had grown out. My mother didn't like it, of course. "I didn't bring you into this world to satisfy men's lust," was her terse observation. I sometimes wonder if she ever satisfied my father's, poor man. She's mellowed a little since, but not much.

I had made it to university a virgin and was firmly resolved to remain one. The idea of sex seemed demeaning to me. I guess I had got that from my mother. Sports were my thing: running and swimming mostly, although I did work out in the gym twice a week. That's stayed with me. I like to keep fit. But the sexual taboo has long gone. I have Aslan to thank for that, even if it was an approach by Wendy Straker, our best middle-distance runner, that made me sit up and wonder if I wasn't missing out on something, although not with her.

For a time I was able to persuade myself that it was the plight of the Chenchian people that concerned me. Political science and languages were my focus. Aslan chose economics to go with his politics. He said it would be more useful to his people. Russian I could study, but I had to learn Chenchian for myself. Professor Strong saw right through me from the start, I think, although he let me write a paper on politics inside the Federation Empire. Sad are the countries that live along the world's fault lines he would often say, and he was not talking about geology. To be stuck on the edge of empires, between competing ideas of the world, meant to be fought over. His candid advice was to get it over with. Become part of one or the other, preferably the one with the strongest future. As for independence, forget it.

Naturally, as a Chenchian by proxy, this incensed me, but Aslan found his ideas interesting. His country had, after all, passed from the hands of one empire into those of another and been fighting for its independence for centuries.

Looking back, I cannot have been easy company for anyone. I was always arguing and always certain of my point of view. University professors must have strange taste, to want to listen to the same passionate chords, again and again. A song, stuck in a groove, destined never to reach its finale. Aslan and Denis Strong often talked late into the night. I think the older man saw something in the younger that was real, an opportunity—perhaps—to step outside his books into the world as it was. Naturally, I was jealous of their relationship.

It wasn't until close to the end of our second quarter that I was finally tamed. Aslan handled me well, I can see that now. It had been like breaking a horse he said later. I was in his room, ostensibly to discuss a paper. He and the professor had both said that what I had written was naive. I was angry, but more than angry, I was becoming frustrated at my inability to get close to Aslan. The more he gently taunted me the more angry and frustrated I became. That day, on some pretext, I let rip at him and managed to wind up my anger to such an extent that I ended up pummeling his chest.

He just grabbed both my wrists and held me as I cussed and twisted like a doll on the end of a puppeteer's strings. The next thing I knew anger had turned to passion and I was literally devouring him. I hadn't realized how much the smell of him had got to me. To start with his hand movements were sparing and subtle, and I felt like pummeling him again. But then, judging the moment right I suppose, he allowed himself to be overtaken by feelings he too, he told me, had been suppressing for months. Thank goodness no one came to his room. It must have sounded as if a murder was being committed.

At the end I was sore inside, a little bruised and blissfully happy. I couldn't leave him alone for the next several weeks. Even washing his clothes gave me pleasure and I decided to take the contraceptive pill so that I could feel his skin. All my ideas about everything were turned inside out. Never had I experienced greater bliss than when I was lying across his chest with his arms around me. I couldn't stomach going home that break to face my mother's bile. She would have known immediately that I had become a traitor to sterile purity. For the first time in my life I felt truly sorry for her.

Over the course of our university life our relationship mellowed. Knowing that he would go back to a country I was never likely to visit hardened us both, I think. When the time came, we were ready. In a way, parting *was* a sweet sorrow. We imagined we had extracted every last drop from our love. And yet here I was, a decade later, my arm in his.

"Do you have someone?"

We had reached flat ground above the village, which nestled below us. Seeing it and thinking about Argun made me shiver at the impermanence of things. The moon had moved but there was still enough light to see by.

"Not really. You?"

"No. There is a girl I will marry, but we do not know each other yet."

Once, I would have exploded in a fit of self-righteousness at such a remark, pouring all my Western values over him and then wallowing in the result. But if I had learned anything from my time with him, it was that humanity could speak with different tongues.

I suppose that what happened next was inevitable. Bodies develop a yearning for bodies they have known, if no other has come along and taken their place. I felt no sense of guilt towards Dirk who I saw from time to time when I was back in my apartment in the capital, any more than Aslan could have done towards this woman he would marry.

We simply, deliberately found one another again, found what belonged to us and no one else. It was too cold to want to be naked, not completely, just naked enough to get to where we needed to be and touch the places we wanted to touch. The words we placed into each other's ears grew in intensity and urgency and their meaning was not the meaning of tomorrow and the day after, but of now and now for evermore. When we were spent we both realized we had finally left behind the enchanted land of our shared past.

CHAPTER 3

The oil pipe and the road were bad enough, but the stream of Federation soldiers felt like impurities coursing up the country's main artery, poisoning its heart. Any one of the men we saw might have taken part in the Argun atrocity.

"I have to leave you here," Aslan announced as we reached the far side of the valley floor. "The leading families try not to trespass on each other's territory. Khalim will look after you."

I paid more attention to the man who had joined us on the way down. He looked the same age as Aslan, shorter, not so elegant as a result, but wiry with a leathery toughness and a gap between his front teeth that made him resemble the classic Mexican bandit in a western movie. The rifle and two belts of ammunition crisscrossing his chest compounded the likeness.

"When will we be seeing you again?" I asked.

"Tomorrow, all being well."

"All being well?" repeated Michael, echoing my own thoughts.

"Khalim will take good care of you, don't worry. Sergei Kadyrov knows you are coming. I am sure he is longing to impress you with his brave words!"

I let the innuendo pass and followed Khalim as we began our slow climb into Sharosky. After five minutes I couldn't resist turning round. Aslan was still there, watching us from below. Michael was too uncomfortable in his saddle to notice my interest.

"Aren't you sore at all?" he asked, almost accusingly.

"I guess some of the things I sit on in the gym have hardened my ass. What exercise do you take?"

"None, unless you count Cindy and bowling."

"Bowling's good. How often do you do that?"

"Four or five times a year."

"Ah! Not an exercise freak then."

"God, I hope she appreciates all this," he moaned.

"Look upon it as self-improvement," I urged.

Khalim must have had some sense of Michael's problem from the way our cameraman tried to hover above his saddle, as if it was projecting pinpoints.

"He's not used to the horse, then?"

"No. I think he's in agony, poor man!"

"Tell him it won't be quite so bad tomorrow. And the day after that it will be better again. After a week, he won't want to sit anywhere else."

I passed this good news on to Michael who swore that if ever the day came when he didn't want to get off a horse, he'd burn his collection. I suggested that Cindy had probably done that already, but it seems the crafty devil has kept backup copies. Part of me almost wants to see his disreputable merchandise for myself.

Sharosky was south of the Mhemet Valley, so the slopes we were climbing faced north. In summer, like now, I guessed they would get a few hours of warmth every day, but in the winter months, nothing.

They were more barren than the Vorsky slopes opposite and there was no sign of human life, no villages clinging to the sides of mountains glinting in the sunlight. It seemed an unwelcoming place and, of the three regions, it was known to be the poorest with the wildest inhabitants. Although Urus, too, was south of the valley, its mountains were lower and more dispersed leaving plenty of room for its people to build their homes facing the sun. Sharosky seemed to be all mountain, rising in tiers as far as you could see. Good for defense, if there was anything worth defending.

I had gathered from Aslan that competition between the regions was intense and always had been. Like Scottish clans, their identity was woven with the thread of raw emotion and like Scottish clans they would eventually be overwhelmed by the modern world. The young would simply drift away from the harsh life to the imagined luxury of the city, although with Zoldek a permanent war zone, its attractions were surely limited. But I'd seen it everywhere. The lot of the rural poor must be a long way from the rural ideal, if scavenging for food on the rubbish tips of the world's great cities was so often considered preferable.

"We'll stop here for a short rest," Khalim announced.

I told Michael, who lowered himself to the ground with an indulgent sigh.

"Perhaps I should stay here until you return," he suggested, hopefully. "I don't imagine the station needs pictures of two burned out villages."

Khalim told us to look at a far ridge on our right. At first I could not see anything unusual. Michael followed my gaze and saw them before I did.

"Perhaps not," he said.

Three armed horsemen were looking down at us.

"Friendly?" I asked.

"Kadyrov's men," Khalim explained. "They'll follow us all the way now."

"What's he like, Kadyrov?"

Khalim reflected before answering.

"He may not be the brightest of men, but he's honorable, he's brave and he understands the old ways. He just tends to over-react, if you know what I mean, to act without thinking, well, without thinking as much as Alu Dudayev or his son."

"So you approve of thinking?" I questioned.

"Oh, very much. But it depends on what kind of thinking."

His answer intrigued me. I hadn't imagined there were kinds of thinking.

"What is the right kind of thinking?"

"You, in the West, think that only your kind of thinking is the right kind of thinking, and that we are merely a primitive version of what you once were. The Federation is no different. In its communist days all our traditions were considered reactionary. Many of our people were shipped off to work in Federation labor camps. Now, the Federation is mostly interested in power. At least we can understand that."

"If the right kind of thinking is your kind of thinking," I suggested, "that would make you no better than us!"

"I didn't say your kind of thinking was wrong for you. I just meant to say that it was not right for us. Thinking does not come from nowhere. It comes from experience over a long time. I have two young cousins who both live in Zoldek. One is fighting for Western democracy, the other for Faith fundamentalism. They are both passionate, they are both convinced they are right, they will both cause us trouble and probably, they will both die young."

"So you did not approve of Aslan going to university in the West?"

Khalim looked at the ground.

"Aslan and I grew up together. Until he went away we shared the same experiences, we talked the same language. Now it is different."

"His father said the same."

"His father is a great man. He understands many things."

"His father also agreed that his son should go to the West, to understand its ways."

"Just so long as he hasn't forgotten ours," Khalim said wistfully. "I would die for him, because that is my tradition. I wonder if he would remember to die for me?"

I was more upset by Khalim's remarks than I expected to be. This wild-looking mountain man had a deeper understanding of political reality than many who had taught me, although he and Denis Strong would have got on, I thought.

"Let me tell you something, because you obviously love him," I said with surprising forwardness. "For the best part of four years, I loved him too and never once did he stop thinking about his country and his people."

Khalim just looked at me and then continued to peel the orange he seemed intent on eating.

"Here, take a piece," he offered, after the skin had been neatly separated from its flesh. "Give some to your friend, too."

SERGEI KADYROV'S village appeared to be wholly intact. Perched on the side of a cliff face, it looked impregnable. Our three shadows had drawn ever closer and rode in just ahead of us along a narrow path that ended in an open area overhung by rock, in front of the first houses.

"Welcome!" boomed a large, powerful-looking man, about six foot three or four, as he approached us, his voice amplified by the cavernous walls.

Ignoring Khalim completely, he came straight up to me.

"I am pleased to have a famous American reporter as my guest. The Sharosky region welcomes you with open arms."

As I made to dismount, he almost lifted me to the ground.

"I thought. . . ."

"You expected devastation," he interrupted, "but you see that my village is in good order."

"That's right. I was led to believe…"

Again he interrupted me.

"They couldn't land their helicopters here. Even the village they picked only allowed for one. Tomorrow we will visit it. Sharosky may be poor, but we have advantages."

He summoned men who took away our horses and Khalim. Michael, unsure who to follow, was hobbling badly.

"Not used to the saddle, eh?" Sergei guffawed. "I have just the remedy for that."

"This is Michael, my cameraman."

"Welcome!" Sergei said to him in broken English. "I fix you buttock good, OK?"

Michael, clearly unnerved by his host's offer, miraculously stopped hobbling and said he was pleased to be in Sharosky. I was impressed by Sergei Kadyrov's obvious powers of healing. We were taken to our rooms and told that we would eat in twenty minutes. One of the men who had taken the horses brought our bags.

My room was not large and felt warmer than it probably was. The one window was open and looked across a narrow ravine towards cliffs as harsh as our own. I peered down into the fading light and could just make out the white foam of a fast-flowing stream several hundred feet below. Jumpers' paradise I thought, if one could squeeze through the window. There was no glass and I closed the wooden shutter so that the small fire in the corner would not be wasted.

The floor was natural stone, but swept. My bed was covered in furs which I was sure would be warm. On a table had been placed a bowl and a large jug of water. The oil lamp gave off a comforting glow and a rather pungent smell. I felt around in one of my bags and extracted a towel, a flannel and bar of soap. Quickly I undressed, poured water into the bowl, and daubed myself all over with the flannel, applied a little soap and daubed again to get it off.

"You need more water?"

I jumped and tried to cover myself unsuccessfully with the flannel. In the doorway stood a girl of about fourteen or fifteen.

"I can get you water," she said, smiling at my surprise and attempted modesty.

"Yes. Yes, please. I would like that."

"My name is Sar. I will look after you."

"Thank you, Sar. My name is Orla."

Soon I had a fresh jug of water. It took me a moment to locate the other essential item I required, but I found it under the bed. There was no lock on the door but need overcame inhibition and Sar did not reappear. In the twenty minutes we had been given I completed my ablutions, as best I could, although longed for a hair wash, but that would have to wait.

THE ROOM I WAS taken to seemed unexpectedly large. It could have been the grand hall of an early medieval castle. A large fire burned at one end, its smoke disappearing through a natural duct in the rock. Sergei Kadyrov, looking like a larger version of the French cartoon character, Asterix, stood with his arm around a comely woman who might have passed for a youthful Tina Turner in Thunderdome. Oil lamps burned everywhere, blackening the walls in return for their light. The scene was a journey back in time, except for the guns propped up in a corner and several cell phones lying on a table. A compression of time, more like, reminding me how far we had and hadn't come.

Michael entered just after me through a different door, grinning like a shark and with a pretty girl in tow.

"Ah, ha!" boomed Kadyrov. "I see Nasha has improved you!"

"Much improved!" admitted Michael sheepishly as he caught my eye.

"And famous reporter," he said, turning to me, "did my daughter, Sar, bring you all that you needed?"

"She did, thank you. And my name is Orla Kildare."

"Come over to the fire, famous reporter, Orla Kildare. You and I have much to talk about. Will your friend mind if we speak in my language? I want to be understood."

"I'm sure he won't, especially in your daughter's company."

"I have ten daughters, eight sons and four wives. Nasha is learning English. She says she wants to go to America. I tell her she is crazy, but that is youth for you."

Soon the room was full of what I imagined were most of the Kadyrov family. Close your eyes and it could have been a New York cocktail party, with everyone talking and no one listening. Only one woman looked the same age as Sergei. Distinguished, with pitch black hair combed back and held in a gold tie. Her eyes darted around the room like a sheepdog and everyone seemed aware of her presence. It was she who called us to the table and sat on Sergei's left, placing me on his right. I noticed the woman he had been fondling far down amongst the younger children.

"So, what did you make of Alu Dudayev?"

Sergei Kadyrov's first question, once we had settled into the meal, surprised me.

"It is his son that I know. But he seems a lot like him."

"You knew his son in America?"

"For almost four years, yes."

"What is it like, this America of yours?"

I could see that his concentration jumped from one thing to the next, but suspected it was still connected to a clear vision of his world.

"It possesses a lot of knowledge. Many people specialize in many things and somehow we all work together to put this knowledge to use."

"To what use?" asked the woman opposite me.

"This is my wife, Yana," Sergei explained, with obvious pride and surprising deference. "My first wife."

I acknowledged her and she nodded back.

"To make our lives more comfortable, more interesting," I answered. "And to make us more powerful, more in control of our situation."

"Does too much comfort trouble you?" Yana asked.

"How do you mean?"

"If everyone is comfortable, why do they still work?"

"Yana is very intelligent," thundered Sergei. "She knows the temptations of idleness!"

In a casual sort of way I had often wondered the same thing, but it had never really struck me so directly. Why did we all work our tails off when most of us had far more comfort than we needed?

"I think we work because we are anxious that if we do not we will become nobody. Work is what we are."

"Being somebody is important," agreed Yana. "But for us it is our family, our clan, that makes us what we are. Work is just what we do."

"Surely you take pride in what you do?"

"Of course. That honors ourselves, our family and our clan. But it does not give us our identity."

"I suppose we owe that to the Protestant ethic," I said, without knowing exactly what I meant.

"*Protestant ethic*?" Sergei repeated.

"Oh, it's a religious idea that we have a duty to work and achieve success if we are to find salvation."

"On Earth or in Heaven?" Yana asked.

"Both, I think, but I'm not really religious."

"It must be a powerful religion if even the irreligious are driven by it," Yana observed with a wry smile.

I must have looked puzzled.

"Your work brought you here, to this dangerous place where there are none of the comforts you are used to. When my people want to go to your country it is for the comforts. I can understand that. Although

I tell them that all the comforts of the world are not worth a single soul."

"So, why *are* you here?" Sergei asked.

As I heard myself say, "because I am interested in your struggle," I felt uncomfortable. Was that really the reason? Was I even here because of Aslan, or was I here because I thought I could get a good story?

Yana stared at me with deeply penetrating eyes and I felt like a child caught lying. But like a wise grandparent she said nothing, knowing that the untruth would twist inside my stomach and be expelled in disgust.

"I had better tell you about our struggle, then," announced Kadyrov.

Even though I had heard about Chenchia's struggle a hundred times or more from Aslan, the flickering light, the abundant food we were eating with our fingers, the chatter of conversation and sweet mint tea all made me eager to hear the story again. I also hoped that its telling would distract Yana's attention from my inadequate reason for being there.

"We are the nut in the nutcracker," Sergei boomed, pleased with the precision of his metaphor. "To the north, the Federation. To the south, the Faith. We are the point at which they meet, the place where their soldiers test their strength and their ideologues their ideas. When the soldiers of the north beat the soldiers of the south and we found ourselves inside the Federation, we held onto the ideas of the south. So it was only a partial victory for the north.

"The Faith became part of our independent identity, in a way it had not been when the soldiers of the south prevailed. In fact, when we originally became part of the south, it was many years before we accepted the Faith.

"Chenchia is only a country because the Vorsky, Urus and Sharosky people share the Mhemet Valley. Our leaders would meet every so often to iron out problems—that's when we weren't fighting one another!"

Sergei Kadyrov roared and jabbed a half-eaten chicken leg in the air to emphasize the point. I realized that this fighting he spoke of was akin to a sporting fixture in my country: an opportunity for young men to let off steam and for their supporters to judge the best leaders.

"And what about the capital, Zoldek?" I asked. "Where does that fit in?"

Sergei's expression changed, as if a new body had appeared in the sky between the sun and the moon only to cause puzzlement.

"That is where the thinking men chose to live, and the money men, and the traders, and our conquerors. It is where our young often go to and from where they never return. It is the rotting fruit that attracts the wasps."

"Sergei!" complained Yana. "It is the place where you can get food all year round, where you can live in houses with water and light, where buses take you to where you want to go, where people can meet other people without trekking across mountains, where you can buy the things that you need without having to make them. All you have to do is work for money and the money gives you these things."

"Yana has been to Zoldek," Sergei explained with a hint of pride. "We have a daughter there. But I still say Zoldek will kill off our ways before the people of the north or the south ever do."

"If our ways are so good, surely not?" suggested Yana, provocatively.

"Of course our ways are good!" Sergei countered. "But they are hard and people prefer comfort, isn't that right, Orla Kildare?"

"I think it is," I answered, relieved to be able to agree with him and his wife.

"Too much comfort creates weakness," Sergei asserted. It was clear he had been here before in his reasoning and Yana saw no point in pushing him further. She probably even agreed with him.

"So why do you think the Federation attacked villages in each of the three regions?" I asked. "It doesn't seem to make sense. One would have been enough to claim a great victory."

"That's easy," roared Sergei. "If they'd hit one of us we'd have blamed the other and a war across the valley would have erupted. They don't want that, not with their precious pipe."

"They would rather have you united against them?" I wondered.

"And that's what they'll get!" thundered Kadyrov.

"I don't like it," muttered Yana.

Neither did I.

Sergei then regaled us with tales of battles between Sharosky and its neighbors, such as the time he and a handful of men had stolen a whole herd of goats from under Alu Dudayev's nose, although I had heard a different version of this story. Apparently, after the raid Sergei and his band had celebrated in style. They were snoring their insides out when the Vorsky men came to retrieve their animals and awoke to discover they had lost not only their booty, but their mounts.

The Sharosky men had stolen women from Urus several times apparently and Yana herself was an example. She didn't deny it, so I assumed the story was true. They had even carried out successful raids on Zoldek, but had found the urban geography so inhospitable for their horses that they had largely stopped doing that. Their greatest recent victory had been the destruction of a Federation tank that had got stuck trying to maneuver up the Klist River. They'd simply lit fires around it, pinning the soldiers inside with rifle shot until the wretched men had roasted alive. Kadyrov particularly enjoyed that story and the whole table, who by then were listening to their clan's oral history, doubtless for the umpteenth time, exploded into barks and shrieks of approval like pack animals celebrating a kill.

I, too, found myself cheering. When I eventually crawled under the furs on my bed I fantasized about riding a black stallion at the enemy, I can't honestly say what enemy, and winning a great victory. I think I fell asleep in a state of sublime happiness.

WE LEFT THE capital of the Sharosky region, such as it was, at daybreak. Michael looked exhausted. His treatment had clearly been effective as he sat slumped in the saddle, barely aware of Nasha's furtive wave. His old malady had been replaced by a drained contentment.

Even though the village was high up the mountainside and south-facing, the sun had still not risen far enough to touch it. Sandwiched between the peaks opposite and the ravine, the place felt desolate. A raw cold penetrated everything and I could see how the young might hunger for the convenience of a city. The horses followed each other in single file, along a trail little wider than a man, where a mis-step by one would send it and its rider to certain death. I did not feel in danger, until I thought about it. I suppose it was hardly more hazardous than cruising along one of our busier freeways. Over time you get used to certain risks and they disappear from view.

Sergei Kadyrov led us and I noticed Khalim towards the rear. There were eight of us in all. I think that the three horsemen in front of me were the three who had shadowed our arrival. Apart from us, everyone was armed with rifles and one of the shadows even carried what looked like a ground-to-ground missile launcher. Technology had found its way into the mountains, but not in the form of creature comforts. Even the cell phones I had seen were adjuncts of war, apparently, although useless most of the time and needing a generator to charge them.

I felt apprehensive about what we would find. The images of Argun were still fresh in my mind. Even though I was sure Bernie would not want to expose our audience to any more unpleasantness, I wanted to see for myself what the Federation soldiers had done and have Michael secure a record. With luck, I'd get a documentary out of it. Like it or not, human misery sells.

The path opened up and we stopped. None of us had eaten yet and I was starving. Oranges and cheese were handed round, together with crusty hunks of bread. One or two of the men walked away a few paces to relieve themselves. Khalim came up and asked me if I needed privacy. I didn't, but wondered where I'd find it when I did.

The man at the rear managed to conjure up a fire from nothing but scrub and in no time small cups of hot tea were being passed round. It was hard not to be impressed by the way these people lived; economical and yet complete. Was giving up hardness and economy for comfort and anxiety, self-sufficiency for interdependence, such a good trade? Of course it was! We could all enjoy camping for a few days, but where was the music store when you needed it, or the deli with its special produce?

I thought I had better bite the bullet before we set off again and caught Khalim's eye. He seemed to know exactly what I wanted and led me twenty yards or so away from the others. There was not a boulder, fold in the ground, or tree in sight. With his back turned, he held open a blanket and I took that as my signal to squat. You can get used to anything after a while.

We approached the village of Tisk up a long, gradual incline. I could see how one of the Federation's XK25T helicopters might have put down nearby, but the houses were still pressed hard against a cliff face. That seemed to be the way the Sharosky people built them, more concerned with defense than convenience. I thought I could count ten stakes arrayed in front of the first houses and feared that the objects attached to them would turn out to be villagers. A knot formed in my stomach and I wondered if I really wanted to bear witness to another Federation atrocity.

Sergei Kadyrov lengthened his mount's pace and started to pull away. The line stretched as each of us noted the change and urged his horse on. He was now approaching Tisk at a slow, graceful canter and I could see people coming out of the houses to greet him. That there were any, surprised me. They could not all have been collecting berries when the attack was launched and anyway, by the look of the terrain, berries were unlikely to be found.

Michael and I gave up trying to follow the others and besides, the packhorse, with all our equipment, could only go so fast. Even the last rider sped past us leaving Khalim, with whom I now had an unusual bond, as our only escort.

"They seem very excited, considering what happened here," I remarked.

"They are excited. This has become a great victory for them."

"Victory? How can a massacre be a victory?"

"It was not like Argun," Khalim told me. "Only eight villagers were killed. I learned that last night. The Federation soldiers were forced to abandon their attack."

"Who forced them?"

"I don't know. They weren't talking to me. I was just listening and that is all I heard."

It was quite clear now that the stakes had bodies on them and by the look of the clothes, they were Federation soldiers, not villagers. The closer we got, the more gruesome the scene became.

"Oh, Christ," moaned Michael. "They've been impaled."

I had read about Ivan the Terrible, but never expected to see what he did to those he captured alive played out before my eyes. The ten Federation soldiers had been kebabbed on the point of the ten stakes which entered their nether regions and came out of their mouths.

"What do you think of that?" roared Sergei Kadyrov, as he approached us and slammed the butt of his rifle against the belly of one.

The man let out the most pitiful groan.

"For God's sake," cried Michael. "He's alive!" and promptly vomited down the side of his horse.

Sergei hooted with laughter.

"Take pictures, cameraman!"

And turning to me said,

"This is what the people of Sharosky do to those who try to burn their houses and rape their women."

It was clear he was comparing his clan with Alu Dudayev's.

A foul stench was coming from the bodies and I could see that several of the houses closest to us had been torched. But this had been a battle, not a massacre.

"Kill him! For pity's sake kill him," sobbed Michael, who had now slithered off his horse.

I couldn't look at the staked soldiers. If I had, I too would have thrown up and I was damned if I would do that in front of these barbarians.

"Here, cameraman. Shoot," goaded Kadyrov handing Michael his rifle.

Michael reached out to take the weapon from the grinning clansman, but Khalim put a hand on his arm and turned to me.

"They are all dead. It was just wind."

I told Michael, who broke down and sobbed uncontrollably. By now a group of villagers had surrounded us and were staring in mild amusement at my crying cameraman. I was just pleased Nasha was not there to witness her lover's humiliation.

"In my country," I shouted at them, "we treat the dead with respect."

"I have read how you treat those you do not like," Sergei countered with real anger. "You fry them with electricity. So don't tell us how to treat our enemies."

I regretted my intervention almost immediately. I was a reporter whose job it was to report, not moralize. But I was starting to like my weird cameraman and had felt protective.

"How did your people do it? How did they beat the Federation soldiers?"

Sergei looked at me for several seconds, weighing me up. In a moment his anger was gone. I had been forgiven. Luckily, he was a man of quick decisions, not one to harbor hidden feelings.

"Let us get away from this stink. I want to show you what they did before our villagers drove them off."

The damage to the village was comparatively slight. The first house had been torched and its occupants, a woman and her three children, burned alive. The next two houses had also been torched but their occupants had escaped. The story that unfolded was this. The Federation helicopters had come up the valley and the villagers had seen them, unlike at Argun where they had been taken completely by surprise. As they approached, the women of Tisk had opened fire. The first helicopter had managed to land and start disgorging its soldiers, but the other two could not find enough even ground.

The people of Tisk had another piece of good fortune that day. Not all of their fighters had gone to the game which was between Vorsky and Urus, Sharosky having already been knocked out of the competition. When the Federation pilots saw a group of men emerge from one of the houses with a surface-to-air missile they suspected an ambush and panicked. In the confusion, ten of their soldiers were left on the ground. The school bully had shown his yellow streak and bolted.

"What do you want me to take?"

Michael was still ashy white and subdued.

"The boy didn't get enough sleep, that's all!" bellowed Sergei, who was clearly in a forgiving mood.

"Take the first house and a long shot of the bodies," I told him. "Vengeance may be sweet, but it sure ain't pretty."

Relieved to have something to do, Michael set about his task.

"If this gets back to the Federation, they will be forced to respond," I told Sergei.

"It already has," he told me. "One of their helicopters flew over later, out of range, but they will have seen their men. We wanted them to see their men."

"I suspect the local commander will keep this to himself," I suggested. "With his president proclaiming a great victory, news of this fiasco would not be welcome."

Torn between a desire to show his people's victory to the world and the sense of what I was saying, Sergei looked disgruntled.

"The Sharosky people will always fight," he announced defiantly.

I didn't doubt it, but against the full force of the Federation it would be a poor contest. These were images I would need to sit on for a while. So much for objective reporting.

With Michael's work done I thanked Sergei Kadyrov for his hospitality and I meant it. I'd experienced some of the richness of these peoples' lives in a way Aslan had never been able to convey. I even wondered if Alu Dudayev's westernized son could ever enjoy the full imagery of his people again. His experience would forever lead him to compare and as the old saw goes, comparisons can be odious.

Khalim led the way. Our early start meant that we would be able to get down to the valley floor before nightfall. When Tisk was no more than a slight shift in color on the mountain landscape and Michael had fallen back out of earshot, I was driven to ask Khalim the question I could not ignore.

"Were those soldiers alive when that was done to them?"

He did not answer at first, and when he did his answer was indirect although perfectly clear.

"Our ways are different to yours."

I shuddered at the thought. But perhaps I shouldn't have. There was a certain symmetry about it. How *could* men who had raped children to death expect better?

CHAPTER 4

*A*slan was waiting for us on the valley floor, where everything seemed different, more civilized. Even the wretched oil pipe and road suggested a comforting modernity.

"So how did you find Kadyrov?" he asked after greeting Khalim and falling in with us as we rode west towards Urus.

"He's a character. A charming rogue. I liked him."

I could see that my answer irritated him, as I knew it would. One does not live with a man for almost four years without unearthing his weak spots.

"Very hot-headed."

His observation was clipped and definitive, and not—I felt—entirely correct. Each of the clans probably saw the other in caricature. Sergei was undoubtedly quick to rouse and hot-blooded, but his instincts seemed canny and sharp.

"He asked me what I thought of your father."

"And what did you tell him?"

"I said it was you that I knew, but that you and your father seemed very alike."

"You think so?"

He seemed genuinely surprised. I suppose we all spend so much time distancing ourselves from our parents, striking out, building new lives, that to discover we are like them in this or that way catches us off guard. I know I am *nothing* like my mother!

"In many ways," I told him, "you are alike."

"In what ways, exactly?"

"Khalim put it well. He said you are both thinkers."

"So, you have been talking to Khalim about me?"

I found his feigned hurt attractive. He was starting to play with me as I was with him.

"He is one of your oldest friends. It was too good an opportunity to miss!"

"What have you been telling this woman about me?" he shouted over his shoulder at Khalim who had now fallen back behind Michael.

"That you are the greatest westernized warrior in Vorsky!" Khalim shouted back.

"But I am the only westernized warrior in Vorsky."

"Exactly!"

"Women! They are the great interrogators," declared Aslan. "Do you have a woman, Michael?"

Michael must have been thinking of Nasha, or remembering I knew about Nasha and Cindy, because he blushed most beautifully.

"It's good to see color back in your cheeks!" I goaded.

Furious with himself, he gave me the finger.

"That's it. I'm asking Bernie for a new cameraman."

"If it wasn't for Cindy, I'd ask him myself," he countered.

"Even after the healing powers of Nasha?"

"One of Kadyrov's daughters?" Aslan asked.

"She eased Michael's saddle sores."

"Lucky man!" he crooned. "Sergei's daughters are known for their charms."

Suddenly Michael was all perked up. The memories of the night must have been obliterating the humiliations of the day.

WE RODE SLOWLY along the north bank. I had noticed that it was pro-tocol for members of each clan to keep to their territory, unless they had been invited, or were on a raid. We passed the confluence of the Klist and Mhemet rivers and so knew we were now opposite Urus, the region I would be visiting in the morning. There was no hurry. We laughed and joked and Khalim treated us to several Chenchian songs. One had a bawdy chorus and he even had Michael hamming it out,

> *Come to my bed if you can, my love*
> *Come to my bed if you can.*
> *Hurry as fast as you can, sweet love*
> *While my husband's heat*
> > *is still here*
> > > *for you to steal.*

although I am not sure he fully grasped the words' meaning.

The setting sun briefly shone straight up the valley from Zoldek, blinding us. And then it was dusk. A cart passed, coming east, loaded with hay. We overtook a man carrying onions and a family, in a hurry, anxious to reach the next village before nightfall. The old track seemed to be preferred to the new road above us. A few Federation trucks sped past along the still incomplete highway and like everyone else, we were pleased to be out of their way.

"Where are we spending the night?" Michael asked.

I wondered if he was hoping to find another Nasha.

"In a village up ahead. A woman rents rooms," Aslan told him. "She has a lovely daughter, too!"

I caught his twinkling eye, and Michael looked suspicious.

"Isn't Ula the most splendid creature?" he called out to Khalim.

"An ocean of love in which a man may drown!" came back Khalim's cryptic reply.

"What did he say?" demanded Michael, sensing a trap.

"Are you a good swimmer?" I asked.

He looked at me, certain he was being set up.

"Don't tell me. She's a mermaid?"

Aslam laughed.

"She has legs, believe me. She has legs," and turning to Khalim, "Isn't Ula known for her legs?"

"Oh, she is. Few men can escape them!"

Again, Michael wanted to know.

"What did he say?"

"That her legs are irresistible," I translated.

With all three of us grinning at him he scowled and scratched his groin involuntarily.

"Yes, you'd better keep that under lock and key," I teased.

Even Khalim grasped my meaning and whooped with laughter.

"Alright! Alright!" muttered Michael.

IT WAS DARK when we reached the first houses, but the night was not black like a sooty chimney. The sky was clear and the air warm. The chill of the mountains had not followed us into the valley. Smells wafted past. The sweetness of jasmine, discharged to attract moths, mixed with the slightly bitter scent of the farmyard and pungent aroma of evening meals being cooked over embers brought back to life from the midday repast. A dog barked, setting off another, and another, until our arrival had been well broadcast. After an impressive crescendo, the mutts' alarm calls—for no obvious reason—petered out. We had passed their test.

Aslan guided us to a house at the back of the village, just above the river, and knocked on the door. A stocky, middle-aged woman in her fifties opened it.

"Welcome! Welcome!" she greeted. "Ula will help you with your things."

A large girl, in her early twenties with straight black hair that clung to her head like pond weed, came to the door and eyed us up over her mother's shoulders.

"Come in! Come in!" encouraged the woman. "I have a room all prepared for you."

We followed her through a front room that had a table, a cooking fire and beds in opposite corners, to a back room divided by a curtain. I imagined that the smaller section would be mine. Suddenly the comforts of Sharosky seemed appealing.

I put some things down and felt the mattress that had been laid out on the floor. Horse hair! It was hard. I just hoped it had been well beaten since the last person slept on it.

Ula brought in one of my bags and stared at me. She had a particularly sullen expression.

"Could I have some water?" I asked.

"You will have to go to the river for that."

"Washing?"

"The river."

I nodded and she left.

At least my section of the room had a window in it. The wooden shutter had been pushed open and I looked out. The sky was full of stars, but there was no moon yet. I wondered if it would be a no-moon night. Bats were beginning to flutter about in pursuit of nocturnal insects, who might or might not have managed to propagate the jasmine before being eaten. The relentless circle of life. There were times when it seemed like a treadmill, activity for the sake of activity without rhyme or reason, save for the banal rationale we often concocted to explain our own existence. I had read somewhere that life was in the moment, no more, no less. If so, I was luckier than most.

I could hear the river, but not see it. Three goats with bulging udders stood tethered beneath my window and I wondered if their bells would clink away jaggedly all night. As I gazed up at the speckled sky, thinking how best to relieve myself, Ula came and started milking one of the goats. If she noticed me, she gave no hint of it. The rhythmic squirt of liquid into her jug crystallized my intent.

"Everything alright through there?"

Aslan's voice was the spur I needed.

"I'm just going out for a moment."

"Round the back," he said with maddening perception.

It was not much. Three wooden walls, with a wooden door, tacked onto the back of the house. It was so dark I had to leave the door ajar so as not to fall down the hole. Next time, I'd find my own place. Rolls of paper were the thing. The best advice I was ever given came from an old hand on my first African assignment. "Always carry a roll of paper," was his somewhat whisky-sodden answer when I approached him at the bar of the InterContinental in Kigali, and asked how I could make contact with one of the rebel leaders fighting the civil war I was supposed to cover. Somehow, he had managed to reduce all the misery and bloodshed he had witnessed in that place down to a single thing—a roll of paper.

His next comment had been even less prosaic. Did I fancy a quick fuck? When I declined his kind offer, he said "Just thought I'd ask," and offered me a drink. We became quite friendly after that and he saved my skin on several occasions when naive enthusiasm might have got me killed. I suppose I am a bit of a danger junkie. I guess all of us are in my line of work, to some extent.

On the way down to the river to wash, I came across a donkey and couldn't resist trying to fondle it. I had just managed to stroke one of its sticking-up ears when it took exception and butted me a'midriff. Knocked over onto my rear end, I found myself staring up at two rows of formidable teeth, like piano keys, jutting out from between curled lips. The wretched beast then let out a triumphant ee-aw and I had to pull myself backwards to escape.

"Found the petting zoo, then?" quipped Michael, who had snuck up and hadn't forgiven me for the ribbing I had dished out earlier.

"It's back that way," I huffed, irritated at being caught at a disadvantage.

"I know. That's why I'm going this way. What a stinkhole!"

"You can say that again," I agreed, pulling myself up.

"Yeah. Sharosky was five star, compared to this."

"I'm glad to see you haven't got your camera."

"How do you know I haven't?" he challenged and stumbled off into the darkness.

I stepped cautiously towards the river, giving the donkey a wide berth and trying to avoid its deposits. The pesky animal seemed intent on getting me one way or another. My stomach felt tender and was probably as bruised as my ego. All I had wanted to do was stroke it; ungrateful beast!

The ground was dry and hard but the river had been eating into the bank, making it unstable, so I walked some distance further down until I came to a pool protected by a plug of land that jutted into the flow. A patch of sand fell gently towards it and I was able to crouch and cup my hands in the water, raising a little to my cheeks. Bliss! This was the spot. I would come back later. Not quite Cleopatra's fabled bath on the shore of Hamam Bay, but good enough.

THE JUG I had watched being filled under my window sat on the table, together with a basket of bread. Ula handed round bowls that the woman had filled with a ladle from a large pot, suspended over the fire. The room was hot. Beads of sweat were falling off the girl's chin into the stew of vegetables and a small amount of meat that had been prepared. We each had a spoon. In the mountains, fingers, in the valley, spoons, in Zoldek—no doubt—a knife and fork. The march of progress. The woman kept up an incessant chatter, like an unstoppable brook. How pleased she was to have us. How she knew Aslan's father and had had him in this very house, a man of dignity, great wisdom—a credit to the Vorsky people.

Wasn't it terrible what the Federation was doing to the valley? It would never be the same again. The clans from Urus, Sharosky and Vorsky had lost, or would soon lose, the places where they came together. It was all in Zoldek now, where people met, traded, and played. Wasn't it terrible about the attacks? What had been the point? Killing the innocent, for the sake of what? So President Nitup could claim a great victory and win back the affection of his people? Surely no one could be so cynical?

Such wickedness! Where had honor gone? Men like Alu Dudayev were the exception now, save for his son, of course, although honor took many years to show itself. Too often people started down the right path, but ended on the wrong one. You just didn't know until near the close of a man's earthly journey whether he had true honor or not. To lose a wife after 44 years, what a tragedy! And to keep from swearing eternal vengeance, what self-control. No, there were few men like Alu Dudayev. Chenchia would not be the same place when such men were gone. Martinets from Zoldek would be ruling the roost soon.

Only yesterday, she told us, or was it the day before, four men from the government stayed with us. Martinets from Zoldek, I tell you! It was the day before. Yesterday it was the four Federation engineers who check the pipe. Up and down they go, day in day out, just checking the pipe. They always stay here, of course. Decent men. Clean men. No bother at all and good payers. But the martinets! Fetch this. Get that. Poor Ula was all over the place for them and then they complained about the bill. All right, so I had padded it a little. But people from Zoldek are used to city prices. Why should we lose out!

As she prattled on we spooned our food and dipped our bread. The goat's milk was still warm, like a buttermilk soup. Ula scowled at us from beside her mother and never once said a word, brooding like a volcano. Aslan started by acknowledging the woman's mental evacuation when he thought it appropriate, but his supportive noises declined in frequency, until it was clear no help was needed. Khalim made no effort, and looked like a man quite used to ignoring such verbal onslaughts from the fairer sex. Michael, of course, had no idea what was being said and appeared unsettled by Ula's fixed stare. Every time he looked up towards the woman, there were Ula's eyes burrowing into him like drill bits. I half listened and half thought about Cleopatra's bath, as I had now named the pool in my mind, and imagined two slave girls, who looked nothing like Ula, oiling and scenting my body.

The woman's monologue was not offensive, in fact it was quite restful and almost entertaining, when you took it for what it was: a performance in front of a captive audience. Board and lodging, show included.

Of course—the woman was saying—it will all end badly, as I used to tell to my poor husband, God rest his soul . . . and it seemed to me the dear departed was well out of it.

"Well, thank you," announced Aslan, rising from the table. "Can we take our tea outside? It is a warm night."

The woman suddenly noticed that her audience was heading for the exit, and a flash of disappointment crossed her face. But she quickly recovered.

"Ula will bring it. You are right. It is too nice a night for sitting inside. As I told one of the engineers just yesterday, or was it the day before. . . ."

But apart from Ula, her listeners had left her auditorium.

We must have talked for two hours or more. Khalim had excused himself after the meal and gone off to visit a friend in the village, so the conversation was in English which kept the woman at bay. Michael was first to make his pilgrimage to the bushes and after he returned I too collected my washing things. Aslan was stretched out on the ground smoking, and observed my departure with a sort of dreamy interest.

"Watch out for the crocodiles," he warned.

"Wrong country," I told him.

"Don't be so sure," he taunted.

I RETRACED MY steps from earlier. The moon had risen and the sharpness of its pale light was almost dazzling. The donkey's ears twitched as I passed, and I wondered how such a stubborn, cantankerous creature could have become associated in my mind with gentle Jesus meek and mild, Mary, and the manger, in that little town of Bethlehem, nestling safe under the star of God's great providence, which had drawn the Wise Men from afar with their gifts of gold, frankincense, and myrrh. Had it been down to this donkey, history would have taken a different turn. This Model T Ford of biblical times would, I fear, have remained resolutely in the garage and King Herod's census would have missed its most important citizen. And, with hindsight, would such an obstinate intervention have changed anything? In spite of the good donkey's best efforts, the donkey of my imagination, kings were still killing babies two thousand years later.

Live for the moment. That was the way. Right now nothing mattered more to me than Cleopatra's bath. Perhaps, after tonight, the pool I was looking for would be known as Orla's bath. And why not?

Light was jumping off the swirling water, as if fairies were dancing on darkness, tempting it, teasing it in their carefree way, certain that their speed and agility would keep them from any harm it might contain. The night had almost become day, minus color, with shades of blackness defining the landscape without the distractions of the rainbow. I have read that certain animals and insects see the world quite differently from us and that what we see as being a three-dimensional universe may have as many as ten.

The shape of the valley was perfectly clear, bound on either side by the high mountains I had begun to know, mountains that contained people who were invisible to me now as I was to them, but whose stories I had started to learn. At what point does 'place' and 'person' merge, so that the latter cannot exist without the former? Place does not need people, but people, it seems, do need place. What is my place? It isn't the little town of Sweetwater, surely? And I have no great love of the capital, although I do love my small apartment. Citizen of the world, that is what I am! This, right here and now, is my place.

Christ! What was that? My heart pounded. It must have been the wings of birds I had startled crashing into willow branches as they made their escape. For a split second I felt that fear which blanks out all thought and turns actions over to instinct, producing the blind panic that causes one to run or be eaten slowly, from toe to head, without so much as a whimper, if one is caught. Before panic sets in, what I normally do when I find myself in a tight corner is call Bernie and expect him to send in the Marines. But I'm not sure I can count on him without reservation. There would have to be a good story in it.

It seemed to be taking longer this time. I hoped I hadn't passed it. Stopping for a moment, to get my bearings, I became mesmerized by the sound of water swishing through the roots of the riverside shrubs. One branch was fighting like a drowning man. The current pulled it under, then some shift in orientation allowed it to spring up in a different place, only to be dragged down again into the watery darkness. Without any reason I found myself willing it to escape this macabre round of submersions. Like those tied to the medieval ducking stool, used to ascertain guilt or innocence—the guilty drowned, the innocent, miraculously, did not—this branch appeared condemned to an endless cycle of repentance, where repentance was not possible. Only when my towel slipped from my shoulder to the ground did I remember that I had an important ritual of my own to perform. I walked on.

Eventually I came to my pool but found it occupied. A lone heron, engaged in a little nighttime fishing, squawked furiously at my appearance and flapped off, leaving a trail of guano in its wake. "Take that!" it seemed to say. The pool was mine now and I didn't intend to let a few extra chemicals spoil my enjoyment.

I took off my shoes and looked around, but the heron hadn't seen anyone else and neither could I. So I removed my robe and laid it and the towel on the ground, and retrieved my precious bar of scented soap from the trusty sponge bag I had brought. Muddy sand pushed up between my toes and the water's coldness lapped against my calves. I advanced a little further until the water reached my thighs. I could see the fast-flowing current further out, but the flow was gentle behind the spur of land that had made my pool. It was now or never. I walked out a few more paces, until the river reached my waist, and then dropped like a stone into the black water.

Christ, it was cold! I sat there gripped in a thermal vice. Bending my head back and holding my nose, I let the current untangle my hair and wash over my face until I could bear it no more. Springing up, with the rush of a jack-in-a-box, I forced the water off my top half, exposing it again to the warm night air. I felt exhilarated and let myself go. For a few seconds my own heat surrounded my loins, until the flow carried it away. Then I soaped with great vigor, soaped and rinsed. The more vigorous, the warmer I thought I might get and besides, I had three days' grime and much horror to expurgate from my body.

In a careless moment, the precious bar of soap slipped from my hands. I reached and probed and even submerged several times trying to find it, but the river yielded only mud. Although I had become more used to the temperature, I couldn't pretend it was anything other than bitter. Much of what moved around me had probably been snow only a short while ago. But the sensation of water, especially when you have been denied it, is special—primal even. So, with quick strokes I swam out to the edge of the fast flow, relishing the freedom. After one last look upstream, and before the current took control, I turned and headed back for the shore.

As I emerged, imagining myself to be some modern day Aphrodite, the sound of a male voice hurled me back into the water with as much force as hands. I collapsed in an undignified heap, clutching at myself pathetically.

"Feeling better?"

It was Aslan, sitting back in the shadows, watching me.

"Jesus! You frightened the hell out of me. How long have you been there?"

"A while."

"I'm sure your faith would take a dim view of such perversion."

"You had better get out. You look freezing."

"I am!"

As I discarded my modesty and stood up, he came down to the water's edge and wrapped the towel and my robe around me. Then, without a word, he peeled off his kaftan and slipped into the water. Within moments he had reached the fast current. I saw his body arch and disappear. His perfect buttocks made me smile with pleasure. Memories of his body mingled with the moment and I stared at the surface waiting for him to reappear. But he did not. I approached the water's edge and strained my eyes to pick him out from the sinuous motion of the river around me. I thought I saw him. But it turned out to be some debris riding the current to Zoldek, or wherever it would end up.

It was one of his tricks. I turned round, but he wasn't there. So silly! I turned again to the water and peered. He could have hit his head and I was just staring, doing nothing. Feelings of anger and anxiousness merged. Surely he wouldn't be so stupid. A river he had known all his life. No, Orla. Don't fall for it. Remember the time when we had gone riding and his horse had bolted and come back riderless? Riderless like hell! How he clung to the far side like that was beyond me. *All the boys learn that trick* was all he said when my anger had subsided. But still I glared at the Mhemet River, challenging it to return him.

A sound behind made me spin round and there he was, grinning.

"Ha, ha!" I coughed out in a childish sort of way.

"Were you looking for me?"

"Lucky you came out when you did," I carped, staring at his manhood which had almost disappeared into itself.

Briefly embarrassed he looked down.

"Give me your towel," he demanded.

"Not sure that I will."

"We'll see about that," he challenged and pulled it from me, wrapping it around both of us. His body felt cold and erotic and quickly what had been non-existent came to life. We began to devour each other as we had in the sunrise of our love, but this was now, in moonlight, beside the river of his birth. I had often wondered what it would have been like to know him, not in my country, but in his, certain that I would have been pushed aside by one of his wild mountain girls, because that was how I imagined them. And yet, here I was, here we were, playing out so easily and so passionately what we had played out before in another place at another time.

Part of me suspected that the impossibility of our situation added to the intensity of what we shared. Doesn't stolen fruit always taste sweeter? When he was with me, our talk had always been about Chenchia and his return. Now that I was here, it was my inevitable return that dominated, not our conversation—so far neither of us had mentioned it once—but our innermost thoughts about the one thing that we shared, a thing that existed in its own world, bound by neither his nor mine. A fact apart we could not deny, even if we had wanted to, more real to both of us than any other, which we knew instinctively would outlast every other aspect of our lives. As the desire to become part of one another became unbearable, he untangled us, gathered up my shoes, bag and robe, and held out his hand.

"Come," he urged, drawing me after him, and we scampered like young lovers up the bank, behind some willows to an array of blankets and coverings arranged upon the ground. I didn't even question his presumption, but fell upon them eagerly and pulled him into me.

For I don't know how long I rode great waves of pleasure, each one more intense than the last. Aslan's body, now warm and streaked in the sweat of his exertions, pushed and pulled mine with all the vigor of youth and cleverness of age. No part of my body escaped the subtle movement of his hands, sometimes harsh and probing, at other times gentle and caressing. As a master extracts notes unimaginable from the instrument he alone has come to fully comprehend, so Aslan drew from me such an exquisiteness of feeling and sound, expression and movement, that we became one and the same, a single act, in a single moment, locked in an infinity of pure feeling, so utterly intense that there could be no other thing so real, so great, so complete. Within the three dimensions that make up most of human life, we had found a fourth.

He and I lay entangled, staring up at the stars, stroking each other gently. There were no words to describe where we had been better than the place itself, so we just enjoyed the proximity of our bodies, the night sky, and the silence. But it wasn't to last.

"Did you hear that?" he asked, suddenly.

"What?" I questioned, a little annoyed at having to leave my dream world so as to think about it.

"Listen," he insisted. "There's someone coming."

I sat up and strained to identify what seemed so clear to him. Sure enough, there were unmistakable signs, but how he had heard them so much before me, I couldn't imagine. The river noise, the noise of water rushing past grasses and twigs and round rocks, was an even noise, a steady noise, but now I could hear a different sound, separate from that of the stream. Something was coming our way. The occasional swish of branches being pushed aside and springing back was becoming more distinct. I hadn't realized he had brought his rifle until he drew it from beneath the blanket beside him. He freed the safety and held it ready and we both stared in the direction of the approaching sounds.

Although we could see no one, a commotion of noises was now coming from the edge of the clearing in front of the pool. Orla's bath was about to be invaded. As we peered, first one body and then another, both buck naked, came into the opening. A large girl was enticing a man into the water.

"B'jeepers it's cold!" the man cried out, and we realized it was Michael.

Aslan and I looked at each other in surprised amusement and he lowered his rifle. The girl was obviously Ula.

Like two voyeurs we studied the unfolding spectacle with rapt attention from behind the willows. The surly individual we had witnessed earlier in the evening was now alive, animated and playful, splashing Michael with both hands, her pendulous breasts swinging from side to side like the udder of the goat I had watched her milk. Michael kept falling backwards as she advanced on him, his feeble attempts at regaining the initiative thwarted at every turn. Up he would struggle; forward she would move, hollering and splashing. He'd wave his arms through the water in a half-hearted attempt to stall her advance, before stumbling backwards and falling, amid howls of laughter. Again and again this was repeated until I worried he might drown.

This thought must have occurred to Ula too, because she stopped splashing, allowing Michael to recover his footing for the umpteenth time and instead of renewing her assault, grasped his member and led him ashore, ignoring his shouts of "Whoa! Steady! You'll pull it off!"

As he lay panting on the sand she bent over him and set about re-kindling his enthusiasm. Her efforts quickly paid off, engendering cries of "God, that's good!", and "For Pete's sake, stop!" Satisfied she had produced what she wanted, she climbed on top and rode him with the volcanic energy of a wild animal.

Just when it seemed her pumping and pounding might go on for ever, she let out a fearful shriek. Her body convulsed several times and she fell forward. Moonlight spread across her large back which rose and fell very slightly with each exhausted breath. Michael was almost lost underneath the pile of requited flesh. Still we watched, utterly riveted by an act that had directed so much energy towards a single end. Without warning, she pulled herself up and gazed down at her conquest for several seconds with what seemed like affection. Then she turned towards the willows and was gone. Michael clambered up calling out "Hang on!" and followed her. We listened to the noises we had heard coming disappear and fade, and then laughed and laughed, until we could laugh no more.

For the rest of the night we stayed there, wrapped in the blankets Aslan had brought. It was a perfect night. The moon followed its arc. Several shooting stars streaked to their spectacular end above us. The Milky Way shone like a great city, beckoning us. The heavens seemed to be ours for the taking. We shared that tenderness we had once known, when the rip tide of passion has come and gone and a gentler, deeper, ebb and flow takes hold. At some point in the early morning, when dawn was just beginning to turn off the night and Aslan lay beside me, breathing gently, I cried. I knew it would never be as good as this again.

CHAPTER 5

The following morning we rode to our meeting with Malik Bassayev who had assumed his father's role as head of the Urus region. I could tell that Aslan was anxious. He was close to his sister, Roaz, but I don't think he had ever felt completely comfortable with her husband. The union was meant to cement relations between the Vorsky and Urus regions, but Malik and Aslan were direct contemporaries and, I suspected, considered themselves competitors. Alu Dudayev and Malik's father, Akhmad Bassayev, had developed an understanding, certainly, but neither man had wanted to step outside his region, and each respected the ability of the other. It was as much down to what Aslan had not said about Malik that suggested to me the two men were rivals. Although rivals for what, I had never been able to work out.

Doubtless the fact of Aslan's American education as against Malik's Russian one had done little to dampen any sparks of enmity that might have existed between them. His sister's wedding to Malik had been arranged, but that was not uncommon. However, whenever he spoke about Roaz I felt he did not think Malik made her a particularly good husband. It was not a question of cruelty, or anything like that, I didn't think, but something more subtle. A lack of affection, possibly, even a deep-seated incompatibility. Aslan had told me many times that members of the Bassayev family were well known for the deviousness of their intelligence—"students of Machiavelli, every one," he once asserted. In the father, this characteristic had never undermined his and Alu Dudayev's mutual respect. So far, the two sons had failed to achieve a similar understanding. Perhaps they would, given time.

"We wait here," Aslan shouted out when we came to the main river crossing between Vorsky and Urus.

None of us had been keen to make much eye contact that morning. The secrets of the night, and its not so secret secrets, belonged to a different place. Even Khalim didn't reappear until after the three of us had sat in silence while surly Ula had put plates of egg and bread and mugs of goat's milk before us, without so much as a look at Michael, or word to her mother, who stumbled half-heartedly into another monologue about the changes overtaking the valley.

There appeared to be more Federation vehicles plying the incomplete highway. Their presence lent an air of menace to a day that already felt out of sorts with itself. Before we had time to dismount, a Federation jeep, amid a cloud of dust, approached us along the riverside track and two men climbed out and addressed us.

"Papers," the older of the two demanded, although he couldn't have been much over twenty-five.

"This is my country. You should be showing me your papers," countered Khalim, revealing a side of himself I had not seen before.

The younger of the two men made as if to strike him, but Khalim turned his horse and the young man stepped backwards.

"We shoot horses as well as people," he mocked, attempting to disguise his fear.

"Papers," the older of the two repeated, trying to regain control of the situation.

Aslan felt inside his cloak, causing the two soldiers to reach for their guns and Khalim to grip his rifle.

"Do you want papers, or not?" Aslan asked quietly.

The older soldier held out his hand and made an impatient gesture.

"Give me," he said.

Aslan handed over a tattered document.

The younger soldier, with a gesture of contempt, then took a similarly battered item from Khalim.

"You will have to get these renewed in Zoldek," the older man announced. "They are barely readable." And then turning to Michael and me, "You two. Papers."

We handed over our pristine permits, secured after much haggling in the Chenchian capital. It was obvious neither soldier had seen anything like them before, because they stood in a huddle, uncertain what to do. Eventually, the older soldier spoke.

"These are not papers. You will have to come with me to Zoldek."

"These are western journalists, accredited by our government," Aslan pointed out. "They have every right to be here. I suggest you radio your commanding officer."

The older soldier looked rattled.

"Our radio is out," he admitted.

As the two rookies stared at the documents they had been given, no doubt wishing they hadn't asked for them in the first place, a posse of five horsemen plunged into the crossing opposite us and splashed their way across to our side of the river.

Suddenly it was nine against two, and the two lost their nerve immediately, which was not surprising as the Urus fighters were armed to the teeth and looking vicious. Without even a comment, the two young Federation soldiers returned all four documents to Aslan and hurried back to their jeep. If I hadn't realized it before, I realized it then: power and freedom are closely allied.

"IT SEEMS I came just in time!" greeted a young man, shorter than Aslan and darker, with penetrating, restless eyes, who I took to be Malik. "I was sorry to hear about your mother."

"These blockheads will never learn that this is not their country," Aslan replied. "It was lucky Khalim here didn't shoot both of them."

Malik acknowledged the other man and turned his attention to me.

"I take it this is your American journalist?"

"Yes. Orla Kildare and her cameraman, Michael Zill."

Malik steered his horse up to mine and offered his hand.

"I am sorry you are seeing our country at such a bad time."

"From what I know," I answered, shaking his hand, "your country has had few good times!"

"Is that what Aslan has told you?"

I shrugged.

"He is probably right. Now we have a long way to ride," he explained, looking anxiously at Michael and the animal loaded with all our equipment. "Dujs is only a small village and it is not close."

"Why do you think the Federation picked it?" Aslan asked.

"It is isolated," Malik conjectured.

"The Sharosky village got off lightly," I stated. "It was inaccessible."

"So I heard," Malik acknowledged. "You can say that about all Sharosky villages. That is why we call the people mountain goats! No one else would want to live the way they do, tucked into the side of cliffs."

"It served them well this time," I pointed out, feeling unexpectedly protective towards Sergei Kadyrov's rugged kingdom.

"Let's get started," he ordered. "Aslan, come and ride with me."

We set off at a fast pace, across the river and into the Urus region. Malik and Aslan were soon way ahead, with two of Malik's fighters keeping a discreet distance behind their leader, and the other two guarding the rear. Khalim rode behind the first two Urus fighters, no doubt watching them and *his* leader. The politics of Chenchia were intricate. It all seemed a long way from campus life, but perhaps Aslan had seen subtleties I had been blind to. It is invariably the tourist who notices things the resident does not.

"How's that back end of yours?" I inquired, as Michael pulled level with me, still looking, I felt, not entirely comfortable in the saddle. "I don't think Malik Bassayev will be offering you the same in-house facilities!"

"No daughters?"

"Aged two and four, I believe." I had had a lingering interest in Aslan's sister. *My* sister-in-law? Dreaming the impossible dream was almost one of my country's national anthems.

"Pity!"

"So how is it?"

"How is what?"

"Your ass, dear."

"Since you ask, my ass is a lot better than some other parts of my anatomy," he confessed.

"Ah!" I conceded. "That may be a good point at which to change the subject."

The image of Ula's aggressive lovemaking flashed into my head, and by the pained look on Michael's face, its lingering sensation was flashing repeatedly into his.

Urus was as different from Vorsky and Sharosky as those two regions were from each other. South of the Mhemet River, the country seemed to tilt up in the east with its sunless mountains, gorges and inaccessible cliffs and down into Urus in the west where the landscape appeared to be dominated by smooth-sided valleys, that curved upwards into a hinterland of rounded mountains, decidedly more ordinary than the jagged peaks of Sharosky or majestic highlands of

Vorsky, crowned by Mount Abochevo. But with its comparative dullness came a less hostile environment and I could see from the map that the region wasn't isolated from the Zoldek plateau, in the same way as the other two regions were. As we climbed higher, Zoldek itself was visible in the distance.

We rode for two hours, stopped for thirty minutes, and rode on again for another two hours. Even I was beginning to feel saddlesore, so I hardly dared imagine how Michael was faring. His martyrdom for Cindy, however, was impressing me less and less, although I was beginning to understand that male sexuality was a good deal more freewheeling than that of my own gender, notwithstanding the impressive show of independence in that department given by two of my Chenchian sisters.

After Aslan had returned to his country, and I had given up feeling sorry for myself, I suppose I too had freewheeled a bit. But the pleasure component had been less important to me than the prospect of finding a mate, and when I realized casual dining wasn't going to produce another Aslan any time soon, I'd pretty much given up on the dating game and hurled myself into work and onto the not-so-tender mercies of Bernie Eisner and DEMOS-TV. I didn't have to sleep with Bernie, just find him stories that would boost his ratings. It was a kind of prostitution, but one I'd been only too happy to engage in. Fearless Orla Kildare, seeker of truth, exposer of evil!

Dirk Ford had drifted into my life unannounced and almost unnoticed. His marriage had imploded many years earlier and he did not appear keen to repeat the experience. His two children were both making their way in the world so he was a free agent, apart from the long hours he spent working the political system for his wealthy clients as one of DC's top lobbyists. Whenever I was in town, we'd have dinner a couple of times a week and perhaps spend some of Saturday or Sunday together. It was almost as if we had slipped into an easy-going relationship without any of the passionate preliminaries. What we did when we were not in each other's company was our own business, unless we wanted to talk about it, and we often did. His antennae were sensitive to the nuances and wind shifts on Capitol Hill and I knew more than most about the uglier imbroglios in the world, which he described as those fly-infested wounds in the human body that some part of our government was invariably trying to feed off.

Pushing sixty, I guess Dirk was something of a father figure for me. So, I was living a cliché—part of the time, anyway. But it suited me. After spending weeks away in some godforsaken part of the world, in which human depravity, as often as not, had become the norm, a spell of solid ordinariness was a gift not to be sniffed at. And I think it suited him too. I blew in and out of his domain and perhaps disturbed the cobwebs of cynicism that might otherwise have engulfed his life.

"Where the hell is this place, Orla?"

Michael's tone had a belligerent, I'm not going another yard, ring to it. I could see him getting off his horse and just sitting right there, in the middle of nowhere, certain that whatever might befall him could not possibly be worse than the unpleasantness of continuing.

"Cheer up," I told him, rather half-heartedly. "It can't be that much further."

"But we still have to go all the way back!" he almost moaned.

I had been thinking about that myself.

"Let me go and ask Malik," I proposed, anxious to stall his intentions. "Now for God's sake hang in there. I don't want to arrive and find I have no cameraman."

He muttered something about all burned-out villages looking much the same, and I spurred my horse forward into a trot so as to close the gap between us and our leaders. The trot quickly turned into a canter and Khalim whipped round in his saddle at the sound of my approach, a move quickly copied by the two Chenchian fighters and then by Aslan and Malik themselves. For a few seconds I felt like a young cavalry officer about to race into enemy lines.

As I came level with the Chenchian fighters, something spooked my horse and it accelerated into a full gallop, so that I hurtled past Aslan and Malik quite out of control. A feeling of panic and utter exhilaration took hold of me as I raced forward, pulling on the reins, with wind pounding my face and forcing tears from my eyes. The power of the animal astonished me. My attempt to pull it up had no effect whatsoever. It even seemed to be going faster. I bent forward, gripping its body tight with my legs and held onto its mane with my hands, praying that I could stay on until it tired. Orla Kildare approaches the winning post at the Kentucky Derby! But where the hell was the finishing post?

Mercifully, the ground was quite flat and grassy, but it had become misty and the compressed moisture poured off my face in streams, making it hard to see. Ahead I could just make out the shapes of houses and I thought I saw three riders disappearing into the haze. As I blinked, to clear my vision, hands grasped my reins from either side and I found myself sandwiched between Aslan's and Malik's racing animals. Quickly, all three of us started to slow and when we stopped amid a flurry of shouts, reins, hooves, spray and horse sweat, I realized I had arrived in Dujs.

"Quite an entrance!" remarked Malik, who was wreathed in smiles.

"I take it you are alright?" grinned Aslan.

"I'm sorry about that," I panted. "Something must have startled her."

DUJS WAS A ghost town. I had Michael follow me in with the camera and, although hobbling, he was clearly glad to be on terra firma. As before, the houses had been torched. I entered the first, prepared to be sickened, but only found the charred remains of the building itself. *Only* someone's burned home. That should have been sickening enough, but the horrors we had seen had lifted our threshold of disgust. With the mist clinging to everything like a soggy blanket, we worked our way from house to house. There were only ten and each had received the same treatment. When we reached the end, we both had an identical reaction.

"Why are there no bodies?"

Michael's question was the one I wanted to ask. We looked at each other, puzzled.

"Terrible, isn't it?"

Malik loomed out of the gloom with his comment.

"Yes, it's terrible," I agreed. "But there are no bodies. Argun was a charnel house and the Sharosky village was awash with human horrors."

"I heard about those," Malik noted, impassively. "And as for Argun, I have been told that what they did was utterly loathsome. We were lucky. We received a tip-off just before the raid and were able to get everyone out."

"That certainly was lucky," I agreed.

"Have you got what you needed?" he asked.

I looked across at Michael and knew he would be thinking "all this way for ten burned houses!", so didn't push him for a comment.

"Yes. I think we have everything we need."

"Good. Then I will say goodbye to you here. I have business to attend to in Zoldek. Aslan wants to visit his sister, so you will be spending the night with her."

We shook hands, Malik nodded at Michael and disappeared, leaving us alone again in the mist.

"We are not going back," I told him.

"Staying here?" he questioned, uncertain as to whether it would be much better than struggling back.

"No. Aslan wants to visit his sister. We will be staying with her."

Michael's brief smile quickly evaporated.

"How far?" he asked.

But I didn't know.

"Three hours if we go the slow way. One if we are up to some climbing."

Aslan's answer almost preceded his materialization and I wondered who else might be close by inside this fog.

"How much climbing?" I queried.

"Most of it the horses can manage. But when we get to the pass," and he gestured behind him into the vapor, towards some mountain range none of us could see, "we will have to lead them on foot."

"Oh, I think I can handle that," Michael responded, visibly bucked up.

"Good. Then we best get going. There's nothing to keep us here."

Malik had left us only one of his fighters as a guide and we had barely started out of Dujs, after repacking our equipment, when we heard it. The unmistakable sound of an approaching Federation gunship.

"How the hell can that thing see to fly?" I shouted.

"This is just cloud. We're in the cloud belt. Twenty, thirty feet above us it could be clear. Now hurry, quick!" Aslan urged.

Sticking close to the animal in front we followed the guide at a trot away from the village as the sound of the rotors thundered closer. We had barely put fifty yards between us and the village before the gunship opened up, terrifying the horses and spraying what was left of the houses with shot. For good measure, incendiaries were dropped sending flashes of light and sound pulsing through the water vapor. The ground was rising steeply and as Aslan had surmised, the cloud belt we were in started to thin.

"Get off the horses and stay put," Aslan shouted. "We don't want to break through the cloud cover."

I quickly dismounted and noticed that Michael was already off and pointing his camera towards Dujs, his instincts as a cameraman drowning out all other considerations.

The bombardment only lasted for five minutes, at most, and soon the sound of the gunship was retreating back down the valley. Had anyone returned to that wretched place, they would have experienced a few minutes of hell. But as it happened, all its spitting and belching had been full of sound and fury signifying I didn't know what. Could its appearance at the same time as us have been mere coincidence? It hardly seemed likely. And what was the significance of the horsemen I thought I had seen?

"Khalim. Help me. This man's been hit."

Aslan's call for help sent a chill through my already cold body. Michael was walking towards me, so I knew it couldn't be him. It had to be our guide.

"What's up?" Michael asked.

"I think the guide's been hit."

"Oh, fuck!"

We walked in the direction of Aslan's call for help and found him and Khalim kneeling next to the Urus fighter who was lying stretched out on the sodden ground.

"Bad?" I asked.

"Dead," came back Aslan's reply.

"How?"

"A piece of shrapnel through the head."

I could now see a hole in our guide's forehead and blood oozing out from behind his skull. Michael stood next to me filming.

"We'll have to take the long way," Aslan announced, in a loud voice. "Without a guide we wouldn't be able to find the pass. As soon as Khalim and I have buried this man we must be off."

The stillness of the place felt razor sharp after the cacophony of the gunship. Even the clink of stones being piled on top of our dead guide sounded intimate and unreal.

"Do you think you got enough?" I asked Michael.

"For a broadcast?"

"Yes."

"Probably. Do you want to try and send it?"

"Later. I'll need to prepare a voice-over when I've seen the images."

"Here. Let me show you what I've got."

I peered into the camera's small screen. The burned houses did not amount to much after Argun, and Michael had lost interest anyway. But what he had managed to capture of the Federation attack was almost surreal. The pyrotechnics flashed through the haze, creating ghastly shadows that hung ferociously for split seconds before collapsing in on themselves, only to be replaced by yet more diabolical shapes. It was as if I was peering into the underworld. We even had a body. The vacant eyes of our guide, whose forehead had been anointed so precisely by death, stared at me as the last image.

"I think Aslan and Khalim, with their backs to the camera bending over the body will be enough," I suggested. "That close-up's too much. Bernie would axe it anyway."

"I guess," conceded Michael.

"You did well to get that attack. Quick thinking."

"So I might make a good field cameraman yet?"

I was warming to this perverted wonk, who had been allocated to me at the last moment because my regular was off, and who wanted to make a point to his tight-ass girlfriend.

"Yes," I agreed. "You very well might."

As soon as the Urus fighter had been buried, we were off. Our horses had drifted back to us after the commotion had died down, and I think even Michael was pleased to see his. Only the dead man's did not reappear. Aslan kept inside the cloud belt and set a fast pace, with Khalim in the rear. I didn't ask how he knew which way to go. I could barely see five feet in front of me.

After ten minutes or so, I found we were following a stream. The water splashed up around the horses' hooves and I remembered being told that if you were ever lost, follow a stream, and it would eventually take you to civilization. We hadn't been going for more than a couple of hundred yards, I would guess, when Aslan suddenly veered right, up a much smaller tributary. The stones were awkward and I wanted to climb out, but we were sandwiched between two sheer rocks. Our horses struggled up the narrow cascade of tumbling water, slipping on the rocks as they went and I was certain one would break a leg. But with several heroic lunges that seemed to require the full force of their bodies, our animals managed to pull us clear of the cut and we found ourselves above the cloud.

Aslan gestured to us to keep quiet and our horses stood in a huddle on a grassy knoll next to the wild little stream that was being filled by a waterfall above us. Where we had come from looked impossible: a narrow gorge full of white foam and angry water. Aslan and Khalim appeared to be listening out for something, but I could hear nothing above the torrent. Suddenly the two Chenchians relaxed.

"They fell for it," Aslan announced cryptically. "Let's go."

He turned his horse and started to back-track along a shoulder of the mountain. Khalim saw my puzzled expression.

"It wasn't shrapnel," he explained.

"The dead man?"

Khalim pointed a finger at his forehead, dead center.

"A bullet," he added.

Michael, who had been trying to make sense of what had just happened, asked me what was going on and I told him about the guide.

"You mean they shot their own man?" he asked, looking visibly shaken.

"It seems so."

"And they were following us?"

I nodded.

The poor man's face turned pallid and I suspected he was seeing himself impaled on a stake.

"All part of the fun when you're a field cameraman," I told him. But I didn't have my heart in the joke and his weak smile was no consolation.

Aslan was moving fast now and we had a job keeping up. The ground was saturated and the horses found it hard to maintain a secure footing. We almost lost our pack animal, when a section of turf it was crossing broke away. Somehow it managed to regain its balance and Khalim, grabbing the reins, hauled the startled beast to safety. Backtracking was the worst. The angle of the slope was horrible and we were not on any sort of path. But eventually we found the trail Aslan was looking for and began to climb straight up the mountain. The brute strength of the horses was incredible. In places the incline was as bad as it had been cutting up the gorge and our animals had to thrust forward with all their strength until the slope became less severe.

I lost all track of time, so absorbed was I in the exertions of my animal, willing it on at every step. I didn't even look back, fixing my gaze instead on what I imagined was the ridge of the mountains, for it was a range we were attempting to cross. The closer we got, the more impossible it seemed. The ground rose steeply ahead and was covered in shale all the way to sheer cliffs that rose up to the ridge itself. I could see no way out and the shale looked impassable. But on we struggled.

At the edge of the shale field we stopped at last and Aslan ordered us to dismount. Only then did I turn around. Far below were the clouds and beneath them what I supposed was left of Dujs. For several seconds I felt sick and scared. I could not believe we had come up a face so steep. Michael was shaking and I thought would throw up at any moment. All Aslan and Khalim were concerned about was that we had not been followed.

"It's best not to look down."

Aslan's quiet words had an instantly calming effect.

"But I can see no way out," I blurted.

"Oh, there is. If you know."

"How on earth *do* you know?" I asked. "This is not even your region."

"As children we used to raid each other's territory and try not to get caught. You learn a lot that way."

After a short rest we started again, this time on foot, leading our horses by the reins, although I am sure they could have led us. Khalim had tied the pack horse to his own horse's tail. The shale was foul to walk on and even worse for the animals. We struggled forward, slipped back and struggled on some more. It was exhausting. My legs were aching and my heart was pounding as we approached the rock face, and I could still see no way out. I looked to see how Michael was faring and when I turned back, Aslan had disappeared.

Only when I was there, with nowhere else to go, did I realize that the cliffs hung like two curtains, with one slightly in front of the other, leaving just enough room for a horse to squeeze behind onto a narrow path which, although steep, was quite manageable and ran at right angles all the way to the top of the ridge. In less than a minute we had reached the top. To my great relief, the ground fell away gently on the other side through a stand of old pine trees and on towards a grass-covered valley. In the middle of this valley nestled a substantial village.

"Lapsi," pointed out Aslan, with evident pleasure. "We will be there in no time."

Which was just as well, I thought, as the light was beginning to fade. I could hardly believe that we had not yet been going for an hour. Our pursuers would barely be a third of the way.

As we approached, a small group of riders came out to meet us. At its head was a striking woman who I took to be Roaz. She and Aslan broke away to greet one another. By the time I reached them she was asking Aslan about the guide.

". . . he was one of my most trusted men. How did it happen?"

"A Federation gunship returned to strafe the village. He was hit by shrapnel," Aslan told her.

She looked concerned and I caught Khalim's eye, but he gave no hint of wishing to refute Aslan's inaccurate account.

THE MEETING BETWEEN Roaz and Aslan, the first since the death of their mother, was more moving than I had expected. I had never met her and so had not seen brother and sister together. She looked like him in so many ways. Beautiful, with thick black hair that fell down her back and a look that suggested great strength. They shared a particular intimacy which was instantly deep and timeless, and I might have felt jealous if Roaz had not come over and welcomed me like a long-lost friend. I suppose we did each know a lot about the other. I could see that they needed time together and so said I had to work with Michael on our next broadcast which, anyway, was true.

I had been going over in my head the words I wanted to attach to the images. Michael and I went through the whole sequence several times, cutting out bits that seemed redundant, until we were both satisfied. I would crouch on the ground under Michael's lights and introduce the piece. Then I would talk over the images as they played on the monitor and were beamed all the way to the DEMOS-TV studios in America. Wonderful! That was assuming we could make the link. Luckily, it didn't take long.

"Steve, this is Mike. How are you doing, fellow?"

"Where the hell have you guys been? We were worried."

"Working, which is a lot more than you've probably been doing."

"Go to hell! Bernie's a red hot trouble spot all on his own. I should get danger money for just being here!"

"That I can believe, although I think these Chenchians could teach him a thing or two. Look, Orla wants a word."

"Hi Steve."

"Orla."

"Did Bernie put out that last piece?"

"More or less."

"What the hell do you mean, more or less?"

"Well, we tamed it down just a bit."

"How much of a bit?"

"A bit. You know how apoplectic he gets about upsetting our sponsors. We can't go showing too much blood and guts to the good people of America. It upsets their TV dinners!"

"God, Steve. Aren't we supposed to be showing the world as it is? Aren't we the real reality TV?"

"I don't make the rules, ma'am. Now you'd better give me what you've got before the nickels run out."

"Alright, you apparatchik. Here goes."

I got into position, Michael hit the lights and my broadcast began.

"I have just come from Dujs, a small village in the Urus region devastated by Federation soldiers. Miraculously, the villagers were tipped off and had made their escape, but every dwelling was destroyed, as you can see.

"Thankfully there are no bodies. Just the charred remains of peoples' homes. Dujs was shrouded in low cloud and felt utterly desolate.

"As we were preparing to leave, a Federation gunship returned to strafe the village. Perhaps they had posted lookouts and mistaken our arrival for the villagers' return.

"Those flashes are incendiaries and the popping you can hear are shots being fired indiscriminately from above the low cloud into the hamlet. It was lucky for the villagers that they had not returned, otherwise there would have been carnage.

"It was lucky for us too that we had just left. Although it was not soon enough to prevent our guide from being killed by a piece of flying shrapnel. It is impossible to see what purpose these brutal attacks can serve.

"This is Orla Kildare for DEMOS-TV, reporting live from the Urus region in Chenchia."

"Did you get that Steve?"

"Yeah. We got it."

"Only one body for Bernie to fret about this time!"

"Very tasteful. We like tasteful wars."

"We try to please!"

"Bernie needs to speak to you, by the way."

"Now?"

"He's not here right now."

"What about?"

"I think he's got some travelling planned for you."

"Where?"

"I'll let him tell you. He's still got some details to iron out. Keep your cell on."

"I can't recharge it here. You know that."

"I do. But keep it on Orla. This is important . . . That's the money running out. Stay safe, you crazies."

At that, the connection broke up. Satellite time was expensive, and Bernie minded the pennies.

BEFORE WE ATE, Roaz took me to see her father-in-law. I found Akhmad Bassayev propped up on the floor of his home against a mound of colored pillows, his body covered in furs. A low fire filled the room with warm light. A lady, much younger than him, sat close by working on some piece of clothing. Akhmad's eyes were closed when we entered, but quickly opened and alighted with pleasure on Roaz. I could tell immediately that the two had a bond.

"This is Orla, father-in-law. A friend of my brother, Aslan."

The old man turned his attention to me and I felt my character being dissected, as if by some infernal machine that could read one's innermost thoughts. He waved his companion away and beckoned me to take her place.

"I'll leave you two to talk," Roaz told him and he smiled at her and nodded.

I settled down beside him and with a weak hand-movement he gestured towards a silver pot containing dried fruit. I took some.

"You speak our language well, Roaz tells me."

I still felt he was weighing me up.

"Quite well, I think."

"In a world of Russians and Americans, one's language is important. It is good that you recognize that."

"I think love recognized that!"

The old man smiled.

"Love is often wiser than we are!"

He closed his eyes and I looked over at the fire.

"What do you make of our tortured land?"

I turned but his eyes were still closed, so I turned back to the fire.

"Against all this interference, I think it is struggling to find a new identity," I told him.

"Did Aslan gain more than confusion from America?"

"I hope so," I answered, feeling somewhat defensive.

"You know how it was decided?"

"How what was decided?"

"Who should go where."

I didn't know what he was talking about, so I said nothing. The fire's gentle puttering noise was comforting and there seemed no need.

"Alu and I tossed a coin," he continued. "Aslan or Malik to America. Aslan or Malik to Russia. So if the toss had been different, your lover might have been my son."

The old man's face was wreathed in smiles.

I felt angry that one of the most important things in my life could have been decided by the toss of a coin.

"I thought Aslan's mother settled it," I told him.

"She probably did. It was as well the toss worked out the way it did," and this time he laughed.

"We knew, Alu and I, that the future of our country would be decided by one or the other, by America or Russia, so we thought we had better get both covered."

"It looks as though your luck was the better," I said.

He didn't respond immediately.

"Perhaps," he continued. "But it has implications. I regard Alu Dudayev as my friend, so his family are also my friends. I have grown especially close to my daughter-in-law. And I must tell you, she may need your help one day."

"She has her husband to help her," I stated, "and Aslan."

"My son must do what he has to do and so must my friend's son."

Akhmad Bassayev closed his eyes again. He seemed to have exhausted himself, looking into the future. I studied his lined face for some time, until I was aware of a sound behind me. It was Roaz standing by the door and my time to leave.

WE ATE WELL and talked late into the night, but the conversation had a strangeness about it. Never once did we mention the guide or the fighters who had tried to follow us, and both brother and sister refused to discuss the present situation, preferring instead to savor shared memories from their rich past. Some things Aslan had told me about, but I enjoyed hearing Roaz's version of events. The many things I had not heard, reminded me that no matter how close you were to a person, there would always be much you would never know.

I CAN ONLY have been asleep for an hour or two, before I found Roaz bending over me, telling me we had to go.

"I am sending twenty fighters with you. They are all loyal to my husband's father. You will be safe."

"But what about you?" I coughed out, from my interrupted sleep.

She gently placed her fingers on my lips.

"Hurry. You must go."

I don't think Aslan and Khalim had slept, because I found them ready. Michael was in a worse state than I, although for once, he was alone, and struggling to gather his things.

Roaz had not slept either, I am sure of it. As Aslan was about to ride off she approached his horse and the two held hands for a brief moment. We clattered away from Lapsi under a full moon. Aslan did not turn, but I couldn't resist and saw Roaz watching us.

We made rapid progress. In less than an hour, I could see the Mhemet Valley below us. Our escort of twenty fighters took us to the crossing and waited until we were safely on the other side. It was then that my cell went off. I'd set it on a silly croaking frog sound and felt embarrassed. Bernie wanted me to fly immediately to Moscow to interview President Nitup. I guess it was only nine in the evening his time and Bernie never was one to pay much attention to time zones.

CHAPTER 6

$\mathcal{I}$ had been to the Russian capital only once before. At the epicenter of a vast empire that stretched east and west, Moscow was a blend of architectures. Gilded domes and spires, buildings painted in colors many Europeans considered garish and North Americans would have consigned to a theme park, mixed with the drab utilitarian functionalism of the communist era. At its heart, a square of such brutal pretentiousness and scale that few observers could have had any doubt that this was a state whose ultimate god was power.

As tends to be the way with false gods, theirs had proved illusory and the communist hierarchy had collapsed as spectacularly as the Romanov dynasty before it. Although to be fair to the Romanovs, they had lasted much longer, perhaps because they had at least paid lip service to a god other than themselves. A new breed of ruler had emerged, jealous of democracy's success, but reluctant to abandon the old ways of barbarous power politics.

President Nitup had been elected after systematically eliminating his opponents, using all the tricks he had learned during his previous career in the Federation's secret police, a technique that had earned him plaudits from most of his people. The young wanted democracy, without knowing much about it, while the old longed for a return to the familiar ways of mass murder and authoritarian rule. The great thing about mass murder, I suppose, is that the dead can't vote—or complain. The middling people, as far as I could tell, like most middling people, just wanted to get on with their lives, be paid, buy food, live in homes near schools and take a holiday. Whoever could deliver that, no matter how it was achieved, they'd vote for. Esoteric concepts like freedom and democracy were luxuries they felt they could not afford.

The Federation government regarded Chenchia as being part of its empire and the stubborn resistance of the Chenchian people something to be crushed, although with the oil pipeline to protect, an all-out war was now considered too risky. The steady loss of Federation soldiers to Chenchian guerrilla tactics within Zoldek had started to make itself felt. So long as those killed came from out-of-the-way parts of its domain, the ruling hierarchy was not much affected. But when mothers inside the elite began to lose sons, members of the government were forced to think.

I had heard that a sizeable minority wanted to give Chenchia independence, but that a hard core were violently opposed to this, believing that Faith Radicals would encroach into other parts of the Federation. From what I knew of Chenchia, its people's adherence to the Faith was largely pragmatic, and most had as little time for Faith Radicals as for Russians. After all, the Faith was a lingering relic of their earlier enslavement from the south.

As the plane landed, I wondered how I was going to structure my interview with President Nitup, assuming he'd even agree to one. He would certainly have been told about my broadcasts from Chenchia. But he was trying to portray Chenchian resistance as part of global terrorism, something my own president was anxious to eliminate. So he might go for it. Bernie clearly thought so, otherwise he would not have sent us.

"*WELCOME TO MOSCOW,*" greeted a pleasant-looking young man, as soon as I recognized my name on the sign he was holding. "I'm Andrew Meadows, from the embassy."

"My cameraman, Michael Zill," I said, turning.

Our greeter was clearly amused by all the equipment Michael was struggling to trolley across the arrivals hall.

"I see you're the pack animal!"

"Don't talk to me about animals. I've been sitting on one for the entire week!"

"Yes. I gather you guys were roughing it. Good broadcast, by the way."

"Thank you," I acknowledged. "But how come the embassy is doing the honors? We're normally met by an agency driver."

"You have stirred up quite a hornets' nest here," Andrew Meadows explained. "Your boss, Bernie something…"

"Eisner. Bernie Eisner."

"Yes. Quite forceful. Well connected too, I think."

"That's Bernie," I confirmed.

"Well he had to pull a few strings to get you in. The Federation was all for denying you entry."

"On what grounds?" I asked.

"That you were connected to Chenchian terrorists."

"Jesus!"

"They think you lived with one for several years," Andrew Meadows explained, with a knowing smirk on his face.

"Is there nothing you spooks don't know?" I complained, with as much hurt as I could inject into the question.

"Diplomat. I'm a diplomat," the man from the embassy clarified. "And yes, we know absolutely everything except the one thing that is about to happen tomorrow. That will take us completely by surprise!"

"Are we staying in the embassy, Mr. Meadows?" Michael asked.

"Andy, please. No. I've booked you into the Regency. It's not the greatest hotel, but it's clean and your man Bernie said the tariff sounded right."

"It's good to know we're valued," Michael noted, grinning at me.

"I expect he thought any bed would seem like a luxury to us after the last few days," I speculated.

"Yes," agreed Andy. "He did say something about needing to acclimatize you to the modern world gently. A careful decompression was one of his expressions."

"He's all heart!" I mocked.

"Actually, it's quite a nice little hotel. Doesn't attract so much attention as the smarter ones, either."

"So they are still up to their tricks?"

"'Fraid so. Although they are a bit short of money at the moment, which is curbing their activities. It's no longer one minder for each citizen and two for every visitor."

After loading us into his car, Andy Meadows chatted away amiably as he drove us to the hotel. I wasn't sure what to make of him. Casual and friendly could have been casual and friendly, but more likely it disguised an agenda. My country was terrified that Faith Radicals would take control of Middle East oil, so on this issue our government saw President Nitup as an ally. I suppose that meant Andy would serve as 'minder' for both countries.

"Alright, here we are," he announced. "As you can see, it's in a quiet street."

"When do you think I will get to interview the president?" I asked, as I hauled myself out of his front seat. Tiredness was beginning to catch up with me.

"We're working on it, Orla. I'll let you know just as soon as it has been arranged. Now, if there is anything I can do for you both, just give me a call. Here's my card. That's my direct number."

"What daily allowance are we getting?" Michael asked.

"That's a matter for your station," Andy told him. "But I was asked to give you this. Nearly forgot!"

He passed Orla an envelope.

"It should help to ease the wait."

Michael's eyes lit up.

"Let's have my share, then," he demanded.

"Who says you've got a share?" I countered.

"On that note of discord, I think I'll leave you," Andy announced. "Now, as I said. Call me any time."

AFTER REGISTERING AT the desk, I opened the envelope and gave Michael some funds. There were a lot of notes, and I didn't really know their worth, so was rather sparing, but he seemed happy. I knew it wouldn't be long before he was back for more. We agreed to meet up later for dinner.

The Regency was like one of those mid-priced Parisian hotels: genteel in a quaint sort of way, but where you half-expected to find Inspector Maigret investigating the brutal murder of a nondescript, middle-aged man who, only that morning, had been seen talking to a distressed young woman in the lobby. Michael and I were on different floors, which was just as well. I already knew more than I wanted about his private life and suspected he knew more than enough about mine. Besides, I had a personal mission, and wanted no interruptions. Even though it was only the middle of the afternoon, I was going to have a long, luxuriating bath.

My room was on the top floor, overlooking a small, unadorned courtyard, where a member of the hotel cleaning staff was indulging in a quick cigarette. I was surprised that the developed world's blitz against tobacco had spread to the Russian capital, where vodka, apparently, still sent more people to an early grave than any other indulgence. In a place where indulgence was in short supply, unless you were a member of the new rich, it seemed a little churlish to use the word vice. I suspected the fatwa against nicotine was not widespread. Leave those parts of the capital exposed to Western eyes and people would be extracting whatever pleasures they could from life, with the blessing of a state anxious not to succumb to the West's predicament of a steadily aging population. However, in the matter of passive smoke, I must confess to being a Jacobin. The guillotine is barely good enough for anyone who lights up next to me in a restaurant.

The bath was in the old style, with feet. The taps were worn and the water clattered out of the pipes, the cold with a rush and the hot at first with a dribble and bursts of steam until the system coughed itself clear. The luxuries were not generous, but I poured in something that claimed to be for the bath and soon had the beginnings of foam and an OK smell. While the water ran I inspected my belongings and laid everything out on the bed. It was a sorry sight. Even when they were clean, clothes suitable for the Chenchian mountains would hardly do for a capital city. I inspected the contents of the envelope again. There had to be enough for some shopping.

I sank beneath the bubbles and let out an audible sigh of pleasure. With my chin at the waterline, and the rest of me almost floating, I just lay there for so long that when I eventually felt compelled to move, it was because the froth had collapsed and the water become tepid. While I stood and soaped, I ran more hot. In the mirror opposite, I noticed a bruise on my right buttock that I must have picked up while cavorting with Aslan in Orla's pool, or was it really the heron's pool, or even Ula's? The thought of that time made me want him with a great eagerness and wish that the hands caressing my body were his and not my own.

THE SHOPS WERE better than I expected and after I had got the hang of the currency, I realized our envelope contained more than I could have hoped. Bernie was not usually this generous with his allowance, but then I did not know how long we were likely to be there. After buying one summer frock, one black evening dress and one power suit, appropriate for interviewing presidents of the Russian Federation, together with three pairs of shoes and various other necessities, I returned triumphant to the Regency with my haul. The envelope was certainly lighter, but it was not empty. To my surprise, I found that my old clothes had already been laundered.

Even after admiring my purchases and putting them away, it was nowhere near dinner time and I decided to go for a walk and find a cafe. I had noticed a park with one adjacent and headed for that. It was still pleasant and the cafe was doing reasonable business, although most people had left the park for the evening. I'd had a hankering for some iced tea, although didn't really expect to find any. The last time I had been in Moscow, the pleasures of the West had been largely absent.

The young man at the kiosk appeared eager to please, which in itself was an improvement from before, when Ula's surliness would have stood out as charm.

"Do you have iced tea?" I asked.

"Of course. Take a seat and I will bring it to you. Is there anything else you would like?"

I told him, no, and sat down at a table near a pond which was home to a group of overfed ducks that nonetheless approached me in the hope of some scraps. They struggled out and quacked in my direction for a while, but I ignored them and they eventually left like disgruntled waiters without a tip.

"They eat too much," the young man said, placing the cold drink in front of me. "People feed them and they can't resist."

"Do you mind me asking, is this your cafe?"

"Not mine, exactly. But my brother and I own the franchise. Whatever we make after paying the rent, we keep."

"When I was last in Moscow," I told him, "the service was terrible. It now seems much better."

"Many of us are working for ourselves now," the young man explained. "So it's worth making the effort."

"That's capitalism for you," I remarked.

"A lot of the older people don't like it. You have to work harder now and there are no guarantees."

"I can imagine. I have another question for you."

The young man looked around.

"We're not that busy now. Ask it."

"What do people think of this war with Chenchia?"

"Why do you want to know?" he challenged, looking suspicious for the first time.

"I'm a foreign correspondent, trying to do a story for my people back home."

"America?"

"Yes."

He seemed to relax.

"The Chenchians are terrorists. They blow up things in our cities. So we have suffered, like you. But I don't like this war. Too many people my age are getting killed. Getting drafted into the army. That's what I fear most."

"Is that likely?" I asked.

"Well, my brother and I run a business so we wouldn't be first on the list. But who knows? Anyway, I must get on. It was nice talking to you."

I was pleased my Russian had not deserted me. If I had a gift, it was for languages. The young man, it seemed to me, had said it all. For the Chenchians, their terrorist attacks were proving counterproductive, but their success against Federation soldiers was not.

I drank the tea slowly and looked into the park. Its few lights were on now and the remaining people were walking fast, anxious to get from one side to the other, not stay as they had wanted to earlier when the sun was out. Parks, all parks I think, become different places at night, inhabited by different human animals, or perhaps by the same human animals but with different human needs. This was not a big park and might soon be locked, denying itself to the night crowd. I remember driving through the Bois de Boulogne after dark for the first time with some friends. The horror and excitement, the sheer force of it, had startled us all.

It was as if we had passed into Dante's Inferno, where strange creatures in human form sought to entice us into their games. From open mouths, flesh waggled at us like vipers' tongues. Every movement offered a promise of extreme sensation, with male female and female a parody of itself of such power and provocation that escape, if you had allowed yourself to look, to become drawn, to feel the pull of its enticement, would have been impossible. We tried to laugh and joke, but when we had passed through, we were subdued, and not one of us, I think, had failed to recognize that part in ourselves from the darker side.

"Is there anything else you want? I'm closing up now."

The young man's voice pulled me back from a world I had unwittingly slipped into.

"No. Thank you. How much do I owe?"

"Sixty roubles."

I paid and he gave me a receipt.

"I don't want to startle you," he said, "but I think there was someone at that table over there watching you."

I *was* startled and looked across but could only see empty tables.

"He's gone now. I could be wrong, but you notice things when you have been doing this for a while. In the bad old days, everyone watched everyone, and you developed an instinct for it."

"What did he look like?" I asked.

"About my age. Longer hair. Darker skin. But we have many people like that. He wasn't unusual."

"Secret police?"

"Who can say? But I don't think so. He seemed nervous."

I left a generous tip and walked quickly back to the hotel.

IT WAS AFTER nine when Michael and I eventually headed out of the hotel for something to eat. The Regency did not even pretend to provide food, other than a continental breakfast. We found a small restaurant in Krimsky Street, only a ten minute walk away. I half-expected him to have picked up a companion already and want to cry off, but he seemed pleased to see me and I was even pleased to see him.

"New dress?" he asked, as we sat down and were given menus.

"Not bad," I commented. "Most men would have got through the entire evening without noticing."

"I was thinking about our allowance, actually."

"I should have guessed!"

"It is nice, though," he conceded.

"There is still some money in the envelope," I reassured him, without being too specific. "What did you get up to?"

"Not much. I read a bit, until I dozed off. All that rough living. I was more tired than I realized."

"Rough living?" I repeated, with just a hint of a smile.

"You can get used to anything, I suppose," he demurred. "But I would hate not to have a comfy bed ever again."

"Even one with only you in it?" I couldn't resist.

"Alright! So the Chenchians are a hospitable people."

I didn't let on that I knew just how hospitable. The waiter eventually came over and I gave him our order and asked for a bottle of red wine.

"So what have you made of it all so far?" I asked him.

"You mean the job?"

"No. Not specifically, more the situation we're dealing with here."

"I try not to think about politics," he confessed.

"You must have some thoughts, surely?"

Two bowls of broth and a basket of bread appeared and then the waiter opened the wine. There were only three other people besides us: a middle-aged man reading a book at a corner table, just the type I had imagined might have been found murdered in the Regency hotel, and a middle-aged couple whose enthusiasm for each other suggested they were not married. A meeting place for the young crowd our restaurant was not.

"I wouldn't want to live there," Michael proffered, after thinking about it.

"Because their customs are different, or because of the situation they are in?" I was determined to get something sensible out of him.

"Both, I suppose."

"So what do you make of the situation?"

"Look, I'm a cameraman," he insisted, showing signs of irritation. "I'll leave the politics to you."

"At home. Do you vote?"

"I guess. But there is not much point, is there? It doesn't change anything, does it?"

"What would you like to change?"

"I'd like to fix it so that Cindy never found my stuff."

"You've got me there!" I laughed, recognizing defeat. "That's probably not a matter the political process can help with."

Our bowls were cleared and something close to the boeuf bourguignon we had chosen was placed before us in their place. The waiter refilled our glasses. The lone man got up and paid and the male half of the couple looked spare while his companion visited the ladies room. I was almost becoming fond of the place. The wine was working.

"There is one thing bugging me," Michael suddenly said. "I just can't see why the Federation wanted to destroy those villages."

"To show the folks back home what a great job they were doing?" I suggested.

"Yes, but why three. What was the point in destroying three?"

That was only one of the things bugging me. I said nothing as I wanted to see where he would go.

"And one from each region," he went on. "That was so precise. I doubt most Russians know there *are* regions in Chenchia, let alone three. So what was the point? If all they had wanted was TV footage and a headline, any one would have done."

"Perhaps they just wanted to be fair," I proposed, my tongue firmly in my cheek.

He looked at me as if I was daft.

"Look at it this way," I suggested. "The Federation believes that the forces attacking its troops in and around Zoldek come from the regions. So on a day when most men in all three regions are expected to be watching the football match in the valley, they courageously launch simultaneous attacks on a village in each region. Not only do they want to make some easy headlines, but they want to force their opponents to the negotiating table."

"I'm not sure I'd want to negotiate if my family had just been massacred," Michael huffed.

"So the Federation leaders are stupid?" I offered.

He shrugged his shoulders dismissively at the suggestion.

"Perhaps they wanted to provoke," he speculated.

"And increase the attacks against them?"

I could see that the apparent cul-de-sac into which his mental processes had led him was now causing him the sort of pain I experienced at school, when my teacher told me to recite the thirteen times table after I had just managed the twelve.

"When do you think we'll be going home?" he asked.

"Homesick?"

"I think I prefer the easy life," he admitted. "When you shoot celebrities, the most you have to fear is being called a jerk. In this line of work you could end your days with a pole stuck up your rectum and out your mouth."

I grimaced.

"But isn't the real world more interesting?" I suggested, although I could see he was distracted.

"That's the fourth time that guy's walked past," he suddenly said.

I turned round in my chair and thought I saw someone.

"What did he look like?" I demanded.

"Scruffy. Long hair."

"What color hair?"

"Black."

"Was his skin light or dark?"

"Darkish. Hey, has someone been following you?"

"Possibly. I was at a cafe earlier and the owner said he thought someone was watching me."

To our waiter's alarm, we both got up and rushed outside. As we stared at the few people walking the pavement, two police cars sped past, lights flashing and sirens blaring.

"I don't suppose he'll come back after that," I said, almost to myself.

THE FOLLOWING DAY I got a call from Andrew Meadows telling me about a woman in the Gorlov district who had given interviews to several television stations. Apparently her son, a young Russian officer, had been killed fighting Chenchian terrorists, terrorist being the term used to describe any Chenchian not loyal to the Federation's puppet regime in Zoldek. As far as I had been able to determine, this applied to almost every Chenchian, apart from the handful happy to work with the Federation in return for lucrative positions or outright bribes, and *their* loyalty was especially questionable.

MRS. VLADIMIR PRESNIAKOV lived in an older block, marked by faded glory, and I wondered how many families that had once prospered under the Romanov emperors had survived communism. Surely they could not all have been displaced or killed? We were admitted by an indolent-looking man on the ground floor and trudged up an ornate, but dilapidated staircase to the fourth.

I pressed a worn bell-push and waited, with Michael panting behind me. It could have been worse. She might have lived on the seventh floor. I had been to a building like this before, except this was different; this was silent. The other had been teeming with people. Children running up and down the stairs. Shouts of anger and laughter pulsing through the air. In that first building, families had literally been stuffed into apartments once occupied by the rich, several to a unit, all waiting to be rehoused in a promised modern block on the outskirts of Moscow, a wait that had lasted twenty years for some.

A shriveled-up lady, poorly dressed, with wayward red lipstick and errant hair opened the door to us.

"Madam is waiting," she said, before I had even introduced myself. It was clear Mrs. Presniakov had few visitors these days.

My first impression was the smell of must and I wondered if Howard Carter had experienced the same when he stumbled into Tutankhamun's tomb. Then, as my eyes adjusted to the dim light, I noticed prints, from floor to ceiling, on both walls of the hallway, all depicting an aspect of military life: uniforms of every sort, guns, swords, cavalry at full gallop, men still whole before the ripping of musket ball and blade produced a winner. The shrunken lady, whose name we later learned was Tania, led us into a sitting room full of red damask, gilded wood and large oil paintings of no value but undoubted impact.

Sitting in a high-backed chair, next to a fire that had not been used for years, was one of those ladies, elegant, powerful, like a bird of prey, with white hair gathered into a bun, and piercing eyes, who would have ruled the imperial world with a rod of iron. In the window was a grand piano covered in photographs of men in uniform and women looking regal. These were family snaps of a different era. They were not designed to show off expensive holidays, graduations, the birth of children or weddings, but to underscore this family's position within the imperial hierarchy. In their midst, a vase containing flowers that had probably been picked furtively from the park that morning, served to provide a punctuation mark of studied informality.

"Please take a seat," she invited, gesturing to a chair opposite her.

She didn't even acknowledge Michael, regarding him, no doubt, as my servant and assuming he would know how to set up his camera without her help.

"You are from America?"

I nodded.

"A very crude country."

"Parts of it have become quite sophisticated," I countered. "Our frontier days are long gone."

She studied me, looking dismissively down her aquiline nose.

"Yes," she agreed, eventually. "The past is gone, but it still informs us. Can I offer you some tea?"

I said I would like that and she instructed Tania accordingly.

"You have come to ask me about my son, Vasilii. As you can see, he is with us."

Only then did I notice that there were pictures of the same, fine-looking young man, in various frames around the room.

"He was the last of the line. For more than three hundred years his family provided officers for the Imperial army. There were compensations, of course. We were always close to power, because we were the power. Even the communists could not do without Vasilii's grandfather. He was one of their generals and just too good to be purged, as many were. Vasilii's father died young, but he was already a colonel in the new communist army. That is the only reason I am here. Only the army could stand as a counterweight to the Communist Party and its secret police. Everyone in this building is connected to the army in one way or another. God willing, I will be left in peace."

"So, have you always lived here?" I asked.

"Oh, heavens no! We had great estates, but they have long gone. This belongs to the army, although I have had the use of it for over twenty years."

Tania brought through the tea, together with some small cakes. I was pleased to see that she included Michael and had already poured his cup, knowing that her mistress would never do so.

"What age was your son when he died?"

"Forty."

"And he had no children?"

"No. He was not yet married. He was in no hurry. I did not have him until I was forty. I had almost given up hoping for children when he arrived. He always took his time."

I turned to make sure that Michael was filming.

"Coming from such an old military family, death in battle must have been something you understood. So why have you been speaking publicly about your son's death?"

"Losing a son is one of the greatest sorrows for any mother. You can never be prepared for that. In this, I am no different from all mothers in similar circumstances. But that is not why I have spoken out.

"Vasilii was a good soldier. He was already a colonel, like his father, and I think would have gone all the way to general. His death was not the result of incompetence, or bad luck. It was the result of political meddling."

"Is that not a dangerous thing to suggest?" I asked.

"It is, and my friends are telling me I must stop. And after this interview, I probably will. My point has been made and other people inside the government and outside it, younger than me, who share my concern, can take up the fight."

"So what happened, Mrs. Presniakov? What was the political meddling that you believe gave rise to your son's death?"

"If you don't mind, my dear, Countess Presniakov. I know it doesn't mean anything any more, but humor an old lady."

"I'm sorry, Countess," I apologized.

And for some strange reason, I truly was.

She nodded.

"How much do you know about Chenchia?" she asked.

"Quite a lot, as it happens."

"Good. Then you will know that our troops have been in that country for some time. Until recently, until this business with the Faith Radicals, there was a reasonable understanding. Our troops remained in Zoldek and left the regions to run themselves. But Zoldek is now ungovernable. Every day there seems to be a new faction on the street. There are pro-Western democrats and pro-Russian democrats —yes, we do have them. There are the Faith Radicals who take their orders from the south and are the most radical. Each of the three regions has its own factions and some of those are split. It's a mess, and it need not have happened.

"Vasilii argued strongly that Chenchia should be granted a high degree of autonomy and left to deal with these problems. His point was that as all we were really interested in was the pipeline, our soldiers should remain in their barracks so long as that was left alone. Only if the pipe was attacked should they carry out reprisals. But our politicians saw it differently. They insisted on absolute political control. They forced our soldiers to fight a guerrilla war for which they were never trained. They even sent in their own secret police. Very quickly, order in the capital collapsed. There is now only anarchy.

"Six months ago, Vasilii was sent down to sort out the mess. He wanted our secret police sent home, our troops returned to barracks, and he began negotiating secretly with the leaders of the three regions. He never completed the job. His car was blown up with him in it. We are still not sure who was responsible. It could even have been elements of our own secret police. There is a lot of corruption. In any event, Chenchian terrorists were blamed—a blanket term for an enemy with many faces—and the situation has gone from bad to worse."

"Did you hear about the Argun massacre?" I asked.

The Countess nodded.

"I even saw your broadcast," she admitted.

I looked taken aback.

"You'd be surprised what finds its way to people. In the communist period, when there was no news other than the news our government chose to feed us, we became very inventive. Those in the military who learned what had happened in Argun found it deeply offensive. We were grateful that you were able to show the truth."

"Why do you think it did happen?"

"We are not sure. The command in Zoldek is split between the military and the secret police. Both are directly accountable to the president, but the secret police is closely linked to hardliners in the government."

"You mean President Nitup is not hard line?" I asked incredulously.

"I'm told the president was furious when your broadcast surfaced."

"Furious at its existence or at its content?"

The Countess shrugged.

"Who knows?" she sighed.

Tania came back in to clear the tea plates and in spite of a withering stare from Countess Presniakov, asked us if there was anything else we wanted. The Countess then asked me if I would like to see some of her old family photographs. I caught Michael's eye, and made an excuse for him to leave, as I was interested and he, clearly, was not. Even if he had been, I suspected he would have had to sit with Tania in the kitchen while the Countess and I enjoyed ourselves. I felt I was coming to understand the protocol of the *ancien régime*.

The photographs were remarkable, capturing the final moments of a ruling system that had been in place for over a thousand years. Armies of servants and relations stood in front of palaces for grand occasions. Hunting days, wedding days, even funerals were captured and frozen onto photographic paper. And, of course, there were the portraits. Men in military uniform, husbands and wives in formal robes looking like the rulers they were, children whose childishness was barely visible behind the stylized poses absolute stillness demanded. I don't believe I saw one smile in the whole lot.

Countess Presniakov showed not one iota of self-pity. "This was the way it had always been," she said. "We didn't know how to change. These people belonged to us, body and soul, and we belonged to them. Almost all of us, in the ruling class, were blind to the opportunities that the modern world was bringing to ordinary men and women. It was the middle class, in the cities, who could see the possibilities, but they did not know how to rule and we were reluctant to let them. The result was a complete collapse of traditional order and its redefinition around a new ideology that had only brute force and terror to underpin it. We had absolutely no experience of the new ways. Perhaps, if we had started long ago to change, a step or two at a time, we could have spared ourselves much misery."

As I got up to leave, she fixed me with her imperial gaze and I thought I sensed a softening.

"Take care, child," she warned. "What you are doing carries great danger."

CHAPTER 7

It was not long after I left Countess Presniakov that I became aware of him. I have often been followed. You develop a sixth sense about it. I think it has to do with patterns, this sixth sense. In the way that blind people take in sounds, levels and other unseen things that previously passed unnoticed, you become aware of an echo. Some movement, not far from you, begins to parallel your own. You may not hear it or see it precisely, but it insinuates itself into your consciousness, if you are alive to it.

The well-trained gumshoe knows that it is not merely a question of keeping hidden. It is the pattern of movement that has to be disguised. That is why agencies use relays, if they can, to break the pattern. No two people move in quite the same way, so that changing tails helps to break the rhythm between hunter and hunted. But this level of professionalism costs money. Mostly those who had followed me were individual men. I don't know why men. Perhaps they could say they fancied me if I rumbled them. More likely it was because agencies tend to be boys-own clubs at heart, except when they need to use the hooker hook. Then we girls have a role to play, although even on these occasions I think half of the men would like to play drag queen.

After his advice about rolls of paper, the next most useful thing my whiskey-pickled friend in the Kigali InterContinental told me was how to deal with tails. "Just remember, sweetie, the poor buggers are trying to do a job. Make it easy for 'em. That way, when you really want to slip away, they'll have got lazy." His own technique was to invite them over for a drink and then drink them into oblivion. I would love to have seen their reports when they tried to extract what had happened from their throbbing heads the following morning: *suspect had a few drinks at the bar and retired early.*

Whoever was after me was not professional. His movements were erratic, even desperate. He moved more like one being followed than one following. My first glimpse of him was at a news-stand. A rack of dark glasses had a small mirror at the top, so that people could check out which pair made them look coolest, smartest or most mysterious. I put one on and saw him looking anxiously about. He was disheveled, with dark skin and unruly hair that hung below his collar.

"They look good on you."

The voice of the vendor interrupted me.

"Thank you."

"You buy?"

I studied the glasses, as if giving them serious consideration. They were quite elegant and not expensive.

"Only 270," he pressed.

"OK. I'll have them."

He beamed and took my money. What the heck. DEMOS-TV could afford it. We were the top-rated news channel and Bernie was raking it in for his owners, and for himself, no doubt.

I walked casually for a while and thought about taking a cab, but remembered the advice: "make it easy for 'em." Besides, I was curious to learn what this young man wanted. He had almost certainly been after me since the previous day. Cutting across the corner of a handsome square laid out with grass and flower beds from which the Countess's maid had probably gathered the fine display that had adorned her mistress's drawing room, I ducked behind a large stone plinth that once might have supported the statue of a Count or Prince on horseback, before the ideologues of the *nouveau régime* had replaced it with a group of healthy-looking men and women, whose pure and eager expressions were clearly intended to extol the virtues of hard labor. Regimes might change, but the purpose of official propaganda rarely did: to make the power structure of the day appear unquestionable.

I waited with my back pressed against the cold granite. Moments later, an unkempt young man wearing a loose-fitting, green windbreaker, army surplus I guessed, stumbled out in front of me looking this way and that. For several seconds he searched, then sensing my presence, turned suddenly and stared at me open-mouthed.

"Alright," I said quietly. "What do you want?"

"What you mean?" he stammered. His voice was nervous and had a thick accent.

"You have been following me since we arrived."

He appeared to be wondering whether to maintain his charade.

"You are Orla Kildare?" he asked anxiously.

"And who wants to know?" I challenged.

"Yorgi."

"Yorgi who?"

"Is not safe we talk."

"So why are we?"

"Why what?"

"Why are we talking?"

"I see you broadcast on DEMOS-TV. You smaller."

"That screen puffs us all up," I told him.

Yorgi obviously didn't understand what I meant.

"But you prettier," he added.

How could I resist that?

"Do you want to come round to my hotel? We could talk in more comfort." As I said it, I hoped he didn't think I was propositioning him. But I needn't have worried. Instead of looking eager, or even pleased, he seemed gripped by panic.

"No time. We talk here. Now. Quick." The words 'now' and 'quick' were fired like cannon balls.

"OK. I'm listening."

"I Chenchian Democratic Movement. America our inspiration, but America no help. She did once help, but not now. Something changed. We not understand. You must find out and report. You report, that what you do, right?"

"Yes, I report."

"Then you report this. America help enemies of democracy."

"I need facts," I told him rather limply. "I can only report facts."

But he was preparing to leave. Like an animal sensing danger, he was anxiously looking about him, almost sniffing the air as his ancestors might have done a million years ago.

"I give you fact," he said, as he turned to leave. "Now you report, Orla Kildare."

I watched him go. He seemed to sidle off at speed not wanting to show the way he was going. A nobody whose nothingness stood out, like a single dried leaf falling from a tree in disjointed arcs. Eventually I lost sight of him within the kaleidoscopic movement of the city. But what he had left me with did not fade. Instead it grew.

At first, I was irritated. My pursuer's naivety was breathtaking! Approaching one of America's top journalists with an assertion and expecting it to be taken as fact. An assertion, moreover, that America was an enemy of democracy. How was I going to report that! And even if I tried, how would Bernie square it with our sponsors?

But there was something about the young man's earnestness, yes, his naivety even, that was persuasive. I'd been doing this job long enough to know that the important stories did not come gift-wrapped. An important story was one that jarred the status quo, unsettled perceptions, altered the way people thought about themselves and had to force its way into the world, into the official world that is.

I knew my country was not as good as it imagined itself to be, nor as bad as its critics claimed. But full-frontal criticism stood little chance of being taken seriously. Would the near genocide of the native American have been arrested if their plight had been better reported? I somehow doubt it. At the time, we white Europeans had our tails up for land and nothing was going to stop what we called progress.

If there was anything in the young man's story, there would be a reason for it. Realpolitik was more the rule than the exception, whatever people's moral claims. At least with realpolitik one could argue in the same vein, about whether such-and-such a course was really in our interests, whereas with ideology you were stuck. Having said that, ideological priesthoods seemed able to split hairs with the best of them, so perhaps there was not a great difference.

I worried about Aslan, though. Part of him was of my country and if we were about to cut loose, or worse, team up with the other side, he, and others like him, would be the losers. All those Americanized Vietnamese had learned *that* harsh lesson.

As I approached Srednij Street, a small group of people had gathered. Two police cars, their blue lights still flashing, were parked nearby. One officer was urging traffic to keep going while another was taking statements. Two others appeared to be holding either end of a measuring tape. I wondered if drivers carried insurance in the Federation.

As I reached the back of the growing crowd, an ambulance arrived, siren sounding, but otherwise at a somewhat leisurely pace.

"Not in much of a hurry," I remarked to the person next to me.

He ran a hand across his throat to indicate that whoever or whatever it was we were all straining our heads to see was past helping.

"What happened?" I asked, now as curious as the rest.

"I didn't see. Hit-and-run, from what they are saying."

'They' was anyone who might have known more than the next person. I pushed forward, hopefully in response to the journalist in me and not the ghoul, although, to be honest, I have always been the curious type. My mother waged a ferocious war against mice and I can remember dragging two of my childhood friends up to our gloomy attic to watch one poor creature haul its trap around the floor, like a convict with ball and chain.

"Hey!"

I was given a death stare by a plump lady who clearly thought my late arrival only entitled me to the cheap seats.

"What happened?" I asked.

Called upon to display her knowledge, she quickly became animated.

"Pow! A direct hit. It was going so fast. He didn't stand a chance."

"A pedestrian?"

"Yes, a pedestrian, but a running one." She seemed amused by this. "Didn't even see it. Instant, that's what I think."

And to emphasize the point, she slammed her chubby hands together with a sharp crack.

"The car. Did it stop?"

"Not likely!"

"Why 'not likely'?"

She looked at me as if I was a simpleton.

"Because he was on the pavement, of course! Joyriders, that's what they were. A stolen car no doubt."

I was about to leave when one of the policemen, anxious to display his trophy to the ambulance crew, pulled away a sheet covering the body. The green army surplus windbreaker was unmistakable. It had to be Yorgi. His untidy hair was now caked in blood and his face unrecognizable, but I knew it was him.

As I moved forward to take a closer look, two policemen began to push me and everyone else back. It was then I noticed that the ambulance was not one of the normal Moscow ambulances I'd seen hurtling about the city on their missions of mercy. The one into which Yorgi's body was being lifted had a nondescript look.

Troubled and a little scared, I pulled myself away from the crowd and started to walk quickly towards the Regency, which was now not far. I hoped Michael would be there. I needed a drink and didn't fancy drinking alone.

"Orla? Orla Kildare?"

I don't know whether it was the shock of what had just happened and hearing my name when I didn't expect it, but for a moment I experienced real fear. Being afraid is one thing, but real fear disorientates you. It makes you lose touch with your surroundings. It makes you fall inwards to a point of stomach-churning intensity that overwhelms all other sensations. Real fear I do not like!

"Orla, it's Andrew. Andrew Meadows, from the embassy."

I must have been walking like a blinkered horse, because he had to race ahead of me to make me see him.

"Andrew!" I blurted out. "What are you doing here?"

"I was on my way to see you," he answered trying to sound reassuring. "Nasty business back there. Did you see it?"

"No, not really. Someone hit by joyriders, apparently."

"Always makes you feel a bit queasy, doesn't it?" he said, clearly not taken in by my poor attempt at nonchalance.

"I guess," I agreed, a little ungraciously.

"Look, Orla, I've some good news. It seems President Nitup is going to agree to an interview.

"*WHAT'S UP?* You look frazzled."

Michael's unruly person, standing in the doorway of his room wearing only a towel, was strangely comforting.

"Can I come in?"

"Sure. Am I about to hit the jackpot?"

I gave him my best schoolmistressy look and sat down on the end of his bed.

"I don't suppose you've got a drink?" I asked.

"Sorry. We'll have to go out for that."

"Well, let's. I need one, a stiff one."

"Do you mind if I get dressed first? I've just been having a shower."

"I can see that."

He stood there, more vulnerable than I might have expected, staring first at me and then at the pile of clothes that were in a heap on his chair.

"I won't look. I promise," I assured him.

Unconvinced, he moved behind me and I held my head firmly to the front, only to find that I had a clear view of him, albeit in miniature and a little distorted, reflected in one of the brass knobs on the cupboard door.

"So what happened, then?" he asked balancing on one foot as he slipped on a sock. I have often wondered why men invariably pull on their socks before anything else.

"There was an accident, not far from the hotel."

"An accident," he repeated, now hopping on the other foot.

"Some pedestrian was hit by a joyrider, apparently."

"Nasty. Were they aced?" he asked, finally getting his shorts on and sounding more confident.

"Yes."

"Wow! Did you see it?" he questioned excitedly, firing a burst of deo under each arm.

"No. I arrived just afterwards."

"Oh."

His disappointment was muted by the T-shirt he had slipped over his head.

"It always shakes you, something like that," I confessed.

"True, although we've seen worse these last days," he reasoned, zipping his pants.

"That's a fact!" I readily agreed.

As Michael moved round to my side of the bed, I watched his image on the door knob disappear, and it occurred to me that his little hobby might have been quite fun.

"Since we are clearly not going to have sex," he proclaimed, "let's go and get that drink. This hotel has absolutely nothing, not even a mini-bar."

WE WERE BOTH relieved to get inside the bar around the corner from our spartan accommodation. It was busy, but we found a reasonably quiet alcove and I was soon sipping a vodka and orange, which was the closest I was likely to get to a cocktail.

"You know that person we thought was following us at the restaurant yesterday?"

"Yes."

"Well, I spoke to him."

"So who was he?" Michael asked, looking surprised.

"He claimed to be with the Chenchian Democratic Movement."

"There is one?"

"Apparently. Aslan talked about it when we were at university. The common belief was that America was behind it as a goad to the Federation. He didn't think much of it himself. A City thing, he called it, for kids who wanted a cause."

"That seems a bit cynical," Michael complained, eyeing up a pretty blond who sassed past us. "Don't we want to bring democracy to the world?"

"Not any more, it would seem. The young man said we were working with the opposition."

"With the Federation?"

"That's what he said."

"Hey, cool! We should get that on camera. There's nothing like poking a hornets' nest."

"Bad analogy. You are liable to get stung."

"Can of worms, then. Worms just slither away. Can you reach him?"

"Unfortunately not. He's dead."

"Jesus! How?"

"He was the one killed in the hit-and-run."

"You *did* say it was an accident?"

"I did. But I don't think it was."

"Oh mother fuck, Orla. What do you think's going on?"

I shrugged.

"Countess Presniakov certainly thought that if we were into lifting rocks we'd find snakes."

"You know her maid?" Michael started up excitedly, clearly anxious to pass on some gossip and change the subject.

"Tania?"

His head rocked up and down like a tremolo.

"I *bet* you didn't realize she was the Countess's cousin? She told me before I left."

"That or the poor house, I suppose."

"But honestly, Orla, would you domestic for your *cousin?*"

"If it was the only way I could stay in anything like the only world I had ever known, I suppose I might."

"You wouldn't!"

"After our civil war, life in the South was destroyed. Many blacks preferred to stay with the whites they worked for, but few whites had the money anymore."

"That's completely different," protested Michael.

"Is it? You saw what traditional life was like in the Chenchian regions. Not what we are used to, certainly, but perfectly real, perfectly complete and perfectly good."

"Aspects of it were pretty good," Michael smirked.

"So, imagine that is the only life you have known and then, it is gone. Suddenly you are told that the Federation way or the American way is the only way. Wouldn't you want to cling to anything from your past?"

"You are not saying we should go back to slavery, are you?"

"Oh, don't be silly! Of course I'm not. I'm just saying it's a lot easier to destroy a way of life than to build one. Change is always hard, no matter what, and we sure need to learn how to do it better."

"Another vodka?" he asked, seeing that my glass was now as empty as his own.

"Why not?"

"That was with orange, right?"

"Yes."

As he went up to the counter I watched him get close to the blond. She seemed interested and I suspected I would be returning to the Regency alone. I envied Michael in many ways. His horizon was short. He seemed to have concluded that the world's wicked ways were beyond his reach and so he'd make the most of what was to hand.

"You don't think we're in danger here?" he asked, returning with our drinks. "I mean, that man of yours being killed and everything. It's a bit, well, scary actually."

"As long as we stay on the right side of the story, we should be fine."

"Right side of the story?"

"Just don't go repeating what I said about the young man being killed deliberately, especially in your room. I know how you like to entertain."

"Bugged?"

"Almost certainly."

"Oh, fuck! I was thinking. . . ."

"I know what you were thinking. Try and go to her place, or just don't say anything about it. She could be one of them."

"Oh, no! I thought she fancied me."

"I'm sure she does."

"So that's why you came to my room? To let them know you suspected nothing?"

"'Fraid so."

"This is very bad for my ego!"

"I'm sure it'll recover. Now try and be a bit sharp tomorrow. It looks as though we've got an interview with President Nitup. Andrew Meadows told me. I came across him just after the 'accident'."

"*He* was there?"

"Exactly. An odd coincidence."

"Holy shit, Orla. This whole thing's beginning to stink. I want to go home!"

"To Cindy?"

He looked across at the blond who was now smiling at him.

"Perhaps not just yet," he grinned.

"Well have all your kit ready in the lobby by eleven tomorrow. Our meeting's set for noon."

CHAPTER 8

Malik Bassayev tethered his horse short of the ridge and crawled forward. Said and Rizvan followed. Far below he could see the man he was going to kill, the man he thought of only by his nickname, *bear*. The two fighters with him were nervous. Neither had met the speck of humanity whose life they were there to take, but both knew his reputation and both understood that, even if they were successful, they would be marked men for the rest of their days.

Rarely did their target travel without an escort, but Malik knew there were times when his adversary preferred to hunt alone, often for several days at a time. Hardly can the girl in the village across the river have realized what she was doing when she told Said, her lover from Malik's clan, that her chief had gone off into the hills alone.

It had taken a day to find him. As a boy Malik had played in these mountains and knew most of the good hunting grounds. With the wind coming from the east, the possibilities had narrowed. Carefully the three men crawled back to where their horses were now grazing and sat in a circle.

"Now listen," instructed Malik. "Our best chance of getting close is if he is concentrating on the hunt. What did you see down there?"

"We saw *him*," Said answered, increasingly worried that his girl would be implicated.

"Yes, I know we saw *him*," Malik snapped, "but what else did you see."

"A herd of deer, perhaps a thousand feet below him," responded Rizvan, a toothy young man with a scarred cheek and a bad character.

"Exactly! My bet is he will be going for them. Now we must try to catch up with our friend unseen by either him or his prey and come within rifle shot as he himself is about to fire. That way we will be closest at the time he is concentrating hardest on his own hunt. The hunter hunted."

Rizvan grinned, clearly impressed by the strategy.

"Now what route will he most likely follow?" Malik asked.

"He'll stick to the stream," suggested Said, anxious to redeem himself. "It'll give him cover all the way to the herd."

"Good!" acknowledged Malik. "But that presents us with an advantage and a disadvantage."

He paused, waiting for one of them to suggest what.

"He will have taken the best cover," asserted Rizvan.

"Precisely. And the advantage?"

Rizvan wanted to answer, but couldn't think of one and it was left to Said, the more measured of the two, except when it came to affairs of the heart, to try his luck.

"A stream like that is hard to climb down," he proposed tentatively.

Malik nodded.

"Which gives us time. We will ride back the way we came, drop down the far side of this ridge and then crawl across until we are opposite the herd. Sooner or later he will appear to take his shot and that is when we will take ours."

"Will we know how far to go down?" questioned Said.

But Malik had grown tired of the tutorial.

"I will know," he answered. "Now eat."

THEY DID NOT sit for long. The way down was steep and a steady drizzle made the ground treacherous. One horse after another slipped, its back legs buckling every time its rigid front legs greased forward, but somehow the animals managed to keep upright. The horsemen almost stood on a startled sand grouse, reluctant to fly on such a sodden day. The bird flapped angrily into the air but soon landed again, only a few yards away.

Each man had time to think, when he was not struggling to stay on his mount. Said wondered how he had gotten into this. It had been known he was seeing a girl in the neighboring region and Malik had asked him, personally, to report on the clan chief's movements. He'd not thought much of it. All three clan chiefs tried to keep an eye on each other. But to kill one. He had not expected *that*. Malik had only told them *what* they were tracking the previous night, when they were already a day's ride from the village.

Rizvan did not think much, if he could help it. He was pleased to have been asked by his leader to accompany him on a hunting expedition. So the quarry was human. That didn't trouble him. He'd killed a Federation soldier once, or at least thought he had. They had never actually found the body. He knew he had an evil streak in him. Everyone told him so. True, he'd stolen stuff from time to time and been involved in countless fights, but you had to make your own way in this world, didn't you? A life killing for his chief—why not? Someone had to do it.

Malik had been locked in thought for months. Sometimes it felt like years, a grand master aware of every piece on the board, planning his moves and countermoves, searching in his mind for the end game, the moment when a new equilibrium would be established and his war-torn nation could enjoy a period of peace. He had decided that everything— friendship, family, loyalty, even traditional agreements—had to be subjugated to this single objective. He minded having such a strained relationship with Roaz, but they sat on opposite sides of a river that ran through their history. Even his father was wedded to the old ways. The great burden he carried, he carried alone.

Judging that they had dropped down far enough, he dismounted and hobbled his horse. The three men trudged towards the ridge, their own feet doing little better than the horses' hooves on the slick and porous grass, itself barely clinging to the rock-strewn mountainside. The rain was falling harder now. Small rivulets trickled down their heads and tried to penetrate their neckscarves. Each man held his rifle tightly in the hand away from the hill, using the other as a third foot, to grasp tufts, steady himself against sharp stones, and catch the weight of his body whenever his two normal feet slipped out from under him.

Close to the ridge, Malik signaled the others to remain while he crawled forward. He had judged it almost perfectly. The herd of deer was opposite, about two hundred yards away, on a flat piece of ground beyond the stream. A few hinds were grazing but most were lying down. Only the stag moved slowly around his harem, alert to any challenge. It would be the stag his rival would go for. As soon as politics invaded a man's life, friendship became a luxury.

He studied the ground. If he were working his way down the watercourse, where would he take the shot? Slightly to his right, he saw that the stream fell off a ledge and plunged thirty feet or more into a pool. At the level of the pool he judged the herd would be impossible to see. So a shot would have to be taken from above the cascade. The ravine, chiseled out by the stream, fell steeply towards the ledge and, although full of awkward boulders, looked deep enough to hide a man from the plateau where the deer were waiting out the weather. A grassy pad next to the ledge, just clear of the ravine, would be the perfect place to take the shot. And even if there was a better vantage point higher up that he could not see, the kill would need to be gralloched, so they'd get a second chance.

He returned to his men and led them, on their bellies, to a point some fifty yards higher than he had been. The deer and the ledge were now in perfect view. All they had to do was wait. He lined up Said and Rizvan six feet apart, whispering into the ear of each where their target would be and telling them they had to fire in unison, but only on his signal. Then he lay between them.

The sound of rain encased the three and the sharp wind from the east carried their dank smell back towards the horses. Malik guessed that it would not be long before the hunter made it down the culvert. They'd had some distance to make up but their speed would have given them an edge. He'd crawled down streambeds often and it was tough. From the plateau, the stag let out a throaty grunt, just to make clear to any young males who fancied their chances that he would be ready for them, but no challengers appeared. The dismal weather had dulled even the imperatives of nature.

Their initial sight of him was almost comical. It looked as if the culvert was giving birth. First to appear was a head of hair. It stopped, becoming indistinguishable from the boulders. Then, cautiously, it emerged, a few inches at a time, and a man's shoulders came into view. He was face down, pulling himself forward on his elbows. Malik knew that every sinew in the hunter's body would be focused on moving without sound and out of sight. Almost slithering over the last rill, his rifle strapped to his back, the man entered the shallow water on the ledge and allowed himself to look up. Satisfied he could still not be seen, he hoisted his upper body onto the grassy pad and gathered his rifle.

"No," whispered Malik firmly. Knowing that both his men would be eager to fire.

The hunter dragged himself onto the pad and, pushing his rifle ahead of him, mounted a small ridge from where Malik guessed he could see the herd for the first time. He would pause, Malik knew, but not for long, to take stock and pick out his target. The stag sensed something and turned. There was a crack from the rifle. The beast quivered for a moment, took a few paces forward and then fell. As the hinds clambered up in confusion and began to scatter, the hunter slowly rose to his feet to survey the scene.

"Now!" urged Malik and two more rifle shots sounded.

The hunter fell forward instantly.

THEY COLLECTED THE horses and maneuvered down to the ledge. Malik crossed the stream and measured the distance to the dead animal: over a hundred paces. It had been a fine shot. As he slit the stag's belly and started pulling out the intestines, he noticed Said and Rizvan standing aimlessly by the corpse.

"Get it up onto one of the horses," he shouted. "And when you've done that, bring the other here."

This was not a time to hang about. Even with visibility as poor as it was, he didn't want to risk being seen any more than he had to. It was Rizvan who eventually came over and the two of them managed to drape the stag over the horse and strap it. Slowly they all worked their way back up the mountainside, Said and Rizvan on foot, a dead man on one of their horses, a dead stag on the other, and were eventually back over the ridge.

Malik knew exactly where he was going and the other two followed. No one felt like talking. After a mile or so, with the rain persisting and the mist starting to thicken, they reached the place he was searching for. It looked as drab and dreary as everywhere else they had passed, but Malik dismounted and began peering about him.

"Here it is," he announced, almost to himself.

Said and Rizvan came over on foot.

In front of Malik was a hole, about five feet in diameter at its widest, but otherwise, nondescript.

"Throw a stone in," Malik told them.

Both young men did as instructed and they could hear the pebbles clatter down, and down, and down.

"What is this?" asked Said.

"It's the shaft to an old mine. An air duct initially, but when the entrance collapsed they tried to use this."

"How deep is it?" wondered Rizvan.

"Deep enough," Malik told him. "Now get that corpse down it."

After heaving and pushing they eventually eased the body off the horse and into the opening. Just when it looked as though its leaden flesh and soaked clothes were stuck, some rocks gave way and the dead man sank out of sight into the ground.

"Brew up some tea," instructed Malik.

While Rizvan searched for anything that might burn, given a flame, Said removed a package of dry twigs and goat's wool from inside his coat. Leaving the two to work on the fire, Malik climbed the hill behind them until they were almost hidden by the pulsing rain. Sitting on a rock, he swung their victim's rifle off his shoulder and began to inspect it. A man's rifle was a personal thing almost as treasured as his wife. It was a fine piece. The sight had been set to a hundred yards, he estimated. He moved it to forty, moved it out to one-fifty and then back to forty. He opened and closed the breech, just to feel the action. He pulled the trigger, to see how light it was. The mechanism could accommodate five shells, so he pressed in five, and put one in the breech.

Below, against the odds, smoke indicated that the two were having some success with the fire. They were both huddled over it, no doubt trying to coax it into life. Malik lowered himself to the ground, rested the rifle on the rock, took aim and fired. One of his targets slumped forward and as the other, Said, turned in horror, Malik fired a second time. At first, he thought he had missed, because the boy stood up and seemed to be staring right at him in disbelief. So he fired again and this time Said was thrown backwards to the ground.

Deliberately, Malik collected the three shell casings and walked back down the hill. As he heaved first one body and then the other onto the empty horse, he saw that his second shot had passed though Said's cheek. Only his third, a heart shot, had killed him. Carefully he dropped the rifle and the spent shells into the hole.

Surprisingly, the fire was still burning. He poured himself tea and savored the heat entering his body. Behind him the horses moved restlessly under their loads. After gathering up the pots, he threw loose sod onto the sputtering fire. Looking around, he satisfied himself that their presence in that place had been disguised. What he couldn't erase, the weather soon would.

Malik mounted his horse and with the two other animals following, started for home. He, Rizvan and Said had been hunting. They had been successful. They had been ambushed. He was lucky to be alive. His tribe would not doubt him. Another move on the chess board had been successfully executed. He hoped he would forget the look on the boy's face.

CHAPTER 9

I tried calling Aslan on my way back to the Regency. The thought of Michael cavorting with the blond made me feel alone. But his cell was not switched on. It hardly ever was. I often wondered why he bothered to carry it. As Western as he had become, his instincts were still those of his people. "If I can be called I can be found," was the reason he gave. And I couldn't deny that he was probably right. So I called Dirk instead, even though it was only midday in the American capital. This time, I was in luck. His clipped "Dirk Ford" was instantly reassuring.

"Dirk, it's Orla. I hope I'm not interrupting anything.

"Good to hear from you, girl. No interruption. I'm at home, working on some papers."

"What papers?"

"Always the journalist!" he laughed. "Just the usual; stuff. Trying to work out how to get one powerful part of our great state to tango with another powerful part. The age-old dating game. How's it going?"

"Same old, same old. Watching humanity get bounced up and down upon the stage while your powerful interests dance their dance, full of sound and fury, signifying I wish I knew what—with apologies to the bard, of course."

"If any playwright understood power politics, he surely did. Great broadcasts, by the way. Causing quite a stir in this cynical old town."

"So Bernie left in some of the good stuff?"

"I should say so. Although I don't know what he cut out, of course."

"Dirk, I've got a question."

"Does that surprise me! Fire away."

"You know we were supporting the Chenchian opposition a while back. Could that have changed?"

"That's not my field, Orla, as you know. But I'll ask around."

"Thanks Dirk, honey. I'd appreciate that."

"Do you know when you'll be returning?"

"No. In two or three weeks, probably."

"Dinner when you get back?" he asked. "Or have old flames been rekindled?"

"I'd like that," I told him. Sure old flames had been rekindled, but I didn't feel like talking about it.

NEITHER DID I feel like staying cooped up in the Regency until sleep spared me from boredom. A disreputable colleague had told me about the *ZigZag* Club in Kuznetsky Street. It was way too early for anything heavy to be going on there, but it might while away a couple of hours.

The place was quite empty when I arrived. A small group were huddled near the bar looking more like refugees than happy revelers, while an illuminated man and woman pole-danced on two small circular stages, some eight feet apart, with greater stoic determination than erotic flare. I'd been told this was a happening space for men, women and all variations in between, but in spite of the art deco mirrors, chrome, and clever lighting, it felt every inch like an Edward Hopper diner.

A waiter showed me to a small booth at the back. It might have been deserted now, but in five hours it would be valuable real estate. I decided to stick with the vodka and orange and pulled out the dog-eared novel I was reading. Well, it was better than reading in my hotel room, surely? At least I could sip my drink and look up at the dancers from time to time. They were not bad looking. The man was black and nubile. The woman had an almost predatory sexuality. The lack of atmosphere was hardly their fault.

I'd read a chapter and was beginning to think I might as well be going back when a husky Russian voice addressed me.

"Why don't you go to a library for that?"

At first I didn't recognize her, all six feet, draped in a hooded, white fur coat.

"I'm too early, I guess."

"Too late for the library? Too early for the fun?"

"Something like that."

"Do you want to come with us? We're off to dance in another club. Smaller. More alive."

I KNOW I am a risk junkie. From my days in Sweetwater, that backwater parody of what its name suggests, I had made up my mind I was going to live. I was not going to lead a life constrained by thwarted ambition. Every corner that came my way I was going to look around. I suppose that is what drew me to journalism, and what drew me to Aslan. I had watched my mother wither on a branch of imagined social obligations, of needing to be the small thing that she was for fear of being nothing and, in consequence, becoming nothing. A fruit, drained of any sweetness it might once have had, through lack of sunlight.

"You speak good Russian, for an American," declared the fur-coated woman, whose name she told me was Liviana, or Liv, as we bounced along in the small taxi that was taking us I didn't know where. Between us was the lovely Sebastian, known, Liv informed me, as Seb, a sweet-seeming creature, clearly floating on a drug-induced cloud of happiness all his own.

"I was always good at languages," I told her, "and I had a Chenchian boyfriend."

"That will do it, every time," Liv acknowledged. "Love and hatred: mankind's great drivers. For the young it is love. For the old it is hatred. They are really both the same, you see."

I looked skeptical.

"They are," she insisted. "They are both ways of abandonment, ways of not having to think, a wonderful immersion in pure passion."

"*He* seems to have found an alternative," I gestured.

Liv nudged him in the ribs and he smiled an utterly contented smile, but said nothing.

THE BROVITSKY CLUB was everything the *ZigZag* was not: small, slightly tatty, packed with people, brimming with atmosphere, and completely Russian. Sebastian and Liviana took on a new lease of life, executing an outrageous routine on the bar top, to whoops of approval and encouragement from men and women alike. I had been introduced to just about everyone as "my friend Orla" by Liv, who I discovered was part-owner of the club. Vodka came at me from all quarters. There seemed to be a shortage of orange.

There are times when I think my white countrymen have forgotten how to enjoy themselves, so programmed are they. Only when a sign flashes laugh, do they laugh, or a book tells them that sex should be fun do they risk its enjoyment, albeit with a pang of guilt. Not so black Americans. We whites envy them for that, I think. But I suppose empires need repression in order to be built, and sacrifice. The Russian people know all about repression and sacrifice, certainly. But pleasure still seems to come to them naturally. I can't imagine communism would have been bearable otherwise.

"You say good things!" an enthusiastic man with a military crew cut shouted at me above the music.

"I didn't say anything!" I shouted back.

"Your broadcasts," he persisted. "I watch them. We all watch them in here."

Suddenly I felt more undressed than either of the dancers.

"I didn't realize I had a Russian audience," I protested.

The man picked me up off the bar stool, hoisted me onto the bar top and joined me. Liv and Seb both laughed and stopped their routine.

"You all know who this is," the man shouted at the amused onlookers. "This is Orla Kildare. The only honest journalist in Russia!"

By the look of it, everyone did know who I was, because they all raised their glasses and shouted 'Live long!', momentarily drowning out the rhythmic beat. Then, amid a clamor of back-pats and sounds of encouragement, the crew cut lowered me to the floor and escorted me to a back table.

"I hope we didn't embarrass you?"

It was Liv, sweat glistening from her body. For several seconds I just stared at her, wondering how someone could look that good wearing no more than a leather thong.

"You recognized me?"

"In the *ZigZag*, straight off," she admitted. "Why don't you come upstairs. We can talk."

I looked at the bar as a waiter brought across her fur coat.

"Time off," she said, reading my mind.

HER APARTMENT WAS small but nicely decorated. The sound from the club below was audible, but I guessed that she would only sleep when it slept. I almost didn't notice Seb sprawled on his back along a sofa.

Apart from a discreet pouch, nakedness seemed to be his natural state, and with a body like his it hardly seemed offensive.

"Away with the fairies," Liv murmured, seeing me studying him. "Such a lovely boy, isn't he? I try to stop him but it's his happiness and somehow he manages to dance. Well, you've seen *how* he can dance!"

I nodded appreciatively.

"Something to drink?"

I held up my hands in mock horror.

"No. I meant something soft. Downstairs is for profits!"

"Why do you dance in the *ZigZag* Club?" I asked. "You surely don't need to?"

She laughed.

"Here. Drink this."

The fruit mixture she gave me was light and refreshing and re-minded me of something I used to have as a child. A blackcurrant cor-dial, I think it was.

"The *ZigZag* is where the politicians go. We like to keep an eye on them in their natural state, as it were. Whenever they want to have a quiet meeting, they come in early. That's when we notice them. That's how I noticed you."

"Surely everyone's vetted?"

"Of course! But how do you vet dancers? And besides, Marco, the manager, has something on most of the powerful men and women in this city and believes, shall we say, in the freedom of information, Rus-sian style. Naturally, we do favors for our secret police occasionally, so we are appreciated. It's all very Byzantine."

"How on earth do you know who your friends are?"

"Believe me, you know."

One of Seb's feet slipped onto the floor with a thump, making him appear even more abandoned than before. Whatever raptures he was imagining inside his dream-filled head, his little pouch was finding hard to contain.

"Would you like to have him?" Liv asked, as casually as if she were offering me a canapé to go with my drink. "He makes love as well as he dances, although you would hardly think it now!"

"Tempting!" I smiled.

"All that beauty," she mused as we both looked at the slumbering Adonis next to us, "and then one day it is gone."

For a moment I was seeing Aslan asleep in my bed. Man-boy, boy-man. So vulnerable and yet so much . . . potential.

"Now, Orla, there is something you need to know."

Liv's words signaled that we were about to return to a less comfortable world. I looked towards her.

"Andrew Meadows, from your embassy, you've met him?"

"Yes. What about him?"

"He's not just diplomatic."

"I didn't think so."

"Good. Because he meets with Yuri Gregor, one of our top security people. And when I say top, he has the ear of President Nitup. They have been seen in the *ZigZag* Club together, several times."

"Do you know what they talk about?"

Liv let out a snort.

"*We* don't have the place bugged!"

"But any idea?"

"Our belief is that your country has agreed to help mine against the Chenchian rebels, as we call them."

"The global war against terror?"

"The global war against the world's two empires, more like!"

"Two? I thought ours was the only one left."

"We may be weak now, but Russia has always been imperial. Just look at our land mass."

"Are you sorry the Soviet Union collapsed?" I asked.

Liv did not answer at first.

"We did have pride then," she admitted after thinking about the question, "and our world seemed much safer, strangely enough. But communism! That was no way to live. Now, though, there are many in our government who fear the Faith Radicals. The war in Chenchia is part of a bigger war, to stop the Faith spreading into our southern states, our oil-rich states."

"Oil!"

"Yes, oil. Useful stuff. But this war is not popular. Too many young men are dying. The one who embarrassed you downstairs, at the bar. He was there for five years. It was not just the friends he lost. It was the things he had to do. Women and children. He wept when he saw your broadcast."

I felt a sudden chill imagining what the hands that had lifted me might have done.

"Did you know someone called Yorgi, a member of the Chenchian Democratic Movement?" I asked.

"The boy who was killed? No, I didn't know him."

"But you knew he had been killed?"

"I knew he had been murdered."

"Why?"

"The CDM are a sideshow. An American thorn in our side which the Americans no longer want."

"The Americans murdered him?" I asked aghast, sensing a good story.

"No. We did. But your people set him up."

"I was the bait?"

"I'm afraid so."

I started to feel sick. Now I was the story.

"How do you know all this?"

"As I told you. We work for the secret service from time to time. There are a sizeable number of people in the government who are against this war."

"And me? What do you want of me?"

"Don't get killed and keep reporting."

"But you might never have met me."

"One of us would. The blond in the bar you and your cameraman visited. . . ."

"Oh fuck! This is sick."

"It's a sick world, Orla Kildare. Now, sleeping beauty and I have work to do downstairs. Do you want to stay, or have you had enough?"

"I'd better be getting back. I have your president to interview tomorrow."

Liv seemed unimpressed, doubtless because she already knew. Instead she was attempting to rouse Sebastian. Miraculously he stood up, shook himself, and appeared ready.

"You'll find a taxi outside the door. Tell him to take you to the Regency. You won't have to pay. He works for us."

"Can I use your bathroom?"

"In there."

When I came out, Liv was replacing the oil on her dancing partner's body that the towel on the sofa had rubbed off. She grinned.

"Just remember what you missed!" she taunted.

"I'll have a hard time forgetting!" I admitted.

"On the table there. I've written out the address of a club in Zoldek in case you have to go back. There's a dancer you can trust. Her name's Amanta."

As I sat in the taxi, speeding towards the Regency, I felt like Alice stepping through the looking glass. Whether it was to or from Wonderland I wasn't sure.

MICHAEL WAS WAITING for me in the lobby shortly before eleven next morning and we were soon on our way to the Kremlin. For once I was not anxious to ask him about his evening, as I felt I had plenty to hide about my own. Going to a club singles-style and then going on to another with two dancers! Somehow I felt that any moral authority I possessed would be dented if I were to confess to that. I could have put it down to journalistic curiosity, I suppose. The fact that I had stumbled onto a golden seam of information by chance was something he didn't need to know. The 'by chance' bit, anyway.

"Sorry I cut out on you last night," he apologized, which made me think his evening had not been an unalloyed success. He often 'cut out' and rarely apologized. Besides, I'd made it clear at the outset that our free time was our own.

"That's alright," I reassured him, resisting the temptation to be drawn.

"So what did *you* get up to?" he asked.

"Oh, I read my book."

The taxi rattled on and Michael's question and my answer hung in the air like two undocked spaceships.

"You know that blond?" he eventually said.

"The pretty one at the bar?"

"Yes. Well, you know what?"

"No. What?"

"She was a boy-girl!"

He fairly spat the words out, as if they tasted foul.

"Dare I ask when you found out?"

"Too bloody late!"

I could hardly contain my mirth. Suddenly my own evening was sounding less bizarre.

"Perhaps you needed to broaden your horizons," I chortled, tears now streaming down my cheeks.

He grunted.

"Judging by that photo you showed me," I taunted, "I thought she looked a lot like your Cindy!"

I couldn't resist it. And anyway, he-she-it did.

I felt him squirm in the seat next to me.

"Not exactly!" he grumbled.

I had to look away. The thought of it all was just too much.

AS WE DROVE alongside the Moscow River, the Kremlin came into view. It is surely true that you can judge a people by how they express themselves in their art, and great buildings are undoubtedly that. The sheer mass and magnificence of this country's political center tells you of a great people who admire strength. But the whites, greens, and bulbous droplets of silver and gold, like upturned Christmas ornaments, wrapped in a wall of red, broken only by occasional pointy-pepperpots in black and green, tell you, also, that these same people have a gaiety about them too. Of the West they are not. No Greco-Roman regularity here. More Eastern, but not that either. These are the Russians. They are themselves. Able to sing and drink and dance. Able to write, paint, and build. Able to survive the harshest winters within a vast landscape. Able, in their millions and if they must, to kill and die.

We entered through a side door and were escorted along many corridors, into and out of several elevators, which took us both up and down, until we reached a large ante-room decorated with burnished gold. In amongst the gilt were mirrors, giving the place an ecstatic look, like a dowager about to receive a birthday cake. At one end was an enormous table with one large chair behind it and one much smaller chair in front.

"You can set up your cameras there," the aide accompanying us said, pointing towards the table.

"Wouldn't the president like a more informal setting?" I suggested.

The aide ignored my question.

"The president will come when he is ready," he said instead, adding, "that's assuming he comes at all."

"He *is* going to come, isn't he?" I asked in far too pleading a tone.

But the aide just shrugged and left us.

"I hate these mirrors," Michael remarked.

"Reflection?"

"I'm going to have to watch the angles. Will you sit in the president's chair, Orla. I'll start with that."

I sat in one chair and then the other, while Michael sorted out his equipment. One camera for President Nitup, another for me. And, of course, the lights. Every time he moved one, its beam bounced around the room like an unruly Tinkerbell.

"Are you going to manage?" I wondered aloud.

"I expect so," he answered rather tetchily, still smarting, I imagined, from the night before.

"Now, I need to do the sound," he told me. "Can you start talking?"

I had been working on my questions all morning.

"Mr. President. Thank you for agreeing to this interview. As you know, DEMOS-TV is America's leading news program. . . .

"Mr. President, perhaps you could share with us your views on international terrorism. . . ."

Like Michael, I was going to have to watch the angles.

WE HAD WAITED almost two hours before a flurry of activity at the door heralded the president's arrival. While he was being prepared for the camera an assistant asked to see my questions. Quickly, he cast his eye down the list . . . yes, yes, yes, no, yes. . . . Suspecting this would happen, I had not included any I thought might be considered contentious, but even so, the aide found several he did not like. Mostly they related to the length of the war in Chenchia and the number of Russian casualties. The president's advisors were clearly aware that my broadcast would not end up in front of American eyes alone.

In my best Russian, I began the interview.

"Mr. President. Thank you for agreeing. . . ."

"No! No! No!" the president exclaimed. "You speak to me in American. I answer you in Russian."

His interpreter shifted nervously and I started again, in my own language.

"Mr. President. Thank you for agreeing. . . ."

"It is always a pleasure when our two great nations speak to each other," and his interpreter repeated the answer, word for word.

"Mr. President. Perhaps you could share with us your views on international terrorism."

"I share the belief of your own president that this is the single most important international issue the world faces. It is vital, in my view, that our two countries work together."

Again, the interpreter repeated the answer in American, almost word for word.

"Are you satisfied with the cooperation between our two countries at this time?"

This question was not on my list, but the aide made no move. The interpreter relayed my question and the president's answer more or less intact.

"We are moving in the right direction," he said.

"Is my country working actively with yours in Chenchia?"

While the interpreter relayed my question, the aide whispered into the president's ear.

"We do not require any direct assistance from your country in that regard," came back the answer.

"Is it not true, Mr. President, that until recently, my country actively supported the Chenchian Democratic Movement?"

Again, the aide leaned forward and said something to the president.

"I am not aware of any such movement," came the president's reply through his interpreter.

"Turning, if I may, Mr. President, to your domestic situation, what is your feeling about the mounting body of opinion in Moscow against the Chenchian war?"

Before the interpreter had even finished delivering my question, President Nitup fired back his answer.

"I must find out who you have been talking to!"

The smile that accompanied his answer was chilling.

"There are strong feelings. . . ." I started, but without waiting for the interpreter or his aide, who was now hopping from one foot to the other, the president elaborated.

"Our soldiers are doing an excellent job protecting the people of Chenchia from the barbarous terrorist attacks that afflict their capital, almost daily. Indeed these soldiers are the first line in the defense of our own capital against such outrages. I don't have to tell you what carnage terrorist attacks against a capital can inflict."

The interpreter was now struggling to keep up.

"If the attacks against your troops are escalating, does this not suggest you are losing this war?"

"We are not losing this war. We are winning this war. And it is important to stress that this is not a war against the Chenchian people, but against the terrorists who are seeking to disrupt their lives—and ours."

"Mr. President. If the terrorists are not Chenchians, who are they?"

"They are the same Faith Radicals who attacked your country," he answered. "I'm sure there are Chenchians amongst them who have been led astray. But are there not American Faith Radicals and British Faith Radicals? This is a shared problem."

"What do you believe motivates these terrorists, Mr. President? Do you see them as being essentially nationalist movements or religious movements?"

At this question, the interpreter labored, as if he was having difficulty and the aide, once more, bent towards his master's ear.

"Whatever the motivation," the president eventually replied, "killing innocent women and children cannot be tolerated."

"I take it, Mr. President, that applies equally to innocent Chenchian women and children?"

I knew this would be my last question. It was inconceivable that the president had not heard about my broadcasts and my bet was he had even seen them. But a flurry of activity behind him, as a second aide rushed into the room with a message, altered the dynamics of the interview entirely. The president read the message and looked grave.

"I have just been advised," he announced, staring straight at the camera, with the words of the interpreter echoing his, "that Chenchian terrorists have taken a whole school hostage in Seblan and that they plan to blow themselves and the children up, unless their demands are met. These, Ms. Kildare, are the sort of people we are up against. This is not a game played out for prime time television, in your country or mine."

The interview was at an end.

Flanked by his aides, the president marched out, leaving Michael and me standing agog in the mirrored room, which seemed suddenly purposeless, now that the power it had been designed to enhance had left. Even the desk and two chairs resembled punctuation marks without a sentence.

"Jesus, Michael. We must get this back to Bernie!" I exclaimed. "Where the hell's Seblan?"

"Don't ask *me*, Orla," Michael pleaded, clearly rattled by the poignancy of the moment.

"It's in the south of the country, close to our border with Chenchia."

Neither of us had noticed the aide, who had escorted us into the building, return.

"You will be wanting to send your broadcast?" he inquired.

"Yes," I readily agreed, taken aback by his apparent willingness to help.

"Let me take you up to the roof. You will get a good signal from there."

Michael and I looked at each other, as if to say, *did we hear that?*

Half imagining we might be about to take the fast way to the ground, we followed with the equipment Michael needed. He checked for a signal. It was good and I called the station on my cell to alert them.

"It will take us a little time to edit the interview," I explained to the aide, "before we can send it."

"There will be no need to edit," he asserted, firmly.

"Not edit," I quickly corrected, realizing by edit he thought I meant rearrange for propaganda purposes, "prepare for broadcast."

He seemed only moderately reassured by that and watched while Michael and I played back the interview, cutting in shots of me with shots of the president. In fifteen minutes we were satisfied and I invited him to watch the finished tape. I thought he would want to cut out my last question, particularly as the interpreter had not even relayed all of it to the president before the news from Seblan had electrified the room. But he raised no objection. The Russians probably felt that one sin could be washed clean by another, and in TV terms, they might have been right. It is usually the most recent image that resonates loudest, although at this point all we had was a chilling announcement. The harrowing images would doubtless follow.

I sat alone for a while preparing my opening and closing remarks and then signaled to Michael that I was ready. He established the connection.

"Steve, this is Orla. Are you set?"

"Hi, Orla, What horrors from the evil empire have you for us today?"

Embarrassed, I looked sideways at the aide, but I don't think he heard.

"I have an interview with President Nitup for you, Steve, and tell Bernie this is red hot. It contains some breaking news, some real big breaking news. Have you got that?"

"Yes. I've got that, Orla. When you're ready. . ."

With world terrorism an issue in every capital and the war in Chenchia showing no sign of ending, there is mounting concern that world leaders are finding it hard to contain the problem. A short while ago I interviewed President Nitup of the Russian Federation.

Mr. President. Thank you for agreeing. . . .

It is always a pleasure when our two great nations speak to each other.

Mr. President. Perhaps you could share with us your views on international terrorism?

I share the belief of your own president that this is the single most important international issue the world faces. It is vital, in my view, that our two countries work together. . .

. . . .and my broadcast continued to its startling conclusion. . . .

What do you believe motivates these terrorists, Mr. President? Do you see them as being essentially nationalist movements or religious movements?

Whatever their motivation, killing innocent women and children cannot be tolerated.

I take it, Mr. President, that applies equally to innocent Chenchian women and children?

I have just been advised that Chenchian terrorists have taken a whole school hostage in Seblan and that they plan to blow themselves and the children up, unless their demands are met. These, Ms. Kildare, are the sort of people we are up against. This is not a game played out for prime time television, in your country or mine.

As you have heard here first, the cycle of violence contin-
ues and we must ask ourselves a question: are world leaders
dealing with the symptoms of an international disease, or its
cause? This is Orla Kildare reporting live from the roof of the
Kremlin, in Moscow, for DEMOS-TV.

"Orla, this is Bernie. That was great. Just great! Now where the
hell's this Seblan place? I want you down there."

"In the south, somewhere, Bernie. We'll need clearance."

"Don't you worry about that. Now let's quit talking and have you
on your way. Sort it out with Andrew Meadows."

I stood there still staring into Michael's camera. Who the hell was
running who in all of this?

"Orla, its Steve. That's us out of nickels. Good luck."

"Thanks, Steve," I replied but I don't think he heard me. The link
had already been cut.

IN THE TAXI, on our way back, neither Michael nor I talked at first. He
was fiddling with his machinery and I was wondering what had just
taken place.

"See if you can make anything of this, Orla," he said eventually,
handing me an earphone.

I attached it and he slipped a switch on one of his gadgets. There
was some static, two people exchanging remarks in Russian and then
more static. One of the voices could have been the president's but the
sound had a hollowness about it, so it was hard to tell.

I could pick out only two sentences:

"Why the delay?"

"I'll need to find out."

I opened my note pad and wrote *when did you get this?* and then
handed the pad to Michael.

He wrote and handed the pad back.

When they had left the room.

I looked at him. It must have been clear from my expression that I was angry and didn't want to talk about it in the taxi.

When we were outside the hotel, about to haul our stuff inside, Michael asked his question.

"So what did I get, Orla?"

"Are you up to your tricks?" I hissed.

"Just the focus mic, for God's sake."

"Look, Michael. I want to get out of here in one piece. Don't you ever, and I mean ever, try anything without clearing it with me first. **Do you understand?**"

"OK! OK!" he pleaded. "But I take it I got something?"

"You got nothing. Now whatever that is, erase it."

"S-O-R-R-E-E!" he protested.

I don't know why I was feeling so anal. I knew it wasn't just because some amateur voyeur on my staff had tried to spy right inside one of the most sophisticated intelligence networks on the planet, without my knowing. There was something about that one sentence *Why the delay?* that really bugged me. Was I becoming paranoid? Having stood in a room of mirrors for over two hours, was I starting to imagine myself in a world of mirrors? Surely I had played enough party games to know that any sentence could take on almost any meaning if it was placed inside a particular context. And in this instance, the context was my own imagination. I told myself to grow up. But the worry monster wouldn't leave me alone.

There was a message from Bernie waiting for us. We had been booked on an evening flight to Seblan. He must have grabbed seats before our broadcast had gone out. By now every foreign correspondent and his camera crew would be trying to get there. I looked at my watch. It was half three. The flight wasn't until seven. I guessed we should be at the airport around five, to stay ahead of the eager beavers who would be trying to bribe themselves onto the plane. That gave us an hour to get ready.

I lay on my bed exhausted. It didn't do to be too reflective in this game. My task was to report. But report what? What I saw? What Bernie wanted me to see? What Andrew Meadows, President Nitup, or the great American public wanted me to see? Whatever the hell objectivity is, I was having a hard job pinning it down. Perhaps reality is only ever visible in the rear mirror. In the here and now, we are part of the story—part of this person's lie or that person's truth. And always hostage to our own uncertainty.

I wanted to close my eyes. But I needed to pack.

CHAPTER 10

The check-in gate at Moscow's Sheremetyevo Airport was like the eye of a needle through which a caravan of the world's press was trying to pass. A half-full flight was what the airline normally expected, a harassed official told me. Seblan was on the periphery of its vast network, a two-and-a-half hour flight away. But our destination was about to become the center of the media world. The artist Andy Warhol is supposed to have said that in the future, everybody would be famous for 15 minutes. Well, the good people of Seblan were about to have their turn.

Although we arrived with almost two hours in hand, it was already plain the flight was seriously overbooked. Check-in staff were looking for any excuse to bump passengers onto other flights, to almost anywhere. With all of Michael's equipment we were overweight, as usual, and a harassed girl behind the desk said it just wouldn't be possible. A supervisor was working the stations and he asked to see our tickets. I handed them over, together with a large bill, discreetly placed. With the dexterity of a conjuror he returned our tickets, minus the money, which I swear I did not see disappear into his pocket, and instructed the girl to issue us with boarding cards. By the time our flight left, almost an hour late, he must have made a tidy sum.

The aluminum tube was packed to bursting. As the aging Tupolev trundled down the runway, it felt as though the pilot was struggling to haul us off the ground. A hearty cheer accompanied his success. Many of the faces on board were familiar to me. I had avoided the bar at the airport. There would be time enough to fraternize when we reached our destination. Journalists do a lot of hanging about waiting for things to happen.

It's a bizarre system, really. Around the world, twenty-four hours a day, television stations wait, primed for that thing called *news*. At the sharp end are people like me, more often than not twiddling their thumbs waiting for something to happen. It's amazing what you can come up with when your station insists on a report to fit its broadcast schedule. Much of what passes for news is little more than cocktail party chatter, really.

"Oi t'ought it was you, Orla."

I'd seen Desmond O'Connor in the bar. The *New Irish Times* was lucky to have him, a fact he regularly pointed out to them. His ancestors and mine had fought a centuries-old duel against the English occupiers of their land and Desmond had an instinctive suspicion of all authority. He had a nose for the political lie. For some reason this did not apply to his own country. He treated every scandal that slipped out of his young republic with fatherly indulgence. "Boys will be boys!" he would say whenever a politician was caught with his hand in the cookie jar. An avuncular "Well, what do you know!" would exonerate any barefaced lie, diligently uncovered. No doubt this small failing was why his editor sent him to report on events abroad.

"I see you managed to get a place, Desmond," I observed, as he grinned at me from the slender push-down seat opposite the galley.

"Not'ing but first class for t'is *Times* reporter, Orla," he assured me, his more than ample frame spilling off the reduced structure supporting him. "Here oi have food, drink, girls—oi'm only a shuffle away from t'e exit and from where you're going. Would you loike me to join you, boi t'e way?"

"I think I can manage, Desmond."

"No doubt you can girlie, no doubt you can," he repeated, rather wistfully. "You know, oi've never done it in one. T'ats somet'ing oi must rectify before t'e Grim Reaper cuts me off at t'e knees."

"If I feel the need, I'll send for you," I promised.

"You do t'at. Now what do you know about t'is business?"

"Not much," I admitted. "I was interviewing President Nitup when the news came through."

"Congratulations on your broadcasts, boi t'e way. Do I gat'er a little student nooky has given you an insoid edge on all of t'is?"

"I had a Chenchian boyfriend," I acknowledged "so let's say I know more about that part of the world than ninety percent of the world's media."

"T'an a hundred percent, most loikely."

"So how did you learn about it?" I asked.

"Well, when your latest came out, around t'ree t'at would have been, now wouldn't it, t'ats when t'e excrement hit t'e fan, if you'll pardon me. But oi'd had a call from a contact in Seblan around eleven t'is marning, saying somet'ing was going on."

"Around eleven?" I asked. "Are you sure?"

The door opened and it was my turn.

"It would be about t'at, oi would t'ink. Between eleven and twelve. Oi was taking t'is gargeous girl from Kazakhstan out to lunch. Full of information she was, some of it even printable...."

There was already a line behind me. All that time at the bar, no doubt. My excuse was a compunction to 'go' whenever I had the chance. By the time I came out, Desmond was halfway down the plane, impeding the galley crew and talking to at least three people in three different rows.

Michael is not proving to be a very rewarding travelling companion. He is usually plugged into something. That is better than mindless chatter I dare say and I must admit, trying to have a conversation in a noisy airplane is a struggle at the best of times. Even so, I would have liked to talk. I had things on my mind. The distraction would have been welcome.

Luckily, I dozed off. When I awoke, the atmosphere on board was somber. Even Michael was eager to talk.

"We have been round twice," he informed me. "The captain says the cloud cover is very low."

"Did he mention an alternate airport?"

"He mentioned returning to Moscow, but I think that was a joke."

"Did anyone laugh?" I asked.

"No. There was a groan that just filled the cabin."

I gazed out of the window. We seemed to be skimming across the tops of clouds disembodied by the lights from our plane. Occasional jerks, every time we hit an air pocket, added to the sense of unease. What would happen, I wondered, if the news gatherers became the news? A sort of Socratic riddle. If all the news gatherers were killed in a plane crash, would that be the end of the news?

The voice over the intercom was familiar, although I couldn't place it at first.

"If y're all sitting comfortably," it said, "then oi'll begin."

> *God's plan made a hopeful beginning,*
> *But Man spoilt his chances boi sinning;*
> > *We trust t'at t'e starry*
> > *Will end in great glarry,*
> *But at present t'e ot'er soide's winning.*

"Now t'at oi have y'r attention, oi t'ought you moit enjoy a starry, as we bob around up here somewhere between t'em pearly gates and t'e flames of hell. T'ats unless you wish to contemplate t'at slender t'read we call existence. For moiself, oi intend to confess moi many and grievous sins to a bottle of whiskey, because oi'm hoping t'e whiskey, having had a hand in most of t'em, will be sympat'etic."

"Sir!" exclaimed a harassed stewardess, who had rushed forward from the back of the plane. "I must ask you to put that down!"

Cries of "Shame!", "What's the harm?", and "Let's hear it!" greeted her understandable intervention. With the plane rocking and lurching she looked confused and against whatever regulations were still being applied to our over-stuffed flight, opened the cockpit door and disappeared. We imagined she was summoning the captain. But the captain clearly had much else on his mind, because she was soon out again and saying something to the man occupying her normal seat.

"Oi'm told t'is open moic," announced the voice which I now realized belonged to Desmond, "until t'e captain foinds our runway, which t'is lovely darling here assures me is down t'ere, somewhere."

Nervous cheers erupted down the length of the cabin and the poor stewardess looked flustered, but somewhat relieved, as she returned to the only seat available for her, at the back of the plane.

"Oi'll be having you all strapped in t'en, if y're nat already," instructed Desmond, relishing his new role.

"Now t'is nat moi starry but one told by a great raconteur from moi own country, Mr. David Allan, who sold himself far a ton of money—oi'm pleased to say—to t'e English. Which just goes to show t'at even t'e devil himself can enjay a good laugh.

"T'is, t'en, is t'e starry. An English soldier goes to Oireland for a vacation because he knows he can get t'e best whiskey t'ere."

Desmond supped from his glass.

"Well, after having had quoit a noit of it he foinds himself wandering along t'e soid of an Oirish road at a very early hour of t'e marning."

"You sure he was an English soldier?" an English voice shouted out from somewhere in the cabin.

"Well, let's just say oi know how he felt," countered Desmond, relishing the participation. "Now, coming up t'e road is an Oirish farmer on his way to market. In his wagon is his proize pig and pulling t'e load is his best harse. When t'e Oirishman sees t'e soldier he t'inks, 'Poor soldier. Out t'is early in t'e marning walkin' alone. Oi should offer him a roid.' So, he pulls up next to t'e soldier and asks if he wants a roid into town."

A frightful lurch grabbed the plane sending it up and then down, causing everyone to shout *wow!*

"Oh, Jesus!" complained Desmond, somehow managing to hold onto the mic *and* not spill his whiskey. "Now t'e English soldier isn't too sure about accepting a roid from an Oirishman, especially when he sees, sitting on t'e flarbards, t'e farmer's roifle. But t'e farmer insists and t'e soldier is quoit drunk.

"When t'e soldier is in t'e wagon, t'e farmer realoizes he is running late and coaxes his harse to go faster. Just at t'at moment a woild rabbit runs across t'e road and scares t'e harse. T'e harse breaks into a mad gallop and no matter how hard t'e farmer trois to stop it, it won't slow down!

The plane made another wrenching judder and someone shouted "rabbit!"

"We'll be dodging t'e angels, more loik," claimed Desmond, taking another nerve-settling gulp. "Anyways, t'is harse makes a sharp turn and t'e wagon tips, shooting everyone out. T'e soldier lands in a ditch, face down, and can't move. He knows he's broken at least one arm and a leg. He is feeling dizzy and t'inks he might even have sustained a concossion. He has trouble seeing from one oiye and knows it is bleeding.

"From behoind him he can hear t'e farmer moaning over what has happened. 'Oh, my poor pig! You've got a nasty cut in your soid. Oi'd best be puttin' you out of your misery.' And t'e soldier hears t'e farmer foir his roifle into t'e pig. T'en, t'e farmer sees his harse. 'Oh, my poor, poor harse! You've broken a leg. Oi best be puttin' you out of your misery.' And t'e soldier hears t'e farmer foir his roifle into t'e harse. T'en he hears t'e farmer coming closer to him. T'e farmer turns t'e soldier over and says, 'oh, you poor soldier . . . how are you?' T'e soldier replies, quick as a flash, 'Oi never felt better in me loif!'"

Spontaneous clapping and shouts of "more" erupted all round, helping to strengthen our skin-deep courage.

"No man should doi sober," asserted Desmond, when the applause had reluctantly subsided. "More of t'is sweet nectar is what oi need!" As our transport nosedived towards the ground, he drained his glass and crossed himself.

What the regular passengers to Seblan made of all this, I could only imagine. But they were probably as glad of the distraction as the rest of us. After Desmond's sideshow another voice, with a thick Russian accent, sounded over the intercom.

"This is captain. I am pleased to say we have broken through cloud, as you will see if you have window. I have runway in window. Cabin staff, prepare for landing. Landing one minute. Now I dim cabin."

For some reason, none of us made a sound. The lights below looked unusually close, even though we were barely clear of the cloud base. The plane was jarring up and down. The shapes below were growing larger and rushing past faster. I realized I was gripping the seat for dear life. While we were being entertained, the man who held our lives in his hands had been struggling to bring us in. If the orchestra did play on the sinking Titanic, I now understood why. There was an almighty thump. And then another. And then the sound of engines, flaps, and brakes unscrambling the aerodynamics that had somehow kept us off the ground. This time the cheer was deafening. For once, I doubt if Desmond O'Connor minded being upstaged.

THE TERMINAL IN Seblan was chaotic. Edgy-looking soldiers were everywhere, fingering weapons. The Russian system appeared schizophrenic. Decades of hostility towards anything other than the government-controlled media jostled uncomfortably with the administration's desire to show the world that it, too, was a victim of international terror. We were herded and hassled, but eventually reunited with our luggage and cleared through. Somehow Bernie had arranged to have us met by a woman who introduced herself as Karen. We tumbled into her car along with Kurt, a German reporter from Berlin, who seemed to be going to the same hotel as us.

"They'll be lucky to get taxis," said Karen.

"Why?" I asked.

"Almost everyone is outside the school or at home, waiting for news."

"Everyone?" exclaimed Kurt.

"There are over a thousand people being held hostage," Karen explained, "parents and children."

"Parents?" queried Kurt.

"It was a special day, the Day of Knowledge. Children and their parents come to school dressed in their smartest clothes, to celebrate the academic year. It is wicked, what they are doing."

"Do we know who 'they' are?" I asked.

"Chenchians, of course," Karen informed me with obvious contempt.

"How do we know that?" I pressed.

"Who else?" she answered dismissively. "Thirty of them came this morning, in two trucks. Five of our police were killed, and one of them. They were wearing ski masks and some wore explosive belts.

Imagine what the children must have felt when these animals stormed their classrooms."

"Do you know people in the school?" I questioned.

"Of course. Everyone in Seblan knows people in the school. I have two cousins inside the building right now, just eight and nine. I mean, children? Why would they do this to children?"

"Can you take us there now?"

"To the school?"

"Yes. If that's alright with you, Kurt?" I added, more out of politeness than any intent to change course.

"Sure. We should be able to get a report in before the rest!"

"How are you for power, Michael?"

"OK. I charged up before we left. I'll need something permanent if we're going to stay there any length of time."

"We'll need to fix up a shift system," I admitted, as much to myself as to either of them. "We should be able to work something out with the others. Things could break at any moment. How flexible are you, Karen?"

"I'm to look after you, while you are here."

"Family?"

"Boyfriend. But I live with my parents."

"Good. This could be a long one."

As we approached Seblan's Middle School Number One, the harrowing drama we were becoming part of silenced us. Floodlights made the school look grim. This was not a prosperous town. Its architecture was dated and functional. Army trucks were everywhere. Soldiers and civilians stood in groups. There appeared to be no cordon around the school, just a menacing space, a no man's land of anxiety and dread.

We were stopped. Karen explained what we were. The soldier did not know what to do with us. Nowhere had been set aside for the press. An officer came over and I explained that we had come to support them; to tell the world about this terrible outrage. I asked if the hostage takers had made any demands. Apparently they had not. He told us not to get close. That was it.

I had Michael pick a good background and started my report. We would catch the late afternoon news.

Earlier today, around thirty masked men and women some, it is believed, wearing explosive belts, made their way from two trucks into the Seblan Middle School Number One. In the process, a number of local police and a gunman were killed. Over one thousand parents and their children, many as young as eight, were inside the building. This was to be a special day. A day of celebration for the school year, for which children wear their smartest clothes. Now they are inside the building you can see behind me, captive. Innocent hostages of men and women who have already demonstrated a ruthless determination and disregard for life.

So far, we have not been given any indication what their motives are or who they are, although people here believe them to be Chenchian terrorists.

Naturally, the building has been surrounded by Federation soldiers, but there appears to be little they can do at present. In amongst the soldiers, you will see civilians. These are fathers, brothers, uncles, and friends of those inside. What they, and their womenfolk waiting at home for news, must be going through, is impossible to imagine. Everyone in this town is affected. No one will be sleeping tonight. This is Orla Kildare for DEMOS-TV outside Middle School Number One, Seblan.

"Alright, Steve?"

"Good Orla. Bernie's over the moon with all of this!"

"That's why we do it!"

"Isn't that a fact!"

"Speak to you again soon, Steve. It's coming up to midnight here, so unless something breaks, that'll be it for a few hours."

At the hotel we'd been booked into I tried Aslan, but of course he didn't pick up. I found a text message from Dirk: *it looks as though our policy has shifted.*

WE RETURNED EARLY to the school the following morning. If anything, the scene looked more chaotic than it had the night before. To the groups of anxious civilians and tense soldiers had been added caffeinated journalists pointing cameras at school windows and thrusting microphones towards anyone with anything to say. An irritated soldier was trying to explain a plan that did not exist. A negotiator was coming down from Moscow. Had the terrorists asked for him? Had they said anything else? What was the condition of the hostages? He didn't know. A female journalist and her cameraman, from a Dallas news channel, had cornered a distraught mother, who was being restrained by two men as she sobbed out the words *my Alexei, my Alexei! What do they want with my Alexei?* The wretched woman can hardly have imagined that her grief would end up in the living rooms of people she had never heard of, many thousands of miles away.

I caught the eye of an unshaven man, a civilian, with a rifle in one hand. With his other he ran his fingers across his throat. The atmosphere was explosive, outside as well as inside the school. It became obvious that the soldiers were local. Torn between a desire to storm the building and a dim sense of the implications, they looked like dogs being driven mad by an itch they could not scratch.

"What's with this negotiator then, Orla?" asked a man from one of the London papers, who I remembered was called Henry.

"I've just heard myself," I told him. "The people inside must know him, or know of him."

"So, do we know who they are?" he questioned.

"The negotiator's name is Uri Shakirov," announced Kurt, who joined us. "Apparently he helped release some children from the Moscow siege, two years ago."

"It was Chenchians t'en, so it'll be Chenchians now," announced Desmond O'Connor, who'd been in the capital during that siege and had lumbered over to us.

"That ended badly, didn't it?" recalled Michael.

"T'ese Rossians don't pussyfoot about," maintained Desmond. "Civilian casualties are considered acceptable. T'ey take t'e view t'at t'e captives are dead anyway."

"But these are mostly children," stressed Kurt.

"Which will be jost whoi t'ey've done it," explained Desmond. "Increase te' downsoide far te' at'arities."

"That's more like it," remarked Henry, as several truckloads of fresh troops arrived. They were dressed differently, looked more professional and quickly began to take charge.

"That must be the *Specials* from Moscow," speculated Kurt. "They train for this."

"About bloody time," remarked Henry.

I've noticed that the English always think they can do things better, quicker and more intelligently than anyone else. Sometimes, they are even right.

As the *Specials* started to fan out, moving civilians back as they went and largely ignoring the regular soldiers, who looked bemused, several explosions ripped into the morning like sonic booms. We threw ourselves to the ground. The Specials, regulars, and civilians all dove for cover. We heard shouts coming from inside the building. There were more explosions. More shouts. A rocket grenade whistled over us, hitting one of the trucks and incinerating its driver who had stopped to enjoy a cigarette.

"Jesus!" exclaimed Desmond, whose large frame had come to rest on a particularly muddy patch of ground.

"The poor sod," commiserated Henry, who had happened to be looking at the truck driver.

"Look! Over there," cried out Kurt. "Some children are escaping."

"Michael, get it!" I hollered, not even thinking to ask if he was alright.

He pulled himself onto his elbows, grabbed his camera which had fallen to the ground beside him, and pointed it towards a trickle of stumbling bodies emerging, dazed, from a side building. Three youths scurried into no man's land, followed by an adult. They looked confused. Everyone was shouting at them to run, but the shouts were coming from all around and at first they seemed unsure which way to go. One of the *Specials* got up from the ground and waved them forward. As he did so, six or seven more children appeared, shepherded by another two adults, and raced away from the building towards us. A single shot came from the building, felling one of the adults. The Specials returned fire and more shots came in retaliation. This time, one of the children fell.

The rest all made it to cover, but the exchange of gunfire continued. I could see that the adult who had been hit, was not dead. She tried to raise herself, but a volley of shots from the school building punched into her and she fell forward. I could hear Michael say, "Oh fuck," but he kept on filming. The little boy who had been shot never moved once. Eventually the gunfire stopped.

Realizing that where we had been standing, talking, and capturing grief was a potential death trap and not the reasonably safe place we had assumed, we wriggled backwards into some lower ground and made our way towards the children. A *Special* was asking them questions: how many terrorists were there? What rooms were they using? Had the school been wired? Had anyone inside been killed?

The small group had been hiding in a store room, so they had not seen much. They thought the others had been herded into the sports hall. One of the boys, peering through a keyhole, had glimpsed two women with explosives strapped to them. At least two of the teachers had been killed. But it was when they were asked if they'd heard any names that I felt numb. The name that kept being repeated was Sergei Kadyrov. *Tell them that I, Sergei Kadyrov, have their women and children.* Those were the words they had all heard. A man, who seemed to be the terrorist leader, had shouted them down a telephone located only feet from where they were hiding.

Michael and I glanced at each other. I pulled away from the gathering. Although it was only one in the morning in America, I needed to file a report. The night crew would probably put it out unedited and some of the European networks might pick it up. The tape would be waiting for Bernie when he came in to work, and he could dress it up in time for the morning news—if events hadn't moved on by then.

Michael and I made our way to a spot beyond the trucks that had brought the *Specials*.

"Let's see what you got," I urged.

We crouched down and looked into his small replay screen.

"I thought that jolt might have screwed her," he said as we watched, referring to the rough treatment his beloved camera had just endured. "Seems alright, though."

His almost casual concern helped us both to ignore the horror of the adult, and then the child, being gunned down in front of us.

"Did you get any sound?" I asked.

"Not sure. I think the mic might have got whacked when I hit the deck."

He fiddled with one of the switches and listened to his earpiece.

"It's OK," he announced, handing it to me. "We got sound!"

I listened. The single shot was chillingly distinct. The volley that followed was almost deafening.

I sat writing up some notes and organizing my thoughts, while he tried to get a signal. I wanted to get my report out before the others found us.

"How are you doing, Orla?" he asked, after barely a minute. "I could make the link."

"I want to record this and see how it works before you send it," I told him. "I need to be sure my words do justice to what you captured. You could have been killed."

"We both could have been," he pointed out, with disarming casualness.

I looked at the tape twice more and edited my notes.

"Michael, I am going to do an intro which I want you to tack onto the front end and a close-out for the back. . . ."

"You ready?" he asked me, as I crouched in front of him.

"I'm ready."

The Seblan hostage siege has entered its second day. Forces from Moscow, known as the *Specials*, arrived this morning to take over from the local force, many of whom have family and friends held captive inside Middle School Number One. We understand the terrorists have requested a negotiator from the capital, Uri Shakirov, who was involved in the Moscow siege. This might have been taken as a hopeful sign, but only minutes ago, amid harrowing scenes of gunfire and death, ten children and three adults made a bid for freedom. Two, a nine-year-old boy and his female teacher did not make it. . . .

. . . .From those who managed to escape, we have had confirmation that two of the terrorists are women and that they have explosives strapped to them. According to these brave children and their teachers, all the hostages have now been moved into the sports hall. They have also told us that a man who calls himself Sergei Kadyrov may be the terrorist leader.

We have learned that there are at least two dead inside the school. Temperatures today are expected to rise, and we must imagine what conditions will be like. With over 1000 children, their parents, and teachers held in one hall by men and women who have demonstrated such disregard for human life, they can only be grim. This is Orla Kildare for DEMOS-TV, outside Seblan Middle School Number One, in the Russian Republic.

As I stood up, I wondered about Sergei Kadyrov. Was this the same man I had met? I could see him meting out cruelty to soldiers, but to children? And it had been the Vorsky village, not his, that had suffered most. He did have a reputation for impulsive action, but not for suicidal action, surely? I needed to speak to Aslan so badly, but I knew that I would have to return to Chenchia for that.

From between the trucks, Desmond appeared and ambled over.

"What you op to, Orla?" he called out, as if it wasn't quite clear. We would help each other in lots of ways, but every one of us wanted to get an inside edge.

"Just filing, Desmond. What about you?"

"T'is contraption of moin," he announced a little sheepishly offering up his cell, "I don't know what's befallen it."

I took one look and it was plain to see.

"I think you've befallen it, Desmond dear, when you threw yourself into that puddle."

"Nat moi foinest moment," he admitted. "I don't suppose. . . .?"

"Go on. Use mine," I said, handing it over. "You'll owe me!"

"T'at oi will, girlie. Moi offer of in-flight entertainment still stands, boi t'e way."

"Oh, I'll be expecting a lot more than that!"

"No doubt you will," he acknowledged, with a roguish chuckle as he sidled off to file his own report.

I could see Henry and Kurt coming over. I was pretty sure we were the only team who had captured the children's escape on camera. By the time they knew it for sure, I expected that my report would have played on every leading station around the world and Bernie would be adding up the royalties. I looked over at Michael.

"Sent," he confirmed, reading my mind.

CHAPTER 11

The news that Sergei Kadyrov was leading an attack against the Federation in Seblan spread through Chenchia with remarkable speed. Only in his own Sharosky region was there surprise, and then just amongst his close family. He had told them nothing about his plans. His absence had been causing Yana great concern, and now this. As she waited by the Mhemet River to be taken into Vorsky for her meeting with Alu Dudayev, she wondered if her husband had lost his head completely.

Her escort was not long in coming and it was well armed. Everyone was nervous. The mass of people in the regions were pleased one of their leaders had taken the fight to the enemy. But those willing to think with their heads and not their hearts feared massive retaliation. Yana was led into the foothills, to a small isolated cottage with a clear view of the valley. She had not seen the Vorsky leader since he had lost his wife and home, and was unsure what to expect.

As she dismounted, the old man appeared at the door. He still struck her as fine looking, but he had aged.

"Greetings, Yana," he welcomed. "Please come in. We will be alone. I hope you do not mind?"

"I am sorry about Ran. It will be a great loss for you."

"Yes, a great loss. But I console myself with the thought that I am the one feeling it and not her."

Yana followed him in. There were only two rooms. One had a fire and an oil lamp. Two chairs had been positioned on either side of the fire, with a low table in between. On the table was a brass tray holding some dried fruits in enameled bowls and two glasses.

"Please sit," he invited. "Can I pour you tea?"

Yana sat.

"Thank you, Alu. I would like that."

Alu Dudayev lifted the brass pot from a ledge next to the fire and poured. Returning the pot to the heat, he settled down in front of her.

"These are bad times for us, Yana," he said.

"When do we have good times!" she answered.

Alu smiled. They *had* all known good times, but the continuing battle for their survival sometimes made these hard to remember.

"Did you know what Sergei was planning?" he asked.

"We knew nothing. In fact, he had been missing for several days and we were becoming suspicious."

"Then why?"

Yana pondered the question. She had been asking herself the same one, over and over.

"He often used to say that we should fight back, but that was just his anger speaking."

"Anger we are not short of," Alu acknowledged.

"What does your son think?"

"I wish I knew. I have not seen Aslan for several days."

"You don't think he could be with Sergei, do you?" Yana wondered.

Alu shrugged.

"It would be against everything I taught him," he reasoned eventually, adding, "but we sent him away and he learned new things. So perhaps I do not know him as I did."

"Not Aslan," Yana assured him. "He would not get mixed up in something like this. You don't think the Americans are behind it, do you?"

Alu shook his head.

"Who knows? Americans? Russians? All either mind about is their supply of oil and gas."

Yana nodded and sipped her tea.

"Why a school? Why children?" she questioned, staring into the fire.

"This will do our people no good," Alu emphasized.

"Have you had word from Akhmad Bassayev?" Yana asked.

"He is not well. My daughter, Roaz, looks after him."

"Malik, then. What does your son-in-law think?"

"Roaz says she has not seen him."

"You don't think all three. . .?"

Yana did not need to finish the question. As improbable as it seemed, the possibility that Sergei, Malik and Aslan were all at Seblan could not be ruled out.

"I must go and put an end to it," Alu concluded after they had studied the flames and each other.

"But how?" questioned Yana.

"I must talk to them."

"Will they listen? Will the Russians let you near?"

"I don't know, but I must try."

AS HE WATCHED Yana leave, Alu remembered the first Federation soldier he had killed. So much had come to pass since that day. His father's death, the death of his sons, his daughter's death in childbirth and his mother's eventual death in ripe old age. Hers, at least, had been natural. But there had been much to celebrate, too. His marriage, the birth of each of their five children, the weddings of his two daughters. These had been great moments, happy moments. Then there had been celebrations in the village. Along with the instances of sadness, there always seemed to be events to celebrate. Across all of Vorsky, there were events to celebrate, as well as losses to mourn and he, after he became head, had attended. Theirs might not have been a large community, perhaps 250,000 spread out over a rugged land, but it was tight-knit.

His father had always told him not to provoke Federation soldiers. "The Russian people are not interested in our mountains," he often said. "But we must resist them when they encroach." His strategy had been simple and largely effective, and Alu had seen no need to change it. Whenever Federation soldiers had moved out of the valley into the Vorsky interior, they would be taught a bloody lesson. Risking as few lives as possible, he and his men would use guerrilla tactics to inflict the maximum casualties on their opponents. The garrison commander in Zoldek would soon realize that there was nothing to be gained by sending his men into the mountains. Alu regretted that the Russians replaced their commanders so frequently, as each invariably had to be taught the same lesson.

In the last five years things had changed. The pipeline, and now the building of the highway, was upsetting the natural rhythm of their lives. Strictly, the valley people on his side of the Mhemet River were his responsibility. But increasingly they looked to the capital. Most of their produce was sold there and that was where their children went to find work. The valley markets were in decline and even mountain people from the three regions were conducting more of their business inside the capital. And Zoldek was full of dissent. Although the better-off Chenchians were in favor of an accommodation with the Federation, the poor and extreme proponents of the Faith were waging an unrelenting war inside the capital against its occupiers. This poison was spreading back into the regions with the most terrible consequences and Alu could see no way of stopping it.

He'd been just seventeen when he'd made his first kill. "It's like hunting," his father had said, "except that we don't eat Russians." A new commander had taken over, of course. A young man, in his early thirties, anxious to make a mark. They hadn't known it at the time, but learned later that his name was Andrei Nabokov.

The young commander had doubtless heard, many times, that the mountain people rarely fought a pitched battle in the open. So he had devised a strategy to make them. He had positioned his small force on clear ground, knowing that his enemy would be watching. Giving every sign of being poorly prepared, he had camped for the night. But under cover of darkness he had detached a small group of soldiers and sent them into a village five miles away to take prisoners. It had been a well-executed maneuver. His men had managed to capture a woman and three children from an outlying home without raising any alarm. It so happened that the woman's husband had been one of the fighters observing the Russians' camp. Alu recalled the consternation amongst his people the following morning when they had seen the woman and children tethered outside it.

Everyone had wanted to rush down and attack, but his father had forbidden it. Instead they had made no move at all and, in accordance with his father's instructions, taken great trouble not to reveal their presence. The standoff had lasted for three days. At the end of the third day, when Alu's father saw his opponent instruct that food and water be taken to the woman and children, he knew he had won. That night, the raiders pulled out, leaving behind their tethered captives.

Before they could get back onto the valley road, the Federation soldiers had to pass through a narrow cut. His father had already moved most of his fighters there, anticipating his adversary's actions. Had it not been close to a full moon, Andrei Nabokov and his men would have slipped away unscathed. There had been three covered trucks full of equipment and soldiers, travelling behind the commander's open jeep.

Inside the jeep had been a driver and the commander, with two soldiers in the rear.

Alu's father had issued the most precise instructions. Under no circumstances was the young commander to be killed, just the three other men with him in the jeep. Alu had been given the most difficult shot—the driver.

Shooting at night was tricky. Even if a moon illuminated your target, you could not always see the bead at the end of a rifle from a dark vantage point and a moving target was challenging in any event. In the cut which the Federation soldiers had to pass through, the road took a sharp left turn over a dried-up stream bed and vehicles needed to slow to a crawl to get by. Alu and the two others selected for their skill had been positioned by his father next to rocks, immediately above the turn. All they had to do was wait.

The lunar light had fallen perfectly onto the road at the bend. The convoy would emerge from darkness into the light at the point of the turn, and the driver of the jeep would be too busy negotiating it to see the danger.

The three marksmen had known they would have only moments to line up on their targets. None of the men had tried to lie and balance his firearm on a rock. Instead each had sat with an elbow resting on one knee to act as a pivot for the hand steadying his rifle. They'd often used this technique against wild boar driven towards them through one of the valley cuts.

Unlike animals, which usually appeared without warning, the rumble of machinery had advertised the convoy's progress. Alu could still remember the feeling of excitement and apprehension. He didn't recall thinking much about the fact that he was going to kill his first man until afterwards. A small, solitary cloud had passed across the moon just before the convoy reached the turn. A little later and they would have been thwarted. Events often turn on such things. Instead it had cleared as the jeep passed below them, bathing it in light. At the turn, it had almost stopped. The sound of the three shots had been all but lost within the roaring, gear-changing noise of the trucks.

All three bullets found their mark. The jeep just stopped. Its driver must have been shifting gears when he was hit. The young commander did not lose his wits. Instead of hiding behind his vehicle and firing at the shadows, as some might have done, he had pushed the driver out and, crouching low, driven the jeep out of the turn and down the hill. His three trucks had lurched and bumped and screeched after him like stampeding elephant.

Once in the valley, which was only a hundred yards further on, the Federation soldiers had regrouped and started firing wildly back towards the cut. But Alu's father had not allowed one shot to be returned. Later, he explained his thinking. He had not wanted the young commander killed because that would have brought on reprisals—and yet another commander. Instead, he'd wanted to give his youthful opponent a message. Having held the young man's life in his hands, he wanted him to know that he would prefer to deal with him than fight him. And over the three years that followed, while Andrei Nabokov was commander of the Federation garrison in Zoldek, there had been no more incursions into the Vorsky region. Alu's father had met with Nabokov three times over that period, to discuss common problems and even taken him hunting once, just before the Russian had left for a new posting.

When dawn broke, Alu had been able to see the man he had shot, in a heap by the side of the road, where the young commander had dumped him. Around midday, three Federation soldiers had walked back up the road towards the cut, one carrying a white flag and the other two a stretcher. Unobserved, the Chenchian fighters watched as the dead man had been carried away. It was then that Alu had felt remorse. Later, sensing his anguish, his father had simply said "take no pleasure in the act, but always remember: your freedom may depend on it."

CHAPTER 12

*A*lu Dudayev and his fighters stopped in front of the Russian garrison. Had he not come with forty armed men, he would never have reached it. Zoldek was shot through with anguish. A growing number of Faith Radicals eyed the Democrats, and a diminishing number of Democrats eyed the Faith Radicals. Federation soldiers watched both with nervous incomprehension, while those Chenchians loyal to Moscow watched their backs. The few citizens determined to lead normal lives clung to their mundane chores like limpets, but mostly the capital was a bazaar in which angry young men and cynical old ones traded suspicions, betrayals, quick money, and quick death.

"Wait there!" shouted the guard.

The bluntness of his command belied his fear. Although an armored vehicle had accompanied the riders over the last three hundred yards, and was now positioned at right angles to the horsemen, their rugged presence and contemptuous manner would have unsettled all but the most seasoned soldier.

When he returned, he pointed at Alu Dudayev and called out, "Only you."

Alu faced his men. In the eyes of every one was a silent plea that he should return with them. He nodded, very slightly, then looked down at the silver encrusted saddle that had been part of his life for so long and dismounted, handing his gun to the closest. Briskly, he approached the guard who grabbed him roughly by the arm. The sound of forty rifles being readied startled the guard into releasing the arm.

The sentry made for his weapon but quickly thought better of it. Instead, the confused man turned, and Alu Dudayev followed him inside.

The Vorsky fighters watched the garrison doors close behind their leader. For a moment, none moved. Then, as if on cue, they wheeled and rode for home.

"This is the one who wants to see the commander," the guard announced to two colleagues, who were sitting idly inside the guardroom.

"Is he armed?" asked the first.

"I don't know."

"We'd better make sure," suggested the second.

"Indeed," the first echoed.

"Clothes off then, big chief," ordered the guard.

Alu glared at them.

"I guess he wants us to undress him," the second man taunted.

The three approached the Vorsky warlord who stood with his arms folded across his chest.

"No point being proud in here old man. Your fighters have gone," mocked the guard.

Just then the new young garrison commander entered the room.

"What's going on?" he demanded.

"Just checking the prisoner for weapons," the guard explained.

"Prisoner? I thought this man had come to see me."

"Yes, sir."

"Well, *is* he armed?"

The three men proceeded to run their hands over Alu Dudayev's body.

"Doesn't seem to be, sir," the guard concluded.

"What's your name?" the commander asked, addressing his stony-faced visitor.

"Alu Dudayev. I am leader of the Vorsky region."

"Of course. I've read your file. Your son went to an American university. Follow me."

"YOU TOOK A risk coming here," the young commander pointed out when they were safely seated inside his office. "The situation in Seblan has made everyone tense."

"That is why I have come. I do not like what is happening in Seblan."

"So why do your people do these things?"

"Why do you seek to control my country?"

"Now that we have cleared the air," the commander continued, "why are you here?"

"I have heard that Sergei Kadyrov is involved."

"Yes. We have heard that he is leading this. . ." the commander paused, ". . .enterprise."

"I know him."

"Do you know anyone else who is involved?"

"I do not know who else is involved."

"Could your son be involved?"

"I do not believe so."

"Then why are you here?"

"This siege will do nothing for my country. I want to stop it."

"We would all like to stop it."

"If I could speak with Kadyrov, I might be able to persuade him to end his occupation of the school. He is not a man who likes to harm children."

"Why should he pull out now? What would be in it for him?"

"He and his men would have to be offered an amnesty."

"I doubt if Moscow would agree to that."

Alu shrugged.

"Are your soldiers going to shoot their way in?" he asked.

"Let me make a call," the commander offered. "Can you wait here? This may take some time. It is not just a military matter. There are political considerations."

"Time I can give you," Alu agreed.

ALU DUDAYEV SAT in the commander's office. He would rather have been on a mountainside stalking game, but waiting, whatever for and wherever it was, required the same thing, patience. The room was quite large. Little seemed out of place. Along one wall was a well-stocked bookcase. The young commander reminded him of Aslan—educated. He, himself, had never read a book. He could not read. Well, he could not read what was written on a page, but he could read faces, the contours of the land, clouds, the sky, the mood of his people.

He knew that his mistreated nation was in the process of establishing a new accommodation with the outside world, a world made manifest by a pipeline. The Mhemet Valley had always been a passageway for trade. In the past, traders using it had needed to reach an accommodation with the valley people, which meant with the people of Vorsky, Sharosky and Urus, who *were* the people of Chenchia.

But now it was quite different. A precious substance flowed from one end to the other without touching Chenchian soil or enhancing its people's lives. It was as if the ancient traders, instead of bringing silks and salts, tools and perfumes, which they would exchange for food, furs, and precious stones mined from the Chenchian hills, had been forced to travel behind armor, guarded by legions. No contact was permitted. No friendships could be made. No mutual benefit secured. Now, a single, desired commodity flowed silently through their land, blighting their lives. It was as if someone had wrapped up the Mhemet River and claimed it for themselves.

He worried deeply about Aslan. Had he and Ran really been wise to send him to America, a country so far away? Hadn't Akhmad been wiser, sending Malik to Russia? Perhaps both families had been wrong and should have sent their sons to the south, to the center of the Faith. Once it had seemed, to Ran at least, that the American way was the best way. How could a country become so successful and so powerful unless it possessed a secret others should wish to share?

But it was not now looking as though his people would go America's way. A metal filing will be drawn towards the closest magnet, when all is said and done. Would his son be a marked man? The young commander clearly knew his history. Or would the things that his son had learned stand him in good stead? He worried. Knowledge was all very well, but like a button without a buttonhole, it was little use away from its context.

"Can I fetch you something to drink, or to eat?"

Alu had not noticed the young woman come in.

"A glass of water, please."

"Nothing else?" she pressed, with obvious concern.

"Do I know you?" he asked. "Where do you come from?"

"I share a small apartment in Zoldek with three other girls, but my parents live in Vorsky."

"Which village?"

"Terek, where I was born."

"What is your name?"

"Surek."

"What are your parents' names?"

"Ana and Andrei Talgayev."

"Ah! I knew it. You look like your mother. A beautiful woman."

Surek blushed.

"Tell me. Why did you leave your village?" Alu asked.

The young woman didn't even hesitate.

"Life is easier here, and more fun. I earn my own money and make my own decisions."

"Do you think your village has a future?"

"Yes," she answered after some hesitation, "but not in the old way."

Alu Dudayev nodded. He had heard this from the young many times before.

"I will be back with your water," Surek told him, as she left the room.

He sat, wishing that he was with Ran. Their time was over. A few minutes later Surek returned with the water. On the tray beside the glass was a plate of cured meat and cakes.

IT WAS OVER two hours later when the commander eventually returned to his office.

"I am sorry to have left you for so long," he apologized. "But you were safest in here. There is much hostility towards your people at the moment."

"There is much hostility amongst my people," Alu replied, "so I understand."

"I see Surek has looked after you."

"Yes, very well."

"She is a fine young lady."

The young soldier looked anxious and paced around his room.

"Can I speak frankly?" he asked, halting in front of Alu.

"Of course."

"They want you in Seblan right away."

"I'm ready."

"But you are expendable. You have to understand that. They will use you as bait."

"Amnesty?"

"Not possible."

"So what can I offer?"

"You can help to save the children, that is all. The hostage takers are dead men and women, regardless."

"They are prepared to sacrifice their own children?" Alu asked in disbelief.

"I am afraid so."

"I will go. But only to show that I am better than those who burned my village, murdered my wife, raped our young women to death and shot our old men."

The young commander looked ashamed. He had read the reports.

"You are already far better," he said, "Now, I have a helicopter standing by. It will get you to Seblan in under an hour."

"What is your name?" Alu asked.

"Leonid Nabokov. Your father took mine hunting when he was stationed here."

"I remember," Alu recalled with a smile. "Your father's driver was the first man I killed."

"Did you mean to kill my father?"

"Not at all. Mine was adamant that yours should not be harmed. He wanted to send a message to him. He wanted to let him know that encroaching onto our land was not the way forward and that he and your father could work together."

"My father understood that message. The two men developed an understanding, I think."

"Yes. We were sorry when your father left."

CHAPTER 13

$\mathcal{I}$nside Middle School Number One, Malik Bassayev's freedom fighters waited. They had been picked because they were the most extreme of the Faith Radicals, the cream of the movement. They had been trained for nine months inside Urus by Malik himself in a camp that did not exist. This was their moment and each man and woman reveled in the purity of it. They were on a mission for God. The Russian infidels would be humiliated, shown to be powerless to protect even their children. And as for escape? That was guaranteed. The kingdom of heaven was theirs.

They had been told to request the mediation of Uri Shakirov, a harmless enough man, trained as a pediatrician. By calling for him, the plight of the children would be emphasized. And their demands? The release from detention of all Faith Radicals captured by the Russians. Over a thousand were rotting in jails across the Federation. One thousand civilians for one thousand men of faith. What could be more reasonable?

Vengeance, the group's leader, paced through the school which was now theirs, looking for any weakness in their defenses, and sloppiness amongst members of his team. None of the fighters used their own names and they always wore masks, not for fear of what might happen to them, but out of concern for their families. Vengeance felt vengeful, hence his name. The Russians had murdered his sister. She had been the victim of an unsuccessful raid on his village to capture Faith Radicals. Realizing their quarry had escaped, the Russians had questioned the villagers. When none agreed to speak they had simply taken one at random and shot her in the square.

This crass act had proved counterproductive in several ways. The person shot, his sister, had been the only one in the village who had actually known where he and his friends were hiding. Never having witnessed such callous brutality before, the villagers became steadfast supporters of Faith Radicals from that day forward. Previously, it has to be said, they had regarded them as something of a joke. For him, the incident was seminal. What might have been a passing teenage fancy became a lifelong quest to avenge his sister's death.

His five closest associates, three men—Wrath, Blade and Death, and two women—Flower and Honey, had their own good reasons for joining. Wrath, he thought, must have been born angry. To have started life in the grinding poverty that had surrounded him, would have been reason enough. But he was able to add zest to his already sour cocktail. His mother had cleaned house for a Russian businessman in Zoldek. To secure her meager salary, she had provided this man with favors his father, an itinerant cobbler, had chosen to endure. The boy might have been none the wiser had another domestic, who lived near them and was jealous of the few advantages Wrath's mother had managed to secure, not referred to her work colleague as the Russian's whore. It hadn't taken long for the boys on his street to work out, in graphic detail, what this epithet meant.

Blade, as far as he knew, could lay claim to no great disadvantage in his early life. Somewhat frail in appearance, a characteristic enhanced by his gangling height, like a plant stretched upwards by competition for the light, his mental ability was robust and had carried him to university. As a beneficiary of the system imposed by his colonial rulers, he should have become a loyal functionary of the Russian state. But the subtleties of the Faith had appealed to his intellect more than the crude—as he saw it—utilitarian nature of the ex-communists who controlled so much of Chenchian life. His only concession to physical force was a mastery of the blade.

Little Gregor, a friend from his school days, had chosen the sobriquet Death because death was something that concerned Gregor a good deal. They had often talked together about eternal life, about whether there really was such a thing, what it would be like, and how one might secure entry if it existed. To say that he was a coward would have been quite wrong, but out of all of them, he undoubtedly felt fear the most. He probably had more imagination than the rest, that was all, and had chosen the name Death to keep his enemy close.

Flower had simply joined the movement one day and was the most fanatical of them all. She would not talk about her past and so he assumed it had been unpleasant and they had all left it at that. Ruthlessly efficient and uncompromising, she had become his second in command. He would like to have had sex with her, as would most of the men, but she had steadfastly resisted his approaches. Instead she had offered him Honey.

Honey was Flower's shadow and, in many ways, alter ego: open, accommodating, generous—Flower's opposite. An otherwise directionless soul, she seemed drawn to her friend's force field in the way a pilot fish is drawn to a shark. But Honey unsettled him. Had Flower not refused to join without her, he would have seen Honey off. Even when he made love to her, he felt her hold back and smile.

They had taken to calling each other by letter. The top six all had one letter, so V (Vengeance), F (Flower), B (Blade), W (Wrath), D (Death), and H (Honey). Those down the hierarchy might have two letters, DT, LM, etc. where the first letter had already been taken, and in the case of further duplication a number was added, such as PR2, or QA1. In this way their personal identity was obliterated, some of the sillier names disguised and the starkness of the system reinforced in them their sense of being a highly-trained force with a singular mission.

The storming of the school had gone better than he could have wished. They had only lost one. Inside, the initial pandemonium had quickly been brought under control. In the process, three adults had been killed, all by Wrath, and two wounded. These last had been quickly finished off by Flower. They could not afford to have the dying making a noise and using up resources. A small group of children and teachers had escaped, although two had been shot before they reached safety. That some individuals would have gotten away was inevitable, but what had annoyed him about this incident was that the group had managed to remain hidden overnight. They would have taken with them some intelligence, for sure.

Everyone, he hoped, had now been brought to the sports hall where they could be guarded by relatively few, leaving the rest to protect the school from the inevitable attack. He doubted if any of them seriously thought the Russians would negotiate. The best they could hope for was that they would take as many of their enemy with them as they could. And what about the children? He didn't feel overly sentimental. They would soon have grown up to be Russian adults.

The smell of fear was beginning to permeate the place. Many of the younger children had relieved themselves in their pants, and everyone was just going to have to live with it. That would only get worse, but it was better than having to set up relays to the toilets. He was not running a humanitarian mission. His strategy was to exert the maximum pressure on the Russian authorities, to force them into a stupid blunder so that public confidence in them would be eroded. It was well known that a growing number inside the Russian capital favored a negotiated peace. If the current leadership became sufficiently discredited, these new voices might assume power.

As attractive as the idea of heaven was, he, himself, did not plan on going there just yet. While his men were fighting a courageous last stand, he and his top lieutenants would slip away to fight another day. They were not far from the Chenchian border, so it was possible. He doubted if Flower would come with them. He knew she had made peace with her maker and seemed ready to face death. Blade would come, and so would little Gregor. In spite of his nickname, death did not become him. He was not sure about Wrath or Honey.

As he walked down the passage towards the sports hall, he lifted up the telephone to check that it was still working. He didn't know why Malik had insisted he use the name Sergei Kadyrov, but guessed it had something to do with Malik's wish to control all three regions. He didn't like Malik, but respected him. He considered the effective leader of the Urus region too close to the Russians. But for now, that didn't seem to matter because in time, Faith Radicals would sweep both him and them away.

"NO! SIT STILL and be quiet."

Flower glared at the teacher who had been presumptuous enough to ask if the children could be escorted, in small groups, to the toilets.

But the teacher, whose name was Larisa, persisted.

"Surely you can't expect the children to sit here in their own filth?"

"Expect!" exclaimed Flower in her harsh, metallic voice. "What I expect is that you, and everyone else in this hall, will do exactly as I say. Do you have a problem with that?"

"Yes, I do," answered Larisa firmly. "These are innocent children. They have no part in your struggle."

Flower advanced towards the teacher, like a panther moving in for the kill, with such anger that every part of her body suggested rage. Even her eyes, staring through the slits in her hood, managed to radiate pure menace. As she came close she raised the butt of her gun and brought it down against the teacher's face with vicious force.

Larisa turned away at the last moment, exposing her jaw to the weapon's full impact and feeling it shatter. Larisa's colleague, Marta, moved to shield her, but Flower bludgeoned her away with a sharp upward movement of the gun.

"These children *are* part of my struggle," the Faith Radical hissed. "They have fathers who are killing and torturing my people, they have mothers who spit on our traditions, and one day, unless they are stopped, these little innocents will grow up to suppress us, just as their parents are doing now."

A boy of about fifteen, incensed by what he had just witnessed, made a move at Flower, but even before he had risen to his feet, bullets from the masked woman's Kalashnikov ripped into his gut, sending him sprawling backwards in excruciating pain. His pitiful cries drowned the shouts and screams that had erupted around the hall. "For pity's sake, do something," someone called out. Flower looked around to see who had spoken before stepping over to the wailing boy and shooting him in the head at point-blank range. Triumphantly she surveyed the hall as the cries faded into suppressed sobs.

"That's better," she snapped. "This is my school now, and you will abide by my rules."

"PROBLEMS?" ASKED VENGEANCE as he hurried back into the sports hall, alarmed by the sound of shooting.

"Just imposing my will," murmured Flower, still scanning the seated crowd for any signs of trouble.

"The shooting?"

"An object lesson."

Vengeance peered into the crush of frightened onlookers until he spotted Flower's handiwork.

"We'd better shift the body."

Flower looked unconvinced.

Vengeance elaborated.

"We could be here a while."

Flower would have preferred her object lesson to have remained in clear view, no matter how unpleasant it became. But grudgingly she agreed to have it moved.

"You and you," she summoned, picking out two of the older boys next to the slaughtered teenager, "pick it up and carry it out."

The corpse was an 'it' now, not a boy, a son, a student, or a friend. The two youths appeared petrified as they rose to carry out their task. One had wet himself and looked in embarrassed disbelief at his stained trousers.

"Never mind about that," screamed Flower. "By the time we are through here, everyone will show the mark of fear. Now pick that thing up and take it out."

At first the boys did not know what to do. One tried lifting under the shoulders while the other held onto the ankles, but the corpse just buckled and the boy at the back lost his grip sending its feet to the floor with a clunk.

"Oh, for goodness sake!" hissed Flower.

The boy holding the shoulders persisted and started to back, leaving a trail of blood across the sports hall floor, until he tripped over a young girl who was too traumatized to pull her legs clear in time. The hall was now silent. Everyone was staring at this macabre farce wondering what would happen next. Flower would have happily shot both stand-in undertakers for sheer incompetence, but even she realized that more bodies would only make matters worse. So, like the rest, she just watched as the two boys reassessed their technique, deciding, in the end, to grab an arm each and just haul their erstwhile friend unceremoniously towards the door. Once there, they looked back at the sea of faces and then at Flower, now imprinted, as youth so easily can be, on their new leader.

"We're going to need a morgue," observed Vengeance tersely.

His remark set off a ripple of sobs, quickly silenced by an unforgiving stare from Flower.

"Why don't I escort them along the passage?" suggested Honey. "They can leave the body near the exit. Death can wire it."

Vengeance grunted, annoyed that he hadn't thought of it himself.

So Honey and Death had the two boys follow them from the room with their burden, leaving behind only a snail like trail of teenage hemoglobin.

"Where are those boys going?" asked a small girl, who couldn't have been more than seven.

No one wanted to answer, so she upped the ante.

"I need the toilet."

There was something about the little girl's statement that cut through the air with more force even than Flower's blunt-nosed munitions had done minutes earlier. In a world of ideological struggle, that pits opposing ideas against one another, with a certainty on each side that defies even elementary logic and draws from a primitive well that defines what 'is' only by what it 'is not', human simplicity, simple human need, strikes a discordant note. It is as if, in the midst of battle, someone says *can we go home now?*

"Set up relays," instructed Vengeance, when the silence, following the question, could be ignored no longer.

Flower harrumphed, but set about organizing three teachers to take two children each which, had she thought—and she probably had, meant that it would take almost three hours to deal with the two hundred youngest.

The two boys returned and hung about behind Flower, waiting for further instructions.

"Oh, sit down, you little fools," she spat out, as soon as she noticed them.

Utterly confused, the two slunk back to the spot within the packed hall next to where their fellow student had been sitting, before honorable instincts had led him to his death, and where now only a solidifying pool of gore remained. While Honey helped to escort the relays,

Wrath and Blade set about mounting a crude explosive device, that Death had armed, onto a wire strung up between the basketball hoop and climbing bar.

"If anyone tries a rescue," Flower announced proudly, "that will go off."

Her proclamation had less impact than she would have liked. Her prisoners were becoming used to horrible things.

THE TELEPHONE IN the office rang. It was now the afternoon of the second day. Vengeance and two of his lieutenants, Death and Blade, hurried to answer it. Vengeance told Death to pick up.

"Hello?" a rather high-pitched male voice asked. "Who am I speaking to?"

"Never mind," answered Death. "Who are you?"

"I am Uri Shakirov. I believe Sergei Kadyrov asked for me. Can I speak to him?"

Death handed the receiver to Vengeance.

"Shakirov," he said, cupping the speaker.

Vengeance drew his breath. He wanted to give nothing away. He knew a whole team would be listening in.

"This is Kadyrov," he stated, in as measured a tone as he could manage.

"Mr. Kadyrov, how are the children?"

"They will be better as soon as you meet our demands."

"They must be hungry, thirsty, do you need food?"

"Our demands, Mr. Shakirov. What about our demands?"

"You must appreciate, it takes time to locate all the prisoners that we are holding. In the meantime, can we send in some food?"

The man had been well briefed, Vengeance thought. Cat and mouse. Develop a dialogue. Establish a relationship. Hint at the acceptance of terms, subject only to matters of mundane practicality. Meanwhile, the crack troops would be appraising the situation, looking for any weakness through which a rescue might be attempted. Wear the hostage takers down, weaken their resolve, attempt to have something sent in as a means of securing fresh intelligence.

"Not good enough!" stated Vengeance in a cold, calm, clear voice, before firing his weapon into the ceiling and then returning the receiver to its stand.

Death and Blade both looked at him. They had discussed their strategy, many times, but now that the situation was real, the knowledge that their terms were virtually impossible to meet and that there could only be one possible outcome, had a chilling effect on the two men.

The telephone rang again. Vengeance lifted up, but said nothing.

"Is that you, Kadyrov? Are you there. We must talk, otherwise nothing can be resolved."

Vengeance waited for several seconds before answering.

"Our terms," he then said simply. "What about our terms?"

"We are working on them, I assure you…."

Like hell you are, thought Vengeance.

". . . .but in the meantime, we would like a gesture, some indication that we can do business with you. How about releasing some of the younger children?"

"How many do you have in mind?"

This question clearly took Shakirov by surprise and he could hear muffled comments in the background as the negotiator was briefed.

"Perhaps twenty?" came back the suggestion.

"Fine. You fly twenty prisoners, whose names I will give you, to Syria and when I know they are safely there, you can have your children."

"But Mr. Kadyrov, that will take time. Could you not make a small gesture, a gesture of good faith, say ten children, even five?"

Vengeance laughed. *Good faith* he repeated to himself. How could anyone talk about *good faith*, after all that had happened. He replaced the receiver.

Ten minutes later, the telephone rang again, as he thought it would. Shakirov's high-pitched voice was beginning to irritate him.

"We have agreed," the negotiator announced. "Give me the names."

Vengeance was ready and read them out, slowly, from a list he was carrying in his pocket. When he had finished, the negotiator read them back. A nice touch that, he thought, appearing to not want to make an error.

"Now how about a small gesture?" Shakirov pushed. "One or two children, at least. Perhaps some are sick?"

Vengeance smiled. What a game this was.

"I tell you what, you send me any one person from the list I have given you and I will let you have one child in return."

There was a confused silence from the other end, but eventually Shakirov said "alright" and Vengeance replaced the receiver.

Death and Blade looked at him, puzzled.

"There'll be no more calls tonight," he told them. "Let's see what food we've got."

They followed him out of the office. He felt anger. Did they honestly think he would give them names of people held in their prisons, people who would suffer in consequence even more than they already were. Every name he had given Shakirov was that of a Radical who had died under torture. He had his sources. Let's see how long it would take them to work it out.

THERE WAS VERY little food, as it turned out. Each Radical had brought some supplies; cured meat to chew on, tablets of candy for sugar. The water into the school still flowed, but they were wary. The hostages could drink it. Indeed it was about all they could have. If the supply was tampered with in some way, the effects would be plain to see on those they held rather than on themselves. But each man's water bottle would not last long. Somehow they had glossed over that detail in planning.

When you are pretending to expect to die, you can't very well dwell on life's basic necessities. Just enough to keep the siege going until the international media was well and truly hooked and then *Wham!* The world could watch the Russian authorities kill their own children.

As Malik had made clear, the trick was to provoke the soldiers into storming the school. Vengeance doubted they would need much provoking. President Nitup was keen to show his people a firm and decisive hand, that was widely known. It was also well known that the Russian president wished to portray the Chenchian resistance, at every turn, as being barbaric, not worthy of sympathy, even amongst its own people. Could a single, horrific act engender in two opposing constituencies, the Chenchian and Russian people, a common desire for peace? Perhaps it could, but Vengeance didn't care. Faith Radicals were playing by their own rules. For them, the *Faith* was everything. There could be no temporizing. Even Chenchia, the country, was unimportant when compared to the *Faith*.

As nighttime reasserted its grip over Seblan, Vengeance did the rounds of his recently-claimed kingdom, a kingdom he, alone, ruled. For the moment, at least, President Nitup, in spite of his omnipotence, was powerless in Seblan's Middle School Number One. That, of course, was the real challenge. The children were incidental, a bargaining chip, a mere component in the matrix of power that both men were manipulating like a 'cat's cradle', the game, using webs of string, the girls of his youth loved playing. It occurred to him that morality was little more than politics, a high-minded name for the balance that existed between people at any point in time. An immoral act was one whose consequences you feared. Change the consequences and you could change the morality. Persuade yourself that such-and-such a group were your absolute enemy and there was nothing you couldn't justify doing to them. Persuade your followers that defending the power structure warranted the greatest sacrifice and there was little they wouldn't accept.

President Nitup must hate the media, he thought. Without its eyes watching, ready to disseminate what it saw around the globe, he could have sent in his crack troops and ended the siege in a matter of hours. The death of a few children would not have resonated outside Seblan and who could give a shit about Seblan? Certainly not the people of Moscow. Only when the media made the children's fate seem like the fate of every watching parent's child, did it carry political weight. Without the media, their own little exercise would be pointless.

He found Flower guarding the sports hall like an angry predator with her prey just where she wanted it. Honey was nearby exchanging peek-a-boo glances with a little boy. What was it with those two? He couldn't work it out. If they were lovers, what was it that appealed to each about the other's wholly different character? Flower could instigate an act of cruelty in an instant. Honey sought little more than to envelop all comers within the natural warmth of her nature. He guessed they liked each other for precisely those things they themselves were not, but there seemed no desire in either to change the other's ways. He'd observed Honey look indulgently at Flower's cruelty, as one might a favorite cat batting a mouse. For her part, Flower seemed utterly indifferent to Honey's random acts of kindness. It was as if kindness and cruelty were wholly equivalent for these two, and perhaps, in truth, they were: different types of act with different kinds of consequences, no more, no less. There were times when he envied Flower for being Flower and Honey for being her friend.

"Do you think they'll come tonight, V?" asked a Radical, hunched, gun at the ready, beside a window at the back of the school.

"Probably not tonight, P. How are you holding?"

"Good. But I don't like this waiting!"

Vengeance smiled and nodded. He knew that applied to all of them.

"Just don't forget," he told his fighter, "that they're having to wait too."

That seemed to buck the man up and he turned back to staring into the gloom for any hint of impending action.

Further down the corridor, Vengeance noticed a skylight no one was watching.

"Think they can't climb roofs, then?" he asked the section leader responsible for that part of the building.

"Shit!" the man exclaimed, wondering how he had missed so obvious an entry point. "I'll have RS watch it."

"You do that," Vengeance told him, with only mild irritation. The approaches to the building were now so well lit by the banks of arc lights the Russians had set up that it would be a feat, indeed, to get anywhere near the roof. Still, when the attack came, all the lights would be cut. And when that moment did come it was going to be a bloodbath no matter where he posted his men. All he needed was enough time to slip away.

As he approached the far corner of the school complex he heard *thump, rumble, rumble . . . thump, rumble, rumble* and found Blade draped languidly over an office chair picking off notices on a cork board. He watched for a moment. The man's accuracy was awesome. After each 'hit' he'd roll forward on the chair, pull out the knife, scoot the chair back and send his weapon of choice flying right into the middle of the next piece of selected administrative information.

"Fuck, V!" he let out. "What are you *doing* creeping up like that?"

"Lucky I wasn't a Russian," Vengeance taunted, closing the door behind him.

Blade flicked his shoulders, angry at having been caught out.

"How's it in the hall?"

"It stinks of piss, shit and fear, and Flower is reveling in it!"

"That woman's something!" Blade uttered. "Isn't she letting them use the toilets?"

"Yes. But in such small groups we're not keeping up. She doesn't want to risk another break-out."

Blade couldn't argue with that and so didn't.

"Thank God she's on our side," he reflected, mostly to himself.

"What do you reckon?" Vengeance asked, nodding towards the window.

"Two or three of us might. It depends where the main attack comes from, and how much confusion there is. They seem to have parked the people from the media over there, so we might be able to slip right past."

"What about the charges?" Vengeance inquired.

"They'll blow as soon as there is any serious disturbance, so you're going to have to get Flower and her honeysuckle out of there, if they're coming."

"I don't think they are."

Blade shook his head. He didn't like Russians, but he didn't like the idea of dying either. Of all of them, he was the one least driven by belief.

"Little Gregor?"

Vengeance scowled at him.

"OK, Death. But it's a damn silly name. And who the fuck's listening? Death is not something I want to be reminded of all the time."

"I want him with us."

There was something about little Gregor that made Vengeance feel protective.

"And Wrath, what about Wrath?"

"I think he's made up his mind that this is his moment."

"So it'll just be the three of us?" Blade queried.

"It looks that way."

"Then we might make it—away from the building at least. With all the anger out there, the tough part will be getting out of Seblan."

Vengeance shrugged. He preferred not to think about that.

THE SPORTS HALL looked like one of those compounds in which animals are tightly gathered before slaughter, for reasons of economy. Being nighttime, the squash pulsed in an almost peaceful fashion. Bodies propped up against one another, for want of anywhere else to go, heaved gently as their lungs inhaled and exhaled the now putrid air. A cough here, a sob there was all that interrupted a rhythm that attested to the presence of life, however degraded it had become. The thought that came to him was of battery hens. Life reduced to a single purpose, in this instance, his purpose. He found it surprisingly easy to detach the individual from the purpose. Could generals dwell on the individuals they sent into battle? Hardly! It became a numbers game. A game of more or less assets than one's opponent, more or less cleverly deployed.

One corner held a group of nursing mothers, their babes held against their breasts. One was even suckling as he looked and the woman stared back at him with dark expressionless eyes. Had he been Flower he would have ploughed his way across and struck her for being so bold. Instead, he let her outstare him and turned away. There was something about eyes that was different from any other part of the body, although he didn't know what, exactly. Of all those people, over one thousand of them, only that nursing mother had looked at him straight on. It was small wonder a hood was placed over the heads of the condemned: to protect their executioners from that look.

Vengeance hurried from the hall, nodding at Flower as he passed. She had now positioned five gunmen at different points around the room and was watching them intently to make sure none dozed off. Her black fatigues and mask made her look like a vulture, waiting, waiting, waiting for that moment to come when she could claim her reward.

On the way out he passed Honey escorting three adults and six sleepy children back from the toilets. Even with her mask she looked like a team leader on a school picnic, the one who sorted things out, smoothed ruffled feathers, anticipated the next need. Of all of them she, surely, was the most out of place. Not driven by faith, nor even, as far as he could tell, by hatred. He knew there was no point asking. She would not leave Flower. Yes, he resented her. Partly it was because she was close to Flower, but mostly it was because she loved Flower. He had not loved anything or anyone for as long as he could remember.

He found Wrath by a window at the front of the building.

"OK?" he asked.

"You'd better keep back. Snipers."

Vengeance nodded, although he doubted the Russians would try that, at least not until an attack was imminent. Any random kill would be matched—more than matched. They surely knew that.

"Is anything going on?"

"Not that I can see," Wrath admitted. "But they'll be planning, somewhere."

"Yes."

Vengeance did not know how to put the question. And he didn't want to be overheard. They had not discussed making a break for it, at least not in so many words. But Wrath answered his unasked question anyway.

"I aim to take as many with me as I can," he said simply. "It will be sweet."

As expected. Vengeance rested his hand on the Radical's shoulder and looked out across the electric wasteland. What was it about raw hatred, he wondered, that could drown out even the urge for life?

THE RING OF the telephone inside the small office was deafening. It jerked him awake, making him realize he'd fallen asleep. He glanced at his watch. 4:30. The perfect time for them to call, the bastards. Across from him, Gregor, Death, was also struggling awake. He had a manic, confused, frightened expression on his face, trying to get his bearings, to remember where he was, to pull himself back into the hellish situation he was in from wherever his dreams had taken him. He looked at Vengeance. Vengeance nodded. He picked up.

"Yes, he's here," he answered in as steady a voice as he could manage, as if he had been waiting peaceably by the phone for just this call.

Vengeance leaned over and took the receiver from him.

"Yes?"

His manner was abrupt, alert, as if to say why are you bothering me? I was in the middle of important business—not fast asleep on one of this hellhole's miserable office chairs.

"Kadyrov, it's Shakirov, I have some good news for you."

"What good news?"

"We have one of the people on your list."

It was not possible. Vengeance was certain none on his list were alive. The man was lying.

"There were twenty names on my list."

"Yes, yes. But this is a good start. It must show you we are acting in good faith. So now, a gesture from you?"

"I said the people on my list had to be flown to Syria and only when I got a call from our contact would I release any of the children. Were you and your minders not listening?"

He could hear the muffled voices of the minders telling the pediatrician what to say next, and wondered if he too had been dragged out of a deep sleep.

"Sergei, may I call you Sergei?"

"No. My name is Kadyrov."

Vengeance was almost beginning to think he *was* called Kadyrov.

"Very well, Kadyrov. We have a problem."

"What problem?"

"The Syrian president does not want his country used in this way."

Tell me something I don't already know, Vengeance thought. Of course the Syrian president didn't want his country used in this way. The man was steering a fine line between the Russians and Americans and was willing to help Faith Radicals covertly but only when they were causing mischief outside his country.

"So who on my list have you got?" Vengeance asked, more out of curiosity than genuine interest.

Again, muffled voices.

"Anatole Zoya," came back Shakirov's answer.

Vengeance shook his head.

"You lying piece of shit. Anatole Zoya was tortured to death by your government on February 1st 2003."

This time the muffled voices were intense. Tell him this. No, tell him that. Keep him talking. Deny, deny. Vengeance was almost amused trying to imagine what they would say next.

When Uri Shakirov came back on the line, his voice was even higher than usual.

"There must be a mistake," he said limply. "The man we have claims to be Anatole Zoya, the man you asked for."

"Well, he isn't. Anatole Zoya was my friend and Anatole Zoya is dead because you killed him. . . ."

"But listen. . ." pleaded the hapless mediator.

"No. You listen," snapped Vengeance. This little game had gone on long enough. "At precisely eight this morning, ten nursing mothers will be released from the west door. They will walk towards the media compound. If anyone comes out to meet them, they will be shot. We are doing this to show that we have honor and that you do not. Is that understood?"

"What about Anatole Zoya?"

"Fuck your Anatole Zoya," Vengeance almost shouted, before slamming down the receiver.

He looked across at Gregor.

"Gather up the nursing mothers and take them to the room next to the west door. You'll find Blade there."

Death gave him a quizzical look.

"Flower won't like this," he suggested.

"No, she won't. But this is a media battle and Flower is not interested in the opinion of others."

"Are you going to tell her, then?"

"In the name of Allah! Are you all frightened of that woman?"

Death looked sheepish.

"I just thought. . ."

"Get on with it. Start getting the mothers, the nursing mothers mind, you know what a nursing mother is?"

Little Gregor made a comical nursing gesture.

"You've got it. Tell Flower I'll be along in a moment."

After Death had left the room, Vengeance tilted his head back and closed his eyes. The media would love it. And that look. He would have got rid of that look.

CHAPTER 14

$\mathcal{H}$e supposed he had expected more. A brusque hearing from the commander of the Seblan garrison at least. Instead his helicopter had been met by a handful of belligerent onlookers and two young soldiers who'd hustled him, handcuffed, into a jeep. The compound they took him to appeared deserted. They knew nothing about the nature of his visit. That much was obvious. "Our commander told us to lock you up until he had time for you, old timer," one had said.

The stifling cell they pushed him into stank of urine. A dim light came down a narrow corridor, mixed with what air there was and the voices of the soldiers. Suddenly he felt utterly alone. He remembered the first time he had experienced that feeling. His father had taken him hunting. He'd been ten and a novice. They had climbed part way up the Abochevo Mountain, the highest in the Vorsky region, in search of chamois. Alu had never seen a living chamois, although he'd eaten its meat which was considered a great delicacy.

It was early autumn and the snows had already dusted the mountain tops, pushing the goat-like animals off their alpine pastures. His father had made him carry the heavy rifle. He'd been allowed to fire three practice shots outside their village, Argun. The local boys had all come to watch. The first shot had missed the target completely. But the second had hit it on one side and the third dead center. "That's enough," his father had said. "Now you know you can do it." To start with, the rifle had felt light and he had felt proud, but after five miles his arm ached and his shoulder hurt. His father must have known this, but never once had offered to help. "If you can't carry your weapon you shouldn't be allowed to use it," he had said before they started, and Alu knew he had meant it.

When he had thought they were never going to stop, they came to an unusual rock formation. Above them had towered a steep cliff of ascending ledges. "The animals feel safe here," his father had said. "I am going around the mountain to find them. You wait ready behind this boulder. You'll only get a single shot." He had pointed to one particular ledge, half way up the cliff face. "Prepare to shoot your animal there." Alu had never thought to ask how his father knew that in all the great wilderness that surrounded them, that ledge alone would be the place where his chamois would stop long enough to be shot.

For quite some time after his father had left, he had lain prostrate behind the boulder and aimed the rifle. With his finger pressed against the trigger he had stared along the barrel, freezing its bead on a point above the ledge. Gradually, as discomfort spread through his body, it had dawned on him that his father would first have to locate the animals and then they would have to come to this spot, all of which would take time. He had relaxed his hold and begun to take in his surroundings.

The boulder he was behind was not one, but two. His father had made him lie in a narrow trench which ran past the large boulder that shielded him from the cliff face. A second smaller, misshapen rock had come to rest against the larger one above the trench, leaving an opening in the shape of an inverted 'v' ^ through which he could observe the ledge and little more. Over the years that followed he had learned how to read the landscape from his father, to see the invisible pathways animals would take, the places where they liked to eat, the resting places they preferred, depending on whether the wind was coming from the east or west. A southerly wind, and you'd most likely find them on a north face; a northerly one and they'd probably have moved to a spot facing south.

"Just remember," he would often say. "These are their hills as much as yours and you must match their knowledge if you want to find them." He would look at the sky, feel the wind and you realized he was slipping into the mind of whatever animal he was hunting. "They will smell you long before they hear you and hear you long before they see you. So use the wind. Work into the wind. It will muffle your sound and carry away your scent." But these were lessons for the future, lessons that would eventually be deployed against Federation soldiers. On that first day, Alu was a ten-year-old boy, with a ten-year-old boy's concentration.

As the minutes passed and nothing happened, he had first balanced the rifle as near to the correct position as he could, and lain on his back. It would be easy enough, he remembered thinking, to turn over. Above him the sky was being agitated by fast-moving cloud and he had watched the muted light strengthen and fade, strengthen and fade, as clouds of varying thickness raced past. But after a while this, too, had lost his interest. First he had sat up and then got up. He didn't think he had strayed far from the boulder. A patch of mountain berries caught his attention. Their blue juice stained his fingers. They were the berries his mother would sometimes give them at that time of year: a little sharp, but delicious!

He had followed the berries until he'd come to a small stream. "Food, and now water to drink," he remembered thinking. "I am independent. I can live!" A good hour or more must have passed since his father had left, but boys, when they are absorbed, are oblivious to time. The dam he built had been a fine dam. He could still almost capture it in his mind's eye. A holding pool. A new channel. Then diverting the original flow and watching the water scour out a fresh path down the mountainside. He and his friends had undertaken many such ventures and they merged in his memory. Once, they had unthinkingly diverted one of Argun's water supplies. Only when they returned from this exploit and found mothers peering angrily at the dry water channel that was supposed to supply their houses did they realize what they had done. Sheepishly they hurried back to undo their handiwork, only to find that several men from the village had got there first. It could have been worse. There was much laughter and joking, but they had not been allowed to forget.

It was while he had been admiring his construction that the first snowflake fell. So gentle, so light, so silent it had been. It had landed on the large round stone he'd used to block the original water course. Around this stone he'd packed earth and moss as a final seal. The water had risen quickly, almost to the top of this stone, before heading off at right angles into the holding pond and then out down the new channel. The flake had settled for only a moment before melting. But then another and another fell, until the large round stone and everything around it was completely covered. So enchanted had he been to see his work transformed in this way, that only then had he looked up.

He'd had his back to the wind and the flakes tumbled away from him in whorls and twists. From a few they had become many, bunched and eager to blanket the world. It was when he turned that he had felt utterly alone. Facing into the wind he had been able to see little and recognize nothing. He also felt cold for the first time. For several seconds, panic almost overwhelmed him, but then he had remembered his father and why he was there. "The rifle. I mustn't lose the rifle!" He stumbled back, trying to recall how far down he had gone. Twice he slipped. The ground under the snow was not yet hard. The light had been eerie and the flakes disorienting. "Go up, not down," he kept repeating to himself, knowing that the cliff face could not have been far away.

The third time he fell he landed badly and winded himself. The ground seemed to hold him, and he turned onto his back to recover. He felt comfortable where he lay and might not have moved had he not started to make out the shape of the large round boulder and mis-shapen rock above him, now coated white. He had fallen into the trench. Turning onto his stomach again he burrowed forward and felt in the snow with his hand. The utter joy he experienced when he touched the smooth shape of the rifle butt was indescribable and prompted him to let go in a strange way. "Now I have not let my father down," he remembered thinking.

He had lain peacefully in the trench for some time, his body white with snow, his head under the rocks and one hand round the stock of his gun. If it hadn't been for the unexpected sound of falling rocks he might have sunk into a deep, contented sleep. The fear he experienced had ebbed away until the sound brought it back. Suddenly he was wide awake, staring out into the snow which was now falling in waves, causing the dark shape of the cliff face to come and go. He was even sure he could make out the ledge. Then he saw it, standing there.

The animal looked so big. Its dark coat stood out against the snow. Moving its white and brown head from side to side it seemed to be searching out danger. Alu aimed the rifle, but a wave of snow obscured his target. He held his breath and kept pointing. For a few seconds the animal shape appeared again. He fired as the snow closed in once more, thicker than ever.

The next thing he remembered hearing was his father's comforting voice. "A nice buck. About 130 lbs. A good pair of horns too. You did well." Stiffly Alu had stood up and watched as his father cut out the intestines with a knife. "You're cold," his father had shouted. "Come and warm your hands in its belly," and he had.

On the way back, his father had carried the chamois slung across his shoulders and had carried the rifle too. The snow had stopped. The night sky had become clear and filled with stars. His father had sung and he had joined in. In the space of a few hours he had experienced the greatest fear and the greatest happiness. Later, when everyone had come to feast on the animal, he had also felt pride. He, Alu Dudayev, had provided for the people of his village. The memory comforted him, and he wondered if he would be able to serve his people once more.

CHAPTER 15

*A*s I had hoped, Michael's footage of the escaping children and my broadcast swept the airwaves. Bernie was ecstatic. I thought of asking him for an improved package. It's always best to hit Bernie when the money's pouring in. But somehow, in the heat of all the praise he was shoveling at me, I forgot. Besides, all the other news hounds, who I had beaten to the punch, were milling around within earshot when Bernie called. So I acted the 'good girl', and made out that our coup was no more than a day's work. Now I was kicking myself for being so supine. Hell, I owed it to Michael, at least, to screw a few more shekels out of the old skinflint. My funny cameraman had kept his cool and got us the prize, after all. I'd just have to face up to Bernie when we got back. But as every good hooker knows, trying to get the money after the event is not so smart.

Karen was proving to be a godsend, bringing us food and gossip from the town. Apparently the *Specials* and locals had almost come to blows. 'It's our children in there'. 'We're the ones who should be handling this' and that sort of thing, with the *Specials* acting all heavy-handed and insensitive as elite corps usually do. One thing she told us especially got my attention. According to her, a Chenchian leader had been flown in from Zoldek to help with the negotiations. At first I thought it might be Aslan, but Karen, who knew someone who had seen him, described a much older man. Whoever it was had not been made welcome. Our guide said he had been surrounded at the airport by an angry mob, before being escorted to the base. She supposed he was still there, but that even the local soldiers were as inclined to shoot him as guard him.

"Jesus, I'm stiff!" complained Michael as he emerged from the bivouac we had made in the press compound, as our patch of mud had seemingly become. "If there's another night, I'm spending it at the hotel."

"Have I missed anything?" asked Henry who strode in looking considerably fresher than the rest of us who had hung around all night, just in case.

"Yes. It's over," announced Kurt, rather aggressively, I thought.

With Henry barely out of earshot, the German informed anyone listening that he disliked the English, especially the supercilious English and most especially so when they had had a good night's sleep and he hadn't."

"Aren't the English always supercilious?" Michael joked, which I thought was quite perceptive for a boy who had only recently travelled outside Los Angeles.

"Since when did you become an expert?" I asked.

"Oh, there's a whole bunch of them in Hollywood trying to turn their innate sense of superiority into an art form, and doing quite well, actually."

"Well, I'm going back to the hotel for a bath," announced Kurt. "Nothing ever happens before breakfast."

"Top o' t'e marning, children," greeted Desmond looking much as always, except possibly more crumpled. "Can oi offer anyone a little pick-me-op?"

He waved his flask in our general direction.

"God, Desmond," I protested. "Do you ever stop drinking that stuff?"

"Not if oi can help it me little lovely."

"You weren't here last night and you don't look as though you've been back to your hotel," I accused him suspiciously. "What have you been up to?"

"Now t'at would be telling, wouldn't it?"

I tried not to be drawn, but he had a glint in his eye. He knew something.

"Well, come on. Tell," I urged. "Payback for the cell I lent you."

Just then the reporter for the Dallas news channel came over.

"Ah heard they'd got someone in custody," she announced tentatively.

"That's news to us," I parried. "We've been here all night and haven't heard a thing."

"Well, ah'll keep y'all posted if ah hear more," she promised, a promise we knew and she knew would not be kept.

"So, Desmond?" I pressed when she had moved on. "What have you got?"

"Not foinding our encampment t'e most salubrious of places, oi took moiself off and as befits me religion, found a place of repose, a quite pleasant little bar on t'e back side of town. Now as lock would have it, oi got to talking wit' a man who works at t'e base out by t'e airpart. He's t'e doctor, actually and says all he ever treats is t'e clap or bosted jaws and broken fingers."

"Spare us the grubby details, Desmond," I urged, fearing he was about to embark on one of his shaggy-dog stories and fancying a bath back at the hotel myself.

"Oh don't you go mocking grubby details, now girlie. More of loife takes place in t'e gutter t'an it does on t'e cross, if you'll pardon me for saying so."

I couldn't help smiling. Desmond's stories had a habit of running to term and I should have known better than to press.

"Onyway, t'is doctor tells me an elderly troibesman has just been flown into t'e base from Zoldec. A distinguished-looking man, he tells me. But t'at's not t'e half of it. What do you t'ink his name is?"

I looked at him, blankly.

"Alu Dudayev," he crowed proudly. "Now isn't he somet'ing to t'at man of yours, t'e one you knew back wherever it was, at university or somet'ing?"

He could tell from my expression that he had scored a bullseye.

"What in heavens name is *he* doing in Seblan?"

"So t'ere is a connection?"

"Father. I met him just a few days ago."

"Well t'is doctor, and oi have to tell you," he continued, tapping his wallet, "a man of considerable capacity, spent some toime wit' your friend's fat'er because no one on t'e base wanted onyt'ing to do wit' him. He was virtually onder arrest, in fact."

"But why is he here?"

"It seems he was furious when he heard about t'e siege and wanted to put a stop to it. T'e yong commander in Zoldek, whose fat'er, boi some strange coincidence, t'is warlord of yours knew, agreed t'at he should be flown here to negotiate wit' t'e hostage takers. He t'inks he knows one of t'em. Unfortunately, t'e yong commander's contacts in Moscow carry no weight in Seblan, and our elderly peacemaker is sitting locked in a room at t'e barracks."

"Did this doctor of yours say whether Alu Dudayev's son was involved?"

"I t'ought you'd be wanting to know t'at," admitted Desmond, pleased that he appeared to be repaying his debt with interest. "All t'e doctor could recall from his conversation was t'at t'e man had not heard from his son and was worried."

I looked at my watch. It wasn't yet seven. Karen would be here soon to run me back to the hotel. I had to have a shower.

"Do you know where I might find this doctor?"

Desmond handed me a card.

"T'at's his sorgery in Seblan. But piece of advoice?"

"Sure."

"T'e doctor said t'e atmosphere in t'e town was explosive. Ony Chenchian, or onyone connected to one, was . . . how did he put it? . . . dead meat." And as he said it he bent his neck and made the hangman's gesture.

While I was taking this in, Karen's car drove up.

"Michael, I want you to stay here. I'm going back to the hotel for a shower and then I must find this doctor and get him to take me to Aslan's father."

"Orla, are you sure that's a good idea?" he questioned.

"No. It's probably a very bad idea, which is why I want you here. Besides, if anything breaks, you can film it."

Michael sniffed under his armpits, a mannerism I have often noticed in males.

"Of course you stink!" I told him. "But that won't stop you filming. I still want you here."

I HANDED KAREN the card Desmond had given me as we drove away.

"Do you know this man?" I asked her. "He's a doctor."

"Certainly. He's well known. He does some work at the army base."

"After you've dropped me at the hotel, can you go to this doctor and say I'd like him to take me to the man they are holding out at the base."

"The Chenchian?"

"Does everyone know he is there?"

"Yes. Everybody!"

I STOOD UNDER the shower and soaked. Mercifully, the water was hot. So, what was I to do? My job was to cover the siege, not find Aslan's father. If I could just persuade someone to take him to the school, to negotiate, then he would be part of the right story, but how? As I watched the water pour off me in rivulets I lined up the options. There was Bernie. He obviously had high-level contacts. But if I asked him he would think my love life was interfering with my work, and for Bernie, there was only work. Another possibility was Andrew Meadows. It would probably be him Bernie ended up speaking to anyway. No. I just didn't trust him. Well, I didn't understand his game, more like, my country's game, that is. If only I could speak to Aslan.

As I washed it came to me: Countess Presniakov. She still had military contacts and this was, mostly, a military problem. I toweled off and leafed through my notebook. Surely I had her number? Would they, whoever they were these days, be monitoring her line? Almost certainly. I found the number on a page of jottings and made the call.

"Countess Presniakov's residence."

I recognized Tania's voice, which reminded me of the rather charming pretence she and the countess maintained.

"I would like to speak to Countess Presniakov, please."

"Who shall I say is calling?"

"Orla Kildare, from DEMOS-TV."

"I will see if she is at home."

That little ritual, the studied politeness, the impenetrable wall if you were the wrong kind of caller. Luckily, I was the right kind.

"Orla, I'm glad you called. I did not know how to reach you."

The countess's concern surprised me.

"I should have left you my number," I told her, although I had not thought for a minute that we would be talking again.

"Never mind. Just listen. The garrison commander at Zoldek was a friend of my son's. It was he who agreed to send the Chenchian, your friend's father, I think, to Seblan. Now he wishes he hadn't."

"But why?"

"The command in Seblan has broken down. The soldiers are local and every one has a relative or knows someone in that school. All they can think about is what might be going on inside, what might be happening to their friends and loved ones. It is not a good situation, Orla."

"What about the *Specials* who have come here from Moscow?" I asked her.

"You must understand, they are not in the chain of command. They report directly to the president and the president will not use a Chenchian to help break this siege."

"Even for the sake of the children?" I questioned.

"You must appreciate the politics, Orla. This is a very . . ."

"Countess? . . . Are you there, countess? . . . Countess, I've lost you. Fuck and damn!"

"Yes, I can hear you, Orla."

"Oh!" I exclaimed, embarrassed. "I'm sorry about the language. I thought I'd lost you there for a moment."

"I must ring off now, my dear. You just stay out of this, do you understand?"

I was about to say that I didn't, when the line went dead and this time stayed dead. I tried to call back but the number was engaged. I repeated the countess's warning. "You just stay out of this." Did she mean it, or did she mean the exact opposite because someone had intercepted our call?

I was getting dressed in an absent-minded way, wondering how best to handle the situation, when there was a frantic rapping at my door.

"Ms. Kildare, Ms. Kildare, are you in there?"

I recognized Karen's voice straight off and rushed to the door. She must have found out something from the doctor.

"Karen, what is it? What's up?"

"Quickly! You must come quickly. Some hostages are about to be released."

"How do you know this?" I asked. "The doctor?"

"Yes, the doctor. Now hurry. We haven't much time. They are coming out at eight."

I glanced at my watch as I gathered my things and hurtled after her. We had just ten minutes.

OUR ARRIVAL AT the press compound, dirt flying every which way, almost had us shot by some trigger-happy soldiers and caused a collective jaw drop amongst my press-jock colleagues who were winding themselves up slowly for another day of idle speculation, false rumors and discomfort.

"What's up, Orla?" called out someone. But I was in too much of a hurry to reply.

"Michael! Thank God you're here," I prattled out, almost tripping into our station, which was no more than a shallow depression in the ground which we had 'furnished' with our things.

"Of course I'm here," he answered rather acidly. "You wouldn't let me go anywhere else."

"Is the camera ready?" I asked, trying to lower my voice and sound less excited. But my arrival had sent a lightning bolt through the media corps. People were now moving, hither and thither, in a state of heightened expectation and looking at us for any hint of what it was they should be expecting.

"Michael's wife is having a baby," I called out.

A wave of disappointment passed through the corps. Mouths opened, shoulders dropped, expressions that had been eager turned flaccid.

"You're shitting me, right?"

Michael's expression was almost best of all.

"Yes, I'm shitting you. Now is that camera ready?"

"Fuck, Orla! Don't DO that to me," he hissed. "Yes, it's ready. But what the hell is it ready for?"

"I don't know, exactly. Some people are coming out at eight."

I looked down at my watch and made it a couple of minutes after. Next to me, a beetle was picking its way across the earth, oblivious to the human drama surrounding it.

"Orla!"

Michael's whisper was intense.

He was glued to his lens and suddenly we were both peering across at the school.

AT FIRST IT was hard to make out anything unusual, but that is probably the wrong word. Everything about Seblan's Middle School Number One was unusual. Troops were everywhere, although with the arrival of the *Specials*, there was less milling around, less intermixing of civilian men with weapons and their military brothers, and the long night had left everyone a little slower and a lot more worn out. It looked and felt not like a school but an army encampment bracing itself for the morning, before a battle that was expected to come on that day, the next, or one after—no one knowing for sure, but everyone knowing that it *would* come.

The crack troops from Moscow had set up a command centre in front of the school. We were off to one side, so had a good view of the battleground. No one I had spoken to thought this siege would end peaceably. The locals were after blood, no question about it. And we knew the *Specials* would want to take out the terrorists first and foremost, saving as many children as they could, but only as a secondary objective. That was how they had acted before and President Nitup's popularity had risen as a result. So that was how they would act now. It is a sorry truth, but a few casualties are just that, a few. The killing of terrorists resonates with many. Democracy, I've noticed, can be as callous as any other form of government.

Perhaps it was because I looked towards the front of the building that I missed the first woman and her child emerge from the door opposite us. They were over fifty yards away and there were some sheds between us and that end of the building, but Michael was onto it.

"Over there, Orla."

When I saw her, the woman, who was holding a baby, appeared to be moving back inside, but very quickly she was joined by another and another, until I counted nine women, all holding babies, standing in a confused state outside the door. For some reason, they did not want to move and were facing towards the school, not away from it. We could hear raised voices coming from inside, but could not make out the words. After what seemed like an age, a tenth woman came out, not only holding a babe in one arm, but with a small boy clutching her hand. Only then did they all start walking towards us.

"Over here!" one of the local soldiers called out.

But the women just kept walking, not running, but walking, straight towards the press compound.

"This is terrific," Michael muttered, his camera turning.

"Whoever's in that building is sure media savvy," I agreed. "Those women are doing exactly what they have been told. They look absolutely petrified."

As the women approached us, the media circus slipped into gear and everyone started firing questions, mostly in English, at the bemused group. "What's it like in there?" "How many are dead?" "Who are the terrorists?". . .

As the women tumbled into our enclave they started sobbing and looking around for any faces that were not ours. I approached the nearest and offered her a drink from the thermos Karen had brought for Michael.

"Here, drink this. It's hot coffee."

Hearing someone speak her own language made the woman less anxious, and resting her baby on one arm, she took the cup.

"Why did you all stop back there?" I asked.

"Renata," she answered, tossing her head in the direction of the woman with the baby and young child. "She wouldn't leave without her boy. At first they said only nursing mothers, but when none of us would leave. . . ."

"Quick. This way. No talking."

A group of masked *Specials* converged on us at the same time as some of the local soldiers and their armed friends, and roughly asserted their authority. The women began screaming and I thought for a moment that the locals were going to lay into the Muscovites who must have looked to the mothers like the terrorists they had just escaped.

"No filming. No camera," shouted one of the *Specials* at Michael, who was pointing his lens right at the scene of panic the man and his elite corps had created. Quickly, the women were herded away, no doubt for a rigorous debriefing. I wondered how soon the doctor would be allowed to check them over. The press corps were left agog, although not for long. Everyone had a report to file.

"*Alright Michael?*"

"Yes, Orla. Go for it."

"We are now into the third day of the Seblan school siege and there has been a dramatic development. At eight o'clock this morning, local time, ten nursing mothers with their babies and one young boy walked out of the school. No reason has yet been given. The atmosphere here is electric. Local people are exhausted and sick with worry. Conditions inside the school must be appalling. We heard shots last night coming from the building but do not know if anyone was killed. If the authorities here are prepared to share with us what they learn from the mothers released earlier, we soon will.

It is believed a senior Chenchian warlord was flown in to Seblan yesterday to negotiate with the terrorists, but so far, the authorities here have been unwilling to use him. The atmosphere is, frankly, explosive, and anyone from that country is at risk. There are rumors that negotiations have taken place between the authorities and the terrorists, but here on the ground, expectations for a peaceful outcome to this crisis are not high. This is Orla Kildare for DEMOS-TV reporting live from Middle School Number One, Seblan.

"OK, Steve. That's it."

"Gotcha, Orla. Take care. That doesn't look like a nice place."

"Bernie doesn't pay us to go to nice places."

"I guess not!"

Or pay us sufficient I thought, and then felt guilty at having had such an unseemly notion, considering what we were in the middle of.

IN THIS BUSINESS, you can move from a state of adrenaline-pumping panic to one of almost total flatness in a blink. After the excitement of the nursing mothers and filing our reports, we were all left sitting around like travellers whose train has departed from the station without them. I tried calling the countess, but her line was busy. That figured. Until this crisis was over, I guessed it would stay busy. I tried Aslan but, of course, nothing. On impulse I tried the doctor using one of the numbers shown on the card Desmond had given me. It looked as though it might be for a cell. After my first two failures, the deep voice that answered almost caught me by surprise.

"Dr. Trofim?"

"Yes. Who is speaking?"

"My name is Orla Kildare. Karen, our driver, might have mentioned me. I'm a reporter for a US station, DEMOS-TV."

"This is not a good time."

I guessed he wasn't alone.

"You are waiting to examine the nursing mothers?"

"Yes."

"I understand you have met Alu Dudayev."

"Yes."

"Is he safe?"

"Can we talk later?"

"You think he may not be safe?"

"That is correct."

"Could we get him into the press compound?"

"I really must go now."

"You don't think so?"

"That would be my view."

"Is there anything I *can* do?"

"I will speak to you later."

With that, the doctor cut off. He had probably told me all that he could.

"I wish I could speak a foreign language," mused Michael, who had been watching me in an idle sort of way.

"Did you ever try?" I wondered.

"Took a shot at Spanish once, but when the Mexican girl I was dating dumped me for a rhinestone cowboy, I lost heart."

"It's pretty much the second language where you come from, isn't it?"

"The first, some reckon!"

"Why don't you go back to the hotel for a spell," I suggested. "You look beat. I don't suppose much will happen here for an hour or two."

"You sure?"

"Yeah. I'm sure."

We called Karen and she appeared in no time to pick him up. While he was collapsing into the back of her car, half asleep, I asked her to come straight back and not tell him. He needed rest.

THE ROAD TO the barracks was deserted. Everyone who had wanted to come to Seblan had done so, and everyone else was either outside the school or at home waiting for news. I felt nervous on two counts. If something happened back at the siege and neither Michael nor I were there, I'd be screwed, big time. That was the first. The second was that I had no idea what to expect out at the base.

When we arrived, it seemed completely deserted. It was not a large base, home to no more than a couple of hundred soldiers, Karen thought, and looked very run down. Doubtless a sop to a local politician and of little real importance to the military, until now, at least.

"I'll just wait for you here, alright?" Karen asked, as we pulled up.

"Yes. Definitely don't leave me!"

I walked across the dirt to the entrance, a large arch with a small door to one side which I opened. It was sweltering. Inside, two startled young soldiers looked up from a small TV set.

"I have come to interview the Chenchian," I announced rather boldly, pushing forward my entry papers and accreditation across a counter. One of the two got up and nervously looked at them, but without the slightest comprehension.

"Stepan, you'd better have a look at these," he said to his friend.

Stepan rose and both of them stared at the papers, unwilling to admit that they could make nothing of them.

"I'm in a hurry. My driver is waiting outside," I flanneled, hoping that they would think it easier to cooperate than have to try and ask someone, when there was nobody there to ask. "One of you can come with me when I interview your . . . er . . . guest."

The two looked at each other and shrugged.

"You take her, Stepan. I'll keep these," the first soldier announced, clearly feeling that by holding onto my papers he was in control.

"Take her yourself, Oleg. The savage stinks," countered his colleague.

"Well, I don't mind which, but will one of you take me to him now, please," I insisted, with as much force as I could muster. Another of the little tricks that wise, liquor-soaked journo I met in Kigali had taught me was *just remember girl, soldiers are programmed to take orders, so command them. You'd be surprised how often it works!*

Reluctantly, it was Oleg who drew the short straw and I followed him down a narrow passage to what was no more than a cell. The air *was* foul and the heat overpowering, but not because of their 'savage'. The place itself was a hellhole. No sooner had my escort delivered me to the bars of the cell door, than he turned and left.

"Is that you, Orla Kildare?"

I recognized the voice, but at first could see nothing. The cell had no windows and the passage drew only a little light from the room in which the two youthful and disgruntled soldiers, Stepan and Oleg, appeared to be overseeing the entire camp.

"Yes, it is. I can't see you."

"I assure you, I am here."

"Why *are* you here, Alu Dudayev?"

"I think, because no one knows what to do with me."

"No. I meant, why did you come?"

"Ah! Probably because I am old and foolish."

"You are not safe."

"You came to tell me that?"

Slowly my eyes began to see. Alu Dudayev was sitting in a corner. He was wearing his customary clothes; a long cloak which loosely covered his body and a turban. In his hands were beads which he was fingering. On his feet were a pair of well-worn boots. As they had the first time, the fineness of his features struck me. In so many ways, he looked like his son.

"I brought some water and a little food, but I wasn't sure if I would be able to give it to you."

"They will be most welcome. The service here is not good. But tell me, Orla Kildare, how did you know I was here?"

"Journalists find out things. The doctor."

"The only intelligent man in the place!"

I pushed the food and water through the bars, worried that one of the soldiers would return and confiscate it.

"Here. You had better take this, before one of them comes back."

The old warlord lifted himself up, collected the food and returned to his corner.

"So, why *did* you come?" I pressed.

"I wanted to show that my people are not savages. I wanted to put a stop to this taking of women and children. Doing so was a foolish act. It brings us down to their level."

"We are being told that Sergei Kadyrov is leading the hostage takers," I informed him.

"That is what I heard, too. But the more I have thought about it, the less I think it can be him. Yes, I have said Sergei is hot-headed, but I have never said he was a fool. There was even a moment when I feared my son might be involved."

"Where is Aslan?" I asked. "I have not been able to speak to him since I left."

"Both Sergei and my son have disappeared from sight. Kadyrov's people thought he might have been murdered, until they heard that he was here. There is great tension in the regions. Everyone is worried."

"What about Malik and Roaz?"

"I have not heard that they have gone missing. But there are always rumors."

"What rumors?"

"Many think Malik is too close to the Russians, just as many thought my son was too close to the Americans."

"What do you think?"

"I think my son was put on the wrong horse."

I didn't know what to say, because I feared he was right.

"So who do you think the hostage takers are?" I questioned.

"Faith Radicals. It has to be. They are the only ones who want Chenchia, and the countries around us, to explode with violence, to become ungovernable, to become—eventually—part of a theocratic south. It is the curse of my nation to have been born on a fault line between two cultures. My wife and I were foolish. The American way was never an option. I see that now."

"Is there anything I can do for you?" I asked.

"Tell the truth, Orla Kildare. Even if no one is listening now, it is important that one day, people know the truth."

"Anything else?" I urged, hearing voices coming down the passage and fearing our meeting was about to be curtailed.

"Yes," he answered rising from the floor and coming towards me. "Give these to Aslan. And if Aslan is dead, give them to Roaz."

Through the bars he passed me the beads he had been fingering and I slipped them into my bag. The thought of Aslan being dead had not occurred to me before. Aslan didn't die. He just disappeared from my life and then reappeared. But I wasn't allowed to dwell on the dreadful possibility of him being gone for good. Stepan and Oleg descended on me with renewed authority.

"What are you doing? You can't be here. Unless you want to join the savage, you must get out."

"Yes, get out right now," the other echoed.

Back in the corner office, I could see, through the open door, that a truckload of soldiers had returned. A group of men had surrounded Karen's car and several were coming our way.

"My papers," I pleaded.

"Here, take them," Stepan instructed, looking nervously over my shoulder.

I turned to leave and almost walked straight into a soldier of higher rank than either Stepan or Oleg. He glared at me, but had more pressing things on his mind than my presence.

"She's just leaving, Sarge," Oleg blurted out.

"If you've been bringing girls in, soldier, I'll cut it off myself, and with a blunt knife, you little pisshead," he snarled.

I couldn't get out quick enough. As I approached Karen's car, the group of men around it began whistling and making lewd remarks.

When I caught sight of myself in the wing mirror, I could see that I was covered in dust, from head to toe, and looking like a pretty good tramp. This had probably saved us a whole bunch of trouble. The sultry smile I gave the men, as I clambered in beside Karen, was duly appreciated.

"What the hell did they think we were?" I gasped as we raced away.

"I told the sergeant we were visiting our boyfriends," Karen giggled.

That was one trick my Kigali friend hadn't taught me.

CHAPTER 16

*O*n the way back, we stopped at the hotel. Michael was dead to the world and I felt harsh having to pound on his door. Eventually he emerged from dreamland, although remained monosyllabic while we drove on to the press compound, just managing the occasional grunt. He admitted he could have slept for a week and asked, as much out of politeness as interest, I think, if I had found Alu Dudayev.

"Sorry you missed the big event, Orla," taunted Henry, which was, to use one of his shooting expressions, a left and right, because Kurt, who was standing nearby, *had* missed the release of the nursing mothers and was still fuming. Luckily Desmond shook his head, so I didn't fall for it.

"Gather round, children," I called out. "I have some ice cream for you. Not suitable for the English palate, though!"

Everyone, including Henry, who was—like the rest of us I suppose —largely without shame, sidled over and I soon had a circle of the world's press around me.

"Try to appear natural, will you," I pleaded. "I don't want to scream out for attention."

A few people sat on what they could find, but I suspect we still looked as though we were about to hold a village meeting, something almost certainly banned by an article of Tsarist legislation that had survived communism and now democracy, or at least Russia's version of it.

"You've all heard, I'm sure, that a Chenchian was flown in yesterday to help with the negotiations," I began.

"Do you know who he is, Orla?" someone asked.

"Yes. He's the leader of the Vorsky region."

"How do you spell that, Orla?" another journalist asked.

His question brought home to me the possibility that almost no one around me knew anything about Chenchia, or its struggle.

"VORSKY, " I spelled out. "Chenchia has three regions."

"Was that three, Orla?" a woman at the back called out.

"That's right. Three. Vorsky, Sharosky and Urus."

"Could you spell them, Orla?"

"Oh, for heaven's sake," complained Desmond, "I don't t'ink Orla wants to teach us all *Chenchia 101!*"

"The three regions," I continued, "are largely self-governing, but there has been a steady migration to the capital, Zoldek. Now it is in and around the capital that most of the country's strife has taken place. The key players are the Russians who have an oil pipe that runs through the heart of the country; the Democrats who used to be backed by the good ol' US of A but are now, I think, on their own; and the Faith Radicals who would like to see the country slip from Russian control and become part of a theocracy centered on the Middle East."

"Wha did we ditch the Democrats, Orla?" asked the reporter from Dallas.

"Officially, I am not sure that we have. But now that our president and the Russian president have found common cause against Faith Radicals, I think we have conceded that Chenchia is in the Russian sphere of influence."

"So we're willing to give t'e Russkies a free hand, t'en," Desmond extrapolated.

"That's the way I'm seeing it," I confirmed.

"So 'ow does deese Chenchian negotiator feet een, Mademoiselle?" a young French reporter wondered.

"Merci à vous pour ne me pas avoir appellée Madame!" I responded.

"Come on Orla," chortled Desmond, "leave t'e innocent alone!"

"As I said, this Chenchian is leader of the Vorsky region. Some of you may have seen my report. It was his village that was burned; the women and girls in his village who were raped and mutilated by Russian soldiers; the young boys who were tortured and killed; the old women, including his wife, who were burned alive in their homes. And yet it is this same man who is utterly opposed to what is happening here and who offered to come to Seblan to try to end it peaceably. And now it is he who the authorities are ignoring and who is being held within an airless cell out at the army barracks."

"Do they not *want* to end this thing peaceably?" questioned the Dallas reporter, indignantly.

"Moscow t'inks t'ere is jost one way to deal wit' terrorists," observed Desmond.

"And they have a point," stated Kurt. "These animals are nothing but killers."

"So who *are* the terrorists, Orla?" a man on the outer ring of our circle called out.

I shrugged.

"Faith Radicals? That, at least, is what the leader of the Vorsky region thinks."

"You've met with him?"

"Yes. An hour ago. It's my belief that the siege here has more to do with Russia's internal politics and her desire to control Chenchia, than it does with Chenchia itself. The battle against international terrorism is about energy supplies, and I think most of us. . . ."

"What the. . . ."

A thunder clap of an explosion enveloped our gathering, forcing us all to the ground.

"Oh, Mot'er of God! Was t'at t'e school?" Desmond spluttered as we all crawled across the ground to our stations.

"I think it came from over there, on the left," Henry coughed out.

And certainly we could see smoke rising on one side of the building, but whether it was coming from outside or inside was impossible to tell.

"How's that camera, Michael?" I shouted as I approached our spot. Following a series of lesser explosions, the sound of shooting had become continuous. Smoke was now everywhere. The battle had begun.

"Rolling," Michael announced, having been well and truly jolted out of his earlier torpor.

"Will you put your fucking hat on," I yelled, even though he was only a foot away.

"Oh, Christ," he said, reaching behind him and slamming it onto his head.

"And your jacket? Have your got your jacket on?"

"Shit. Here, take this," he stammered, handing me the camera "point and press."

And he rolled back into our depression, to grab his flak jacket.

It was hard to make out what was going on. Shots seemed to be coming from all directions. I could see a group of locals—soldiers and civilians—crouching behind a wall, waiting for an opportunity to use their weapons. The *Specials* were also firing into the school, but selectively and I assumed, with the aid of telescopic sights. I could only imagine what it must have been like inside. The sun was now overhead and it was getting hot. The thirteen hundred or however many there were in the hall must have been baking, breathless and terrified. I supposed some of the terrorists were still guarding them although most must have moved to the windows. And what were the *Specials* up to?

Skulking around the back of the building, no doubt, looking for any weak spot, any way to force an entry.

"Sorry about that!" Michael murmured, retrieving his camera.

"I want to get a broadcast out," I almost shouted.

"What, now?"

"Yes. Are you powered up."

"I think so."

"Jesus, what do you mean 'you think so'?

"Well, I left it on charge while I was at the hotel, so it should be alright. But I haven't checked."

I scowled, which was ungracious of me, in the circumstances.

"OK. Let's crawl into the ditch behind us and see if we can get a link."

"Fair enough," agreed Michael. "We're as likely to get shot there as here!"

So we slithered back, hauling our kit, until we flopped over into the ditch, only to discover it occupied.

"Ah, campers! It's noice of yous to join me."

"Bloody hell, Desmond, you startled me. Have you given up on the front line, then?"

"Oi should say so. T'e great beauty of t'e written word is t'at it doesn't have to be introduced to bullets personally. Do you fancy a nip, girlie?

"*I* do," pleaded Michael.

"T'ere you go, yong Michael. 'Tis t'e Almoighty's antidote to hell."

Suitably fortified, Michael started to set up the dish and search for a signal.

"Are you sure you won't, Orla?" Desmond pressed, holding out his flask. "Oi've been ronning on Dotch corage all me loif."

Whether it was out of fraternal feeling for him or to steady my own pumping heart, I'm not sure, but I took a swallow. The burning sensation was quickly followed by a distinct improvement to my state of mind.

"I've got it, Orla," Michael shouted. "Steve's not in yet. We've got Paul."

"Now Michael, I want you to start with me, then pan up and capture everything that is going on at the school until I stop talking. Send Paul the stuff you took earlier and they can use it later if they choose, but I want what we do now streamed into Europe and set up for our early morning news, just as it is. Are you getting all that, Paul.

"I sure am, Miss Kildare. Ready when you are."

Michael and I exchanged looks—*Miss Kildare*. Paul must be new.

"Earlier today, we had a hopeful sign. Ten nursing mothers walked from the school unharmed. As far as we know, this was a gesture by the hostage takers in return for nothing, other than the publicity it gave them. But in the last several minutes matters have deteriorated horribly. There was an explosion. We do not know if it came from inside the school or outside. We do not know if it was initiated by the hostage takers or by the many armed solders, civilians and *Specials*, the crack troops from Moscow, answerable directly to President Nitup, surrounding the school. All we do know is that a fully-fledged battle is now raging and that many people will almost certainly be killed.

"Meanwhile, Alu Dudayev, leader of the Vorsky region in Chenchia, who condemns the hostage taking absolutely and came here voluntarily to help negotiate a peaceful end to this crisis, is being held in an airless cell within the nearby army barracks.

"The impression here is that there exists no clear chain of command. The *Specials* have a history of ending such incidents by killing the hostage takers, even if it means that many hostages die. The local soldiers and civilians, however, appear completely out of control. It is their children, their mothers, their wives, and their friends who are being held inside the school. A more incendiary situation would be hard to imagine.

"This is Orla Kildare reporting to you live for DEMOS-TV outside Middle School Number One, Seblan."

"How was that, Paul?"

"Terrific, Miss Kildare, really terrific!"

Michael and I couldn't help smiling.

"Can I ask you, Miss Kildare, are those real shots I'm hearing, I mean not posed or anything?"

"Yes, Paul, they're real alright. Believe me!"

The signal went dead and we ducked back down into the trench.

"He's probably been playing *Battlefield* on his computer all noight," chuckled Desmond.

"God!" I groaned. "I hope we measure up!"

ALL AFTERNOON THE conflict raged, with alternating waves of intensity. One side would take offense and fire a volley of shots at some imagined insult, and the other would reciprocate in kind. No clear advantage was being achieved, as far as I could see. The hostage takers remained in control of the school. There were occasional lulls, when no one could think of any good reason to squeeze his trigger. At the very least, the Faith Radicals, if that is who held the children, were using up ammunition they couldn't replace.

We stopped filming continuously after my broadcast and just lay there watching. The group of locals in front of us, a mix of soldiers and civilians, kept trying to work their way closer to the school buildings. But every time they attempted to gain ground, they were met with a hail of bullets. At first, Michael and I wondered why they kept trying, their efforts bore so little fruit. Then we noticed, to their left, three men inching up a gully that must have been invisible from the school.

"Do you want me to try and catch that, Orla?" Michael asked.

His question posed a dilemma. We were visible from the school, and it was clear the hostage takers considered us to be an essential part of their offensive. Apart from stray rounds that whined past every so often, they left us alone. The locals, too, largely ignored us. A mixture of being flattered by our interest and insulted at having their anguish exposed was probably how they felt towards us. The *Specials* would just as soon have sent us packing, I think. A few pictures at the end, of them hauling out dead terrorists, might have suited their purpose. But not more. So how neutral were we?

If I let Michael capture the three men working their way up the gully and his camera angle alerted the hostage takers, not very. We were already part of the militants' game plan. Although it was hardly our fault that neither the locals nor *Specials* were media savvy.

"Orla, what about it?"

"We might give them away. Let's hold off for a while."

"Until they are spotted?"

"Something like that."

As we lay there, strangely detached from what was going on around us, I knew Michael was thinking. Back home he might have tried to avoid politics because, as he saw it, the game was a fix anyway, but that hadn't stopped him thinking. I'd learned that about my cameraman since we'd been together, that and a few of his 'little secrets'.

"Is news ever neutral, do you think?"

His moments of gestation had given birth to a powerful question. One that had troubled me, often.

"I sometimes ask myself that question," I admitted.

"And what answer do you come up with?"

"That it isn't."

"That it isn't?"

"How can it be, really?"

"Do you feel like elaborating?"

"Goodness, Michael. We're in the middle of a battle. Is this a good time to be considering the philosophy and ethics behind journalism?"

"I should say so."

I realized instantly that I had sounded unnecessarily peevish, and that his simple answer had put me firmly in my place.

"Yes, you would, wouldn't you! And it probably *is* the perfect time and place."

He smiled at me, indulgently.

"OK," I conceded. "Let me elaborate. For starters, we have an audience of one, Bernie. He has a bigger audience, our sponsors. And what are they interested in? Viewers. But not just any viewers. The interplay between the tone of our broadcasts and the reaction of our viewers has to be in line with the product image our sponsors are attempting to project. So our news must be essentially patriotic; it must appear to possess gravitas; it must, in a subtle way, suggest that we—and so they, our sponsors—know what the hell we are doing, that ours is an ordered world in which their product plays a vital role. And that is just the basics, before we even get close to such knotty issues as objectivity, neutrality and truth."

"So we all have to brown nose," smirked Michael. "Tell me something new!"

"You really are insufferable!" I griped. "You ask a serious question and I'm trying to give you a serious answer."

"Whoa, steady there, Miss Kildare!"

"I hate you!"

I felt my blood pumping. The boy had made me angry. How could I have let him?

"Alright, alright!" he conceded. "So news has to sit within a social framework and that framework determines how we interpret it."

"Yes. And not only that. The framework also determines what is newsworthy. Take this conflict in Chenchia. It has been going on for centuries. But only in the last few years, thanks to oil, the collapse of the Soviet Union and the terrorism of Faith Radicals have we become interested."

"Are you saying that news is essentially self-interest?"

"Of course. Why else *would* we want to know about things?"

"So what on earth are we doing in this dump? It has nothing to do with us, really."

"Ah! Now we come to the good part."

"There is a good part?"

"Yes. It's not all about doing penance in order to get back into favor with demanding girlfriends!"

"Ouch!"

"God, Michael. Will you look at that!"

As we were talking, a man from the group we had been watching suddenly decided to make a break for it. He just started running towards a pile of rubble some twenty yards from the wall he had been sheltering behind.

"The idiot," hissed Michael, who had instinctively started filming.

"Oh, Christ!" I groaned, as he took first one shot and then another, but still managed to drag himself behind the rubble.

"Now what, you moron?" muttered Michael.

"Michael, look! Those three men. They've made it to the school wall."

"Well I'll be damned!" exclaimed Michael. "So that was just a diversion. The crazy bastard."

The next twenty minutes were a confused blur of activity. It was as if the event itself had come alive, forcing its own violent will on all concerned. No one seemed to know what they were doing, but they did it with a ferocity that bordered, at times, on lunacy or extreme bravery, I wasn't sure which. Part of me got caught up in the sheer excitement of it all. Another part recoiled in horror every time a human body was ripped apart in front of us.

We were already coming to the end of the day when the battle entered its final, horrific, crescendo. Nature's dulling was giving way to a shallow glare from arc lights which infused the smoke belched out by spent munitions with an almost biblical glow. The three fighters, two in uniform and one a civilian, who had reached the school wall seemed to have been the catalyst for this final convulsion. We watched them, pressed hard against the bricks, slide their way along to one of the windows from which the terrorists were firing. The first to reach it lobbed a grenade through the opening. It exploded almost immediately, knocking out part of the wall and hurling the first two fighters to the ground. The third, the civilian, clambered through the opening into the smoke and we heard a barrage of shots. It was then that the sports hall went up.

I don't know where the *Specials* were at this point, but some had surely gained entry from the back. As a plume of smoke rose from the hall, the firefight continued unabated. Flames were now coming from several parts of the building. People were running every which way. It was hard to make out who was who. To our amazement, a few children, naked save for skimpy underpants, started to appear at several doors. At first they didn't know what to do, until, one by one, they started to run across the battle zone. A number were felled, almost as soon as they began the perilous crossing, but many more reached safety. Five children and a woman, a teacher or mother, I never did discover which, tumbled into our compound and were quickly gathered up by locals. The young ones looked grimy and vulnerable, more like spirits than living beings, the way their drawn white skins were illuminated under the harsh lights.

All this time, Michael was filming, filming. Neither of us spoke, the sheer horror of it all was too gripping. The destruction of the sports hall had sent the locals wild. The women had begun to gather a short distance away, hoping their loved ones might survive the carnage that was taking place in front of us. Their wails and cries and shouts of anguish mixed with the sounds of gunfire and crackle of burning. The rumble of trucks coming to collect the dead and wounded was all that reminded us that there was somewhere other than this place, such was its intensity.

Two men, carrying a body on a stretcher, moved crab-like from the buildings straight towards our compound. They passed between us, looking straight ahead, as if we didn't exist, and disappeared into the darkness behind. A fire engine approached the school, but was soon forced back by the shooting. Whoever remained inside was either dead, too wounded to flee, or had resolved to fight to the death.

Almost three hours had elapsed between the start of the final conflagration and the emergence of *Specials* from the front of the building, claiming victory. Some of us moved towards the school, but were forced back by the soldiers whose victory it was. Several fires still burned, but less intensely than before. Fire crews were now able to do their job. The Muscovites attempted to prevent locals from entering, but quickly realized that, unless they wanted another fight, their authority held no sway. Michael set up our equipment. We edited his footage. A link was established and I started my report.

> It is after eight o'clock in the evening here in Seblan and the battle for Middle School Number One has finally ended. We do not yet know how many of the more than 1300 hostages have survived their ordeal, but we do know that many are dead.
>
> At around 5 p.m., as local troops and *Specials* probed for any weakness in the hostage takers' defenses, a loud explosion rocked the school. We have learned that the sports hall, in which everyone was being held, had been wired to detonate. If the explosion we heard was the result of these charges being set off, a great many lives must have been taken. In any event, the fire that followed was fierce. A number of children and a few adults did manage to escape from the building. We do not yet know whether any of the hostage takers survived.
>
> This final conflict has brought to a bloody end a siege that began three days ago. It was Lord Wellington, after Waterloo, who said that nothing except a battle lost can be half so melancholy as a battle won. Well, that is how it feels here now: melancholy. But as the people of Seblan come to terms with their loss, a loss that must affect nearly every family in the town, I wonder how long it will be before their sadness turns into an

uncontrollable thirst for revenge. If any of the hostage takers did escape the building, I would not wish to be in their shoes. This is Orla Kildare, for DEMOS-TV outside what is left of Middle School Number One, Seblan.

FOR THE NEXT several hours trucks came and went, ferrying first the wounded to hospital and then the dead to makeshift mortuaries around the city. Slowly the news came together inside the press compound. Well over 300 civilians had been killed and over half of them were children. The *Specials* had lost 11 of their men, mostly shot in the back while trying to rescue youngsters. Of the 32 attackers, 28 were dead, one was rumored to be in captivity and three were believed to have escaped. A massive search was underway.

While we hung around, unsure what to do after filing our reports, desperate women approached the scene in search of loved ones, only to be forced back by men fighting the fires. One of these forlorn souls wandered into our compound, moaning a pitiable lament, *My Irina, where is my Irina?* We just stared at her, open-mouthed, unsure what to do. I knew most of my colleagues would not understand her words but all of us must have felt her anguish. She passed through us like a spirit trapped in purgatory.

THE ENTIRE PRESS corps had decanted itself from the battle zone into our hotel. Desmond claimed our establishment had the most congenial bar. None of us could sleep. It must have been shortly after one when Karen rushed in, almost tripping over in her eagerness to reach me through the crush.

"They've located the terrorists!" she bellowed down my ear, trying to restrict this news to me, but unable to contain her excitement.

Suddenly the comforting burble of well-oiled bystanders, wondering what the next drama would be, stopped. Karen squirmed at the end of forty pairs of hungry eyes and I realized instantly that an attempt to maintain exclusivity would be futile.

"Michael's wife's had another baby," I tried, limply.

"That's the second one in twelve hours," droned Henry.

"I didn't think you English could count."

"We're pretty good up to two."

"Oh, come on now, Orla," chided Desmond, "what's cooking?"

"They've located the remaining terrorists," I confessed.

Shouts of 'where?' ricocheted around the room.

Still slightly embarrassed, Karen looked at me and I nodded.

"In a residential building, close to the school," she announced.

As the press pack thundered from the bar, I pulled out the card Desmond had given me and tried Dr. Trofim's cell. I knew he would be up to his neck in severed limbs, but I was worried about Aslan's father. All I got was a polite message asking me to leave my name and number and the doctor would call me back as soon as he could.

"The man at the base?" Karen asked. "You are worried about him?"

"He's probably as safe there as anywhere," I acknowledged. "Now, where is this building the terrorists are holed up in?"

"They won't let us anywhere near," Karen warned. "Your friends are wasting their time. It's down a side street and the *Specials* have already blocked it off."

"Oh, they're used to that," I assured her. "They'll find the action. They have a nose for it."

"But I mean they won't be able to *see* anything."

"That's never stopped a reporter reporting a good story yet," I explained. "Sometimes I think we possess psychic powers."

I could see that Karen was confused by my humor, the blackness of which was starting to mirror my mood. We seemed to be acting out Hieronymus Bosch's depiction of Man's descent into hell.

"How far can that see," she asked, gesturing towards Michael who had just joined us with his camera.

"A lot further than us," he asserted.

"And in the dark?" she pressed, looking quizzical.

"Yes. With the night lens on. It's not easy to hide these days."

"Uh, uh!" I jibed and he glared at me. I think he likes our guide, or would like her. He rarely seems to worship at the altar of abstinence.

"It's just that I have a friend," Karen continued, "and she lives in an apartment that looks right across at the block the terrorists are hiding in. I was with her when the *Specials* surrounded it. They must have been given a tip-off."

"You honey!" I exclaimed, the scent of combat welling up again and overpowering my earlier feeling of despair. I think we all feel a bit soiled after witnessing horror, like men in overcoats after a girlie show, I guess.

"We'd better hurry," I urged. "I don't imagine the *Specials* will stand on ceremony."

KAREN'S FRIEND LET us in and was understandably nervous at first, but Michael soon had both of them eating out of his hand. There was only the living room with a gas ring and roll-up bed and a shared bathroom on the landing, but the view of the terrorists' hideout was just as Karen had described it. It was so good I was surprised the *Specials* hadn't put a sniper into the room. For all I knew, there might have been one above or below us, staring across at the same target.

At first we could see nothing out of the ordinary. Everything appeared to be dead, lifeless, the way a residential city block looks late at night, with patches of street light here and there revealing only emptiness. A small part of me began to wonder if Karen had led us astray.

"Here we go."

Michael's quiet comment drew us closer to the open window.

"Here," he said, inviting Karen to look into the viewfinder of his camera which was now mounted on a tripod overlooking her small flower box. "About half way up the building."

Karen squinted.

"I think I can see something," she claimed.

"Close one eye," Michael urged.

"Oh yes, I have them now. Three men on the balcony."

"Shouldn't you be filming?" I asked rather tartly, as Karen's friend squeezed between her and Michael to take a look.

"I am filming."

"Come on now girls," leave Roman Polanski to get on with it. And stand away from the window, unless you want to get shot.

Karen and her friend, rather too grudgingly, I thought, untangled themselves from the camera and stood back.

"Do you want to take a look, Miss Kildare?" Michael asked, without turning.

"Up yours," I muttered, straining to see what was going on, over his shoulder.

The three hooded *Specials* on the balcony, pressed back so they could not be seen, appeared to be waiting for a signal. Each man was wearing a breathing apparatus. Suddenly, they sprung into action, hurling flash grenades through the neighboring window and following them inside. We heard a volley of shots and then another. I suspected the apartment the terrorists had taken over was being stormed from the inside as well. In less than ten seconds it was over. A plume of smoke wafted from the shattered windows. In the street below, soldiers were rushing out of the shadows and converging on the building, anxious, no doubt, to claim their place at the 'kill'.

"Is it over?" Karen asked, afraid to look.

"Yes," I told her. "I think it is. You did well, by the way. We must get this on air."

Michael had already transferred his attention to the portable dish and was trying to get a signal.

"It's no good. We need to get to the roof," he complained.

"I have a key," Karen's friend announced. "The door is kept locked, but the building manager lets me hang out my washing up there."

Quickly we followed her.

At first the lock appeared to be jammed.

"It's just fickle," Karen told us, as her friend jiggled the key back and forth. "It can't be forced."

Like a safe-cracker, the girl gently worked the key this way and that, feeling the touch of the lock.

"I don't think my key's a very good copy," she apologized. And then bingo! The door opened and we were through, in amongst water tanks and beneath the stars.

It didn't take Michael long to set up his equipment under the admiring gaze of his two girls. I idly wondered how he was going to choose. Perhaps he wouldn't have to. While he worked I composed my thoughts.

"It's Steve," Michael called out to me.

"That's a relief. I don't think I could handle Paul's deference right now!"

"Hi, Steve."

"How are you doing, Orla?"

"Getting tired of man's inhumanity to man. What time have you got?"

"Ten before six, about."

"Can you get this on the six o'clock?"

"Jesus, Orla. That's tight. We'll get in someplace. Might not be first up."

"Just get it out as near the top as you can, Steve. Bernie's going to love this. It's an exclusive."

"Yeah. Bernie sure loves exclusives. Let's have it then."

I steadied myself.

"Some of the earlier footage first Michael, and then this."

"I'm ready when you are, Orla," he confirmed.

He was learning fast.

"The Seblan siege is over. Initial estimates are that over 300 people died, many of them children. There has been a steady stream of trucks taking the wounded to hospital and the dead to makeshift mortuaries around the town. Mothers have been coming to what is left of the school in search of their loved ones. Many will not find them. At least, they will not find them alive. The grief here is palpable.

We believe 28 of the 32 hostage takers and eleven of the *Specials*, the crack troops from Moscow, were also killed in the final battle. These are just initial estimates. The final total is likely to be higher

Moments ago, following a tip-off, three hostage takers who had managed to escape the siege were surrounded in a residential building not far from the school. A commando unit from the *Specials* has just launched a daring raid. From what we could see, none of those targeted will have survived. A single individual, captured earlier, remains the only hostage taker still alive.

For every one of them killed, it looks as though ten civilians will have lost their lives. A ratio of 10 to 1. An appalling price, by any measure.

This is Orla Kildare for DEMOS-TV, in Seblan.

"That's it, Steve."

"Great, Orla. Now, how sure are you no one else got those last shots?"

"Very sure. I think you can scoop the field with those."

"The boss is going to love it! Stay safe, you two. Where you are doesn't look like a nice place."

We hauled our kit from the roof, relieved we had survived. Could I have guessed that a final act of horror remained? I don't know.

I LEFT MICHAEL with Karen and her friend and took Karen's car. She said she only needed it to pick me up from the hotel and if I had the car, I could pick myself up. A smirking Michael informed me that he thought he'd 'stick around for a while'. I felt like a frump, no longer part of the party set, divorced from the possibility of physical contact, able only to carp and carry my dry self with an air of righteous indignation. Hell, I was nowhere near forty yet. I had no right to be feeling these things. I wanted Aslan. I wanted his teasing eyes, his long fingers, the way he held back, making me desperate for him. I tried to think of Dirk. Dirk was reassuring, calming, like an aspirin. But I didn't want to be reassured, or calmed. I wanted to be set alight. I wanted to be taken out of this hellish place. I wanted it totally blanked out. I wanted to be loved with such a passion that nothing, absolutely nothing, mattered beyond that moment.

I drove, aimlessly. Left here? Why not. Now a right? No. Another left. Assert my independence. The place was deserted, a strange mix: blocks of communist concrete, the creation of a planner's barren mind, ordered lines on the horizontal and vertical in ways no human ever is, nor many things in the natural world, if it comes to that, then down an alley that had escaped the bureaucratic pen, into a jumble of dwellings astride narrow streets fit only for people, real people. But there was no one. I kept hoping that around the next corner I would see a light coming from a door, and inside find Liviana and her Sebastian knocking the socks off everyone the vodka hadn't got to first.

I burst out of the warren of real people back onto a wide boulevard which only had one purpose: to carry cars, except there were none, so that its pillar lamps and starkness made it look like a boundary, a no man's land, a place where people were not supposed to come. It occurred to me that the efficiency of our modern world came at a price. Much of what we did was not just functional, but one dimensional. As drivers, we drove cars to get from A to B, not to socialize, nor to interact with our fellow creatures in a pleasant way, but to get the journey over with as quickly and painlessly as we could.

And I was a journalist, there to report, not to mix with those I was reporting on, not to feel their happiness or sadness, but to send back a stream of words and pictures that would be interpreted by people like me, many thousands of miles away, as a validation of *their* lives. Such indignation as my reports might stir, from time to time, would soon be replaced by another sensation from the merry-go-round of sensations that our media supplied. I hoped it wasn't all pointless, or that its point wasn't only to entertain and earn me a salary. Gradually, slowly, glacially even, opinions did change and the media played its part. That was my justification for leeching off the misery of others. Their misery could become our misery and so we watched, in order to avoid. Rarely was sympathy part of the process. And even when it was, it was more often than not a cover for our own agenda.

At first I didn't register that the lights ahead were vehicle lights. They were just something that didn't quite 'fit' into the static, hollow landscape that mirrored the emptiness I was feeling. But they were moving. There seemed to be a wave of them approaching, like a flood from a burst dam, quicker and quicker, on both sides of the road. I felt my heart pumping and my negative thoughts dissolve into a rush of raw excitement.

I only just managed to pull off the road before a cavalcade of lights and wheels and engines thundered past, so many machines, of all kinds—cars, vans, trucks—I lost count. It looked like the Seblan hunt was in full cry. I turned and followed and was soon at the back of the pack and cursed at not having Michael with me. Whatever this was, it felt like news. It felt like another scoop. It felt like I had landed in the right place at the right time—again, but this time, without my bloody cameraman. My little mobile would have to do. I could get something. Some grainy image onto which I could overlay my award-winning report.

God, Orla, you're despicable! A news junkie. A misery mainliner. Hooked on Bernie's praise. *Good job, Orla.* Ah! What a sweet fix! Send me, Bernie! Send me anywhere you like! Send me to the most sordid human pustule on the planet and I'll vacuum-pack its ugliness, its despair, its cruelty, its utter hopelessness! Set it out in our visual bazaar, Bernie, so that the station's clients can sell a few more cars, computers, health aids, or whatever, to people thankful that what they are seeing has absolutely nothing to do with them.

The cavalcade started to slow. I took a look at the drivers next to me, straddling all four lanes of the highway. They were men. Staring forward, like zombies. Each car was full. It looked as though the entire male population of Seblan had taken to the road. They were on a mission, these men, that much was plain to see. One turned and caught my eye, and as quickly turned away. We began to bunch up. Ahead, I could see why. Our convoy was turning off, in the direction of the school.

We must have been close when the car in front of me stopped, where it was, in the middle of the road. Its occupants spilled out and hurried forward on foot. I got out too and followed. Men hurried past. I thought of the rush before a game. That's what it reminded me of. A crowd, anxious to get to their seats before the start. But what game was this? It was almost three in the morning. I tried Michael's cell as I ran, but it must have been switched off.

The acrid smell of burning was still in the air. I started to take pictures. As we reached the small square that fronted Middle School Number One, the crowd pressed forward. I could now see the few flames that were still coming from part of the roof that had not yet collapsed. I could also see that I was never going to get to the front. Men kept pushing past me, pushing me to the back. Some were now climbing the few trees that had been allowed to puncture the concrete. I thought of joining them. But I hadn't climbed a tree in years. And anyway, I was starting to feel unwelcome, as if I had stumbled upon the supporters of an opposing team.

I moved to the side and up some steps to the door of a building that must have stood as a silent witness to the goings and comings in Seblan for decades, from a time when civic pride was allowed to express itself in architecture, and the joyful exuberance of the rococo was not regarded as bourgeoisie excess. Only when I had managed to haul myself up onto a balustrade high enough to give me a view across the sea of heads, towards the front of the crowd, did I notice that the building I had picked belonged to the police. But it was completely deserted. Not a single light was on inside, not one. It was as if civil society had been switched off and another kind, a dark, instinctive kind, switched on.

The school was no longer bathed in arc lights. They had been removed. They had served their purpose. Now only the flames, still jumping in small bursts from the gutted hall, were providing light for the ritual taking place in the yard across which children and their parents had so recently passed, dressed in their best, to celebrate the Day of Knowledge.

A cheer rippled backwards through the crowd. I could just make out a body being hoisted onto a make-shift rack, propped up in front of the school. There was another cheer, and another. All the time I was filming with my cell in the hope of capturing something. When it rang, I almost dropped it, the sound was so unexpected.

"Michael, is that you?"

Another cheer rose from the crowd and I couldn't make out his answer. I was torn between filming and listening.

Only when the roar of the excited crowd fell back did I become aware of the unfamiliar voice.

"Orla Kildare, is that you?"

"Who's speaking, please?" I wanted to know.

"Dr. Trofim," the voice answered. "Is that you, Miss Kildare?"

Suddenly I remembered Aslan's father, and was annoyed with myself for having put him out of my mind.

"Yes, it is. Thank you for returning my call."

"Where are you?" he asked.

I looked across at the street name and explained that I was in front of the police station.

"It is not safe for you to be there," he urged. "You must leave, immediately."

"I think they have just been dealing with the last terrorist," I told him.

"I am in the area. I will come and get you."

As I was talking I was watching. People in the crowd were now hurling things—stones, cans, bits of wood, anything they could lay their hands on—towards the suspended body. More and more people were joining the horde and I was now surrounded by a heaving mass, all straining forward to bear witness and assuage their fury. I raised my cell back to my ear.

"Dr. Trofim? Dr. Trofim, are you still there?"

But he wasn't. The connection was dead.

For a moment, I felt afraid. The eyes of the men seething past me seemed unnatural, wide with a thirst for vengeance is the only way I can put it, blind to anything but the object of their hatred. They kept pushing forward, like a river in flood. Had I not been on the balustrade I would have been swept up in that current of bile.

IN AMONGST THE hysterical shouting, the jackal-like cries, I thought I heard my name. I don't know how long I had been standing there, rooted to the spot, locked in a surreal dreamworld like everyone else. I looked back down the street. It was now full to bursting. I was in trouble.

"Miss Kildare, over here."

There it was again. I hadn't imagined it. I strained to make out a familiar face, but recognized no one.

"Over here."

The voice drew my gaze towards the entrance into the police station, but it was dark and I could not see.

"Yes. Over here. Come to the door," the voice encouraged.

Gingerly, I eased myself off my perch. The human flow was pressing part way onto the steps. Trying not to get caught up in it, I worked my way towards the door, but still could see no one there. Only as I came right up to it did it swing open. I felt myself being pulled in and heard the heavy metal door slam shut behind me.

"It's a short cut. If they thought they could use it, they would."

The man who had literally pulled me off the street was hard to make out. He seemed well built for a doctor, although why a doctor shouldn't have been, I'm not sure. I suppose I had some avuncular figure in mind: middle-aged, slightly balding, with glasses.

"Dr. Trofim?"

"Yes. We should hurry. There is a rumor circulating about a female American journalist who is friendly with the Chenchian."

I looked at him. His words barely made sense. 'The Chenchian'. What did he mean? The possibilities spun through my head like spider's thread, until one dominated all the rest.

"Good God! Not Aslan?" I pleaded, and felt my stomach retch.

"I thought he was called Alu Dudayev, your friend?"

Dr. Trofim's words were too much for me to take in.

"I tried to stop them," he said. "But I'd been piecing together broken bodies until a short while ago. I drove to the barracks as soon as I could. But they had already taken him from the cell when I got there. There was no stopping them. There were too many with too much anger. I don't think there's a soldier or a policeman who hasn't put aside his uniform for this. That's why the building is empty. Luckily, I have a key to one of the doors. I'm the police doctor, amongst other things."

I was hardly listening. I bent forward and threw up on the floor. All the time I had been wound up with excitement, I had been following a lynching party for Aslan's father. I vomited again and started sobbing uncontrollably.

I let Dr. Trofim guide me along a corridor, down some steps, and into a tunnel. I was barely aware of what was happening. If, at that moment, I had been strung up on the rack alongside Aslan's father, I might not even have noticed. The tunnel must have taken us well clear of the mob, because when we emerged at street level, there was no one.

"I left my friend's car," I whimpered.

"That's not important. My car is here. I'm taking you home with me. For the next few hours those men could do anything."

I suppose it was Dr. Trofim's wife who gave me a sleeping draught and put me to bed. It was five in the afternoon when I awoke.

CHAPTER 17

*B*ack at the hotel I found a note from Michael.

> *I guess you had a night out too!* it read. *A Doctor Tofu said that you were with him and were fine.*
>
> *Michael*
>
> *PS. The doctor also told Karen where to find her car, by the way. Wow!*

God, that boy could make me angry! I imagined him smirking as he wrote it, certain I had been up to the same as him. I felt groggy. As soon as I reached my room I cried again. Pavel Trofim, who confessed he was tired of being called 'doctor' all the time because people expected miracles, told me that I was in a state of shock and should rest. "Cry as much as you can," he said, "which is my prescription for this town."

The drive from his home had been unnerving. Unnerving because everything appeared normal. Cars were moving up and down the roads. People were walking into and out of shops. Police were directing traffic. We even passed two army trucks with soldiers in the back, looking more or less like soldiers. How does a town deal with over 300 dead? How does it face itself when its menfolk, in an orgy of excess, have just taken the life of an innocent man? The answer seemed to be that it moves on, attends to everyday things, closes its collective mind. And what else could it do? I just wished I was able to do the same.

"ORLA, ARE YOU in there?"

I forced myself to look at the clock. Eight something. Was that a.m. or p.m.?

"Orla, it's Michael. Are you alright?"

Only p.m. I'd unplugged the phone, crawled into bed, and prayed for oblivion.

"Go away!"

Two hours of oblivion. That's all I'd got. What did he want, banging on my door and shouting at me? Couldn't he leave me alone?

"Orla, let me in."

"I'm asleep."

Nothing. That was better. He'd gone.

"Orla, I think you should let me in."

"Go and bother someone else!"

Why couldn't he go away?

"Orla, I'm going to get the desk key."

"Alright, alright!"

I struggled up and opened the door.

"Now, what *do* you want?"

"I just heard what happened last night."

"Well, clever you."

"I'm going out for a drink. Do you want to come?"

"What about your harem?"

"Look, I thought we'd finished for the night. It was after two, for Christ's sake."

"Yeah, I guess. Give me ten minutes. I'll meet you downstairs."

He looked at me, unconvinced, and left. The temptation to crawl back into bed was almost overwhelming, but I resisted. I was Orla Kildare, top journalist. I couldn't go cracking up in front of my cameraman, for fuck's sake.

THE BAR WAS another of Desmond's finds, but the press crew seemed to be its only customers. There was an end of term atmosphere. With the siege over, everyone who hadn't already left was due to fly out in the morning. I'd had a shower and was feeling better, although would still have sooner been in bed.

"Orla, now t'ere you are," Desmond greeted. "Will you and Michael not come over and let me get yous bot' a drink. What'll it be?"

Pavel Trofim had said I shouldn't take alcohol for twenty-four hours. Something about it not mixing with the sleeping draught his wife had given me. I wasn't sure I wanted a hard drink, anyway.

"Tomato juice, please."

"Will t'at be wit' Worcestershire Sauce?" he asked, with just a hint of malice.

"They have that?"

"Probably not. Now what about you, yong Michael?"

"Vodka and orange."

"When are you shipping out, Orla," asked Henry who appeared to have attached himself to Desmond's generosity.

"We're going back to Moscow tomorrow morning," answered Michael. "Then it's the evening flight to Washington."

"It looks as though we will all be on the morning flight, then," noted Henry, without obvious pleasure.

"Since when, Washington?" I hissed, into the side of Michael's face.

"Here you are, one tomato juice and one vodka orange. So what did you get up to last noight? Rumor has it you were in t'e t'ick of t'ings."

"What things?" I asked, unsure what they knew and what I wanted to share.

"Oh, come on girlie," chided Desmond. "T'ere's no need to play t'e innocent with us hardened piranhas."

"Piranhas? I like that. It's better than leeches, less passive."

"Fearless fighters for the truth, I thought we were," complained Henry, who had clearly been keeping Desmond company for some time.

"Since when have t'e English ever been interested in t'e trut'?" Desmond taunted.

"You wound me, little shamrock. That'll cost you another drink!"

"'Tis always a great mistake to wound t'e English," grumbled Desmond. "It costs you dear."

"So did you actually see it?" questioned Kurt.

"You mean you missed it?" I countered.

"T'e t'ing of it is," explained Desmond "after t'e t'ree hostage takers were blasted to kingdom come and we saw none of it, we was a bit demoralized. T'en, when we sent in our reports, only to be told that DEMOS-TV had filmed t'e whole darn malarkey, as it were, we was downroight despondent. After t'at we sought solace in t'e traditional manner."

"The whole press corps?" I asked, incredulously.

"Not everyone was quite as traditional as Desmond," droned Henry. "It was late. It had been a long day. The siege was over. Most of us went to bed."

"We only learned this afternoon," admitted Kurt, "that the sole surviving terrorist had been snatched from prison and butchered."

"Quite a ritual killing," elaborated Henry, "if the rumors circulating are to be believed."

"Not just rumors," added Kurt, excitedly. "Have you seen the photographs?"

Henry and Desmond looked sheepish. They clearly had.

"What photographs?" I demanded.

"'Tis alright, girlie. None of os got 'em. One of t'e locals wanted a little somet'ing for his scrapbook, apparently."

"And was happy to sell copies for $10," explained Henry. "The idiot. He could have got several thousand for an exclusive."

"I don't think they were printable," interjected Kurt.

"Oh, one of the glossy news magazines would have gone for it," speculated Henry, "in the interests of objective reporting, you know."

"What I can't understand," wondered Michael, "is why they removed the body so quickly. You'd have thought they might have left it hanging there as a totem. Something for everyone to vent their anger on."

"Charming!" mocked Henry.

"Well, it was dead, for God's sake!" reacted Michael. "I'm just saying that it might have done some good. Sort of like lying in state, or in this case, un-state. If you know what I mean."

"Un-state!" repeated Henry "I like it."

"T'ey always used to leave t'e bodies on the gibbet after a poblic hanging," elaborated Desmond. "A sart of warning and a cat'arsis rolled into one."

"Ah! The good old days," mused Henry.

"It was t'at doctor of yours who took t'e body away, by all accounts," explained Desmond, looking at me.

"You introduced me to him," I pointed out.

"Indeed oi did," he agreed. "So you owe me, girlie. What did you see?"

"That's for me to know and you to find out," I stonewalled.

A chorus of injured feelings followed. The—*What about the camaraderie of the press corps?* and *We'd do it for you, Orla*—from Desmond and Henry appeared quite light-hearted. Only Kurt sounded genuinely peeved, with something about the enemies you make on the way up not being your friends on the way down. It might have sounded lighter in German, but I doubted it.

I noticed the barman leaning towards me, pushing something across the counter.

"You want to see?" he asked.

"No," I told him.

Clearly disappointed, he withdrew his offering.

"Chenchians!" he spat out. "That's all they deserve."

"I think I'd like to leave, Michael," I announced, aware that I must have sounded prissy. But the truth was, I couldn't stand much more.

"Oh, don't mind him," advised Henry. "After all they've been through, its hardly surprising."

To Michael's astonishment, I put my arm through his and said, as cheerily as I could,

"OK. Take me home, Romeo."

As my slightly bemused cameraman escorted me out, I heard Desmond call out—

"You take care now, girlie."

—and I felt he meant it. For all his drinking and levity, the reporter for the *New Irish Times* had a far sharper idea of what was going on around him than most. And we *were* almost kinsmen, after all.

I THOUGHT I was going to faint as we climbed the steps from Desmond's subterranean discovery and found myself clinging on to Michael's arm for dear life. Luckily I had already imprinted myself onto him as a mother figure, and he didn't assume that I'd suddenly taken a fancy, as most men surely would.

"Orla, what's the matter?" he appealed, anxiously.

"Nothing fresh air won't cure," I told him, gulping it in as soon as we reached street level.

"There's something, Orla. What is it?"

"That terrorist they killed. . ."

"Last night?"

"The one whose grisly photographs everyone seems to have been looking at. . ."

"It was pretty foul what they did to him, but I guess he deserved it. . ."

"He most definitely didn't deserve it. *He* was Aslan's father. . ."

"But I thought. . ."

"A mob dragged him from his cell at the barracks. They wanted blood, Chenchian blood."

"But why didn't they go for the terrorist who was captured?"

"According to Dr. Trofim, he was already halfway to Moscow to be interrogated. The *Specials* had seen to that."

"Oh, fuck. And you saw the whole thing?"

"I thought I was watching the terrorist get his comeuppance, until Pavel, Dr. Trofim, found me. When he heard what was afoot, he'd gone to the barracks, but there were just too many of them. He'd also heard a rumor that they were after an American female reporter who was friendly with the Chenchian. If he hadn't found me I might have ended up in those pretty pictures you have all been drooling over."

"Jesus, Orla!"

"Yeah, Jesus indeed! Now, we've got a report to file."

"But what about pictures?"

"Can you download from my cell?"

"You got some?"

"Well, can you."

"I think so."

BACK AT THE hotel, Michael got his equipment together and started working on my cell. I sat in a corner, scribbling notes. I had a choice. I could talk about the mad crowd venting its fury on an innocent Chenchian or I could mention Alu Dudayev by name. All that was holding me back was the thought of Aslan. He was bound to learn about his father eventually, and in the end I felt he might as well learn about it from one of my broadcasts. At least I could tell it like it was.

We'd found a way onto the roof where we could get a good link. The sky was clear and for a moment I felt overwhelmed under the awning of stars. God, the things we humans did to one another. What *was* the point of us? I was still feeling very tired.

"See what you think, Orla," Michael invited. "They're a bit jumpy and grainy, now that I've blown them up some, but there's no doubting what's going on."

My pictures had come out clearer than I expected. The close-ups of men, rabid-eyed with bloodlust, were harrowing and powerful. But it was the long shots that took my breath away. They were horrific, certainly, but they also had a magisterial quality. The distance and poor light hid the indignities that had been inflicted on the warlord's body. Instead, it looked as though he was about to leave behind the flames of hell and hell's baying inhabitants: Christ crucified—Christ ascending.

Michael established the link and Steve told us he was all set.

"Last night, a crime was committed. Last night a crime was committed by at least 10,000 people, and it will go unpunished. Last night the people of Seblan vented their rage and grief upon an innocent man.

"Previously I told you, when the siege was in its infancy, that the warlord from the Vorsky region in Chenchia had come to Seblan to try and end the hostage taking. I met this man on two occasions. The first time was just after Russian soldiers had destroyed his village, butchered its women and children and murdered his wife in a savage and unprovoked attack. I had expected bitterness and anger from this man. Instead I found courage, wisdom, and a deep desire to bring peace to his troubled land.

"The second time I met Alu Dudayev, for that is his name, was when he had been locked inside a putrid cell in the barracks here in Seblan. No one, it seems, was willing to let him try to negotiate with the hostage takers.

"Last night, at three in the morning, he was dragged from his cell and taken to what was left of Middle School Number One. In front of the still-burning sports hall he was tortured, tied to a grill, and hoisted in front of a crowd, wild with hatred. Under a hail of stones, sticks, and objects at hand, he was put to death.

"Knowing what I do about Alu Dudayev, I am certain he would hope the manner of his death helps the people of Seblan bury their anger and ease their grief. That was the nature of the man killed here last night. For DEMOS-TV, I am Orla Kildare, reporting to you live from Seblan."

For several seconds there was just silence, and I was afraid the link had been cut.

"Are you there, Steve? Steve, did you get that?"

"Yes, Orla. I'm here."

"So, did you get it."

"We got it alright. That was heavy stuff. Goodness knows what Bernie will make of it."

"What the hell do you mean, Steve?"

"Oh, it was great, Orla. Don't get me wrong. It just sounded, well, personal."

That was it. Our time had run out. I looked across at Michael.

"I guess he knows Bernie as well as any of us," he shrugged.

"What did you think?"

"I thought it was one of the best pieces you've done."

"So?" I challenged.

"It did sound personal."

I laughed.

"Yeah. I guess it doesn't do for a reporter to get personal. Keep a professional distance at all times. Maintain objectivity—whatever the hell she is when she's at home! I'm turning in. I'll see you in the morning."

"You take care, now," he called out, as I headed from the roof. He was the second person who'd told me that.

I SLEPT A very strange sleep. The faces of the street people, eyes a-glaze, crowded in on me, pulling me forward, shouting, silently, everything was silent, but I could tell they were shouting because their mouths kept opening and closing like fish as they stared, seeing me but not seeing me, in a dead-look from bodies that floated, under strange locomotion, as if on a current of air. I knew the faces. There was Bernie. There was Steve. There was Michael. Again and again I saw them, in duplicate, triplicate, a production line of Bernies and Michaels and Steves. We kept moving forward, but getting nowhere, like those airport walkways that go round and round, although you don't actually see the round.

Then I was facing them, hundreds of them, thousands of them, stretching back as far as the eye could see, all shouting at me, hurling things at me, things that passed through me, around me, over me and under me, but without sensation. I felt my body lift from its place and yet could see it staying where it was. The zombies could not see my lifted self and continued to hurl abuse and more at the part of me that stayed put. Even as I watched, my stationary self began to sweat blood, at first just spots and then gobs and then rivulets until it deflated, like a punctured balloon into almost nothing. This nothingness drove the zombies wild with despair and I felt sorry for them.

Dr. Trofim joined me as I hovered above the wailing horde. He held out his hand and I took it and then he wasn't Pavel Trofim, but Aslan. I tried to hold on, but he slipped from my grasp. He stretched out his hand and I stretched out mine, but the distance between us kept increasing, until he disappeared into the blackness in front of my eyes.

Now the zombies had gone. There was just one old man sitting by a fire, a blanket drawn tight around his shoulders. I dropped down beside him, but he kept gazing into the fire. I tried to speak, but no words came from my mouth. I tried to reach out and touch him, but my arms would not move. Then Andrew Meadows appeared and told me that it was time to go.

I AWOKE DRENCHED in sweat. It wasn't even two. I felt cold and started to shiver. I wondered where I was. Shafts of raw fear shot though my body. I lay rigid, stretched full out, and tried to get a grip on myself. The darkness pressed down on me. My teeth rattled inside my head. I tried to stop them, until I could no longer. I tried not breathing, not breathing, not breathing. . . .

WHEN I WOKE again it was seven. I felt mended. Tired, but mended. I'd been skating on thin ice for a while now. I needed a rest, but not yet.

"STEVE, I NEED to speak to Bernie."

We were at the airport and I had just learned from Michael, who'd been sorting out some travel details with the office, that Bernie hadn't run my piece on Alu Dudayev.

"Sure, Orla. I'll get him."

Part of me was furious. The other part couldn't give a damn.

"So, how's my star reporter?"

Bernie's voice had that, *let's not fight* tone about it. At least he was trying to flatter me.

"Pissed, Bernie. That's how I am."

"Oh, come on! There's no need for that."

"So why didn't you run it, Bernie? Tell me."

"There were issues, Orla."

"What issues, Bernie? Spit it out."

For a man who was as tough as nails, I'd found that he could be surprisingly diffident when it came to giving people he liked bad news.

"Well, for starters, Orla, the piece was a bit biblical. All that about the man being *put to death*. We have some powerful people on our board with strong views."

"All that, Bernie! That was three words. *Put . To . Death.* Since when has the religious right had a lock on those three words?"

"It was more the tone of it, Orla. This man was being portrayed as some kind of martyr."

"Well, he was certainly killed for the sins of others, if that's what you mean."

"That's just it. Biblical. We are not in the business of creating martyrs, Orla."

"Hell, Bernie. On that basis we'd have been on the wrong side at the crucifixion!"

He let out a raucous laugh.

"I wouldn't doubt it, my dear. As you know, our lot are still waiting!"

"Come on, Bernie. It had to be more than that."

"It seemed kind of personal, Orla. We all know you were once sweet on the man's son."

"Of course it was fucking personal, you old hypocrite. What the hell's wrong with that?"

"Objectivity. We can't let our personal feelings interfere with our objectivity."

"Name me one thing about my report which wasn't objective."

"It was more balance, Orla. You can't go feeding our viewers with all that grief about the siege and then show the grief-stricken people behaving like animals."

"And why the hell not, if that's the way it happened?"

"Because we're against terrorists, Orla. Now that's the bottom line."

"You've been got at, Bernie."

"I resent that."

"Bernie, I'm due time off, right?"

I could almost hear him thinking. Wondering why I had changed tack. Worried that I was about to ambush him.

"Sure you are, Orla. You'll be in DC late tonight. Why don't we talk about it tomorrow?"

"Because I won't be in DC tonight, Bernie. I'm not going. I'm taking a break, starting right now."

"You can't do that, Orla. You've only got a short-stay visa. And anyway, that man at the embassy. . .."

". . . Andrew Meadows?"

"Yeah, that's the one. He wants you and Michael out. Says its getting too dangerous."

"I'll see you in a couple of weeks, Bernie."

"Orla. . ."

I cut him off. There was no point arguing with Bernie Eisner. He never gave in. Besides, he was happier if you did what you had to do and then squared it with him afterwards, just so long as it didn't damage the station. He knew I was due time off. How I spent it was my business.

"Are you not even coming to Moscow?" asked Michael, who had been listening to my conversation with Bernie.

"No. And by the way, you did one hell of a good job. I just hope that Cindy of yours appreciates it, although from what I've seen, you might be better off single!"

"Can't live with 'em; can't live without 'em. Pathetic, really!"

"Oh, I don't know. I think it's strangely reassuring."

"Look, Orla. I'm due some time off myself. Are you sure you wouldn't like me to come with you?"

"Why, that's the nicest thing I've heard in a long while. But thank you kindly, no. Besides, you don't even know where I'm going."

"I can guess. Is there a flight?"

"Three hours after yours."

I WATCHED THEM go. It was an odd sensation. Like I imagine an out-of-body experience is supposed to be. The mighty press corps of the world looked like a party of disorganized and rather garrulous trippers continuing on their group holiday without me. When I was on the inside looking out, I felt as though I was at the center of the universe, at the nexus of world power, with my hand on the human pulse, feeding life-giving information to humanity. But as I sat there on the outside looking in, it was our complete irrelevance that struck me.

Did it really matter if a family in Wichita Falls was told about a family in Darfur that had been bombed out of its village and was now living on next to nothing in a United Nations refugee camp? We never seemed to be able to do anything about these problems anyway. As often as not, whatever we did—send a little food, a few tents, some harassed doctors and perhaps a handful of soldiers without the power to be soldiers—appeared to prolong the crisis we had stuck our noses into. Having got rid of the Deity, perhaps our liberal conceit is to imagine we have taken His place.

Several of the 'pack' came to say goodbye. Desmond, of course, urging me not to let this Vale of Tears get me down, "because, Orla, t'e human race has quoit a few good points, alt'ough don't go pressing me to name t'em!" Henry drifted by and said that as Americans went I was alright and should call him next time I was in London. Even Kurt managed a perfunctory—"Goodbye then, Orla"—which I suspect, for him, was as warm as it got. The girl from the *Dallas News*, whose name I still hadn't managed, Janice Stringer or something, everyone just called her Dallas, launched into one of those gushy tributes we Americans are prone to. She said I was a credit to female journalism. I said I hoped I was a credit to journalism, period, which was a mistake, because she then over-compensated, saying that I had been her heroine for years and was the reason she had stayed in the business and that she would be calling her daughter Orla, when she had one, which she didn't, because Randy, the man she was seeing, wasn't ready, and Randy was important to her, even though she was not seeing as much of him as he would like, the work being what it was "but I guess you know all about that, and I just have to ask. How *have* you coped?" I'm not sure my one word answer, *badly*, was the inspiration she was searching for.

ONLY WHEN THEY had finally boarded did I start feeling twitchy. Seblan International Airport was no more international than our gas station back home in Sweetwater, whose main claim to fame, according to its owner, Otis Fitzgerald, was the undeniable fact that it sat just a few miles east of the oil-producing Panhandle. I don't know how many times we'd all heard him tell us we couldn't get fresher gas. I never did know what he meant. I think it might have had something to do with him once being a farmer, because "straight from the cow, straight from the ground," was another of his little sayings.

I started to think that every man who walked past might have been involved in Alu Dudayev's murder, and so might have become *my* murderer, had not Pavel Trofim intervened. I'd called him earlier and asked him to meet me out at the airport, if he could. He said he'd try, but that the hospital was still struggling to keep alive mothers and children hurt in the siege.

The killing of the hostage takers, that had been understandable. But when 10,000 people commit a murder, are they all guilty? Or are there degrees of guilt? Perhaps one or two of the ringleaders can be brought to book, but as for the rest—scot-free. One has to ask, though, would the ringleaders have done what they did without all those people behind them? Almost certainly not. Human society is predicated on structure, so leaders do have particular responsibility. I suppose that means we are entitled to take it out on them if they stir up the worst in us rather than the best, although who gets to decide, is a moot point. I've always felt uncomfortable about victors' justice.

Thinking about it, what I had witnessed had been more akin to a sacrifice than a plain killing. *Lamb of God, who takest away the sins of the World*—Alu Dudayev, take away the pain of Seblan. Perhaps Bernie had been right. I had touched on things best left alone.

"Orla?"

"Pavel!"

"I thought I might have missed you."

I looked at my watch.

"I've still got an hour."

"Good. Let's get some coffee."

I immediately felt lifted by his company. It even seemed as though the few people milling around the terminal were no longer staring through me.

"This is not haute cuisine, I'm afraid," he confessed, as he steered me towards a soiled plastic table in front of a deserted counter. "I'll just see if I can find someone."

As he disappeared I felt my spirits ebb. I needed to be with someone. I just wished that need related to Dirk and not Aslan.

"The others get away alright?" he asked as he returned with a disgruntled lady in tow, who ran a rag across our table without any noticeable impact.

"Yes. Only half an hour late."

"Remarkable! That's classed as an on-time departure here."

"How are things at the hospital?" I wondered.

"Just ten on the critical list now. But that's partly because we lost three last night. Of course critical and non-critical are really only mechanical terms. The hundreds we have managed to patch up are going to be scarred for life. There's hardly a family that hasn't had someone killed or maimed."

"I believe you took away Alu Dudayev's body?"

"Yes. Some wanted to leave it on display. Luckily there were enough who wanted nothing more to do with the whole thing. I dressed it in one of our soldier's uniforms and put it in the morgue, so it should be safe."

I shook my head.

"The uniform?"

"Yes," I admitted. "What an irony!"

He nodded, just as two cups and a rack of condiments were put on our table.

"Milk and sugar?" Pavel queried.

He got the expected 'I can't do everything' look, as a bowl containing crumpled packets of sugar and dried milk joined the salt and pepper.

As soon as she'd turned her back, we both dissolved into laughter.

"We still have a little way to go!" he joked.

The coffee was at least hot and I added more sugar than normal, just to get some taste.

"How long did you know his son for?" he asked me.

"Four years, give or take. We were at university together."

"That was in America?"

"Right."

"So how is your friend finding Chenchia?"

"Difficult, I think. Especially now that the Americans seem to have given up on it."

"Your country should stop thinking it can run the whole world," he commented.

"What about yours!" I taunted, suddenly feeling partisan.

"Mine too," he acknowledged. "I often think most of the trouble today comes down to big countries interfering in the lives of little countries."

"Pavel, I must ask you, what are you going to do with the body?"

"I've been wondering about that. When I spoke with Alu Dudayev, out at the barracks, he mentioned that a Major Nabokov had helped him come to Seblan. He even said that his father, and Nabokov's father, had known one another. I thought I'd ask him to collect the body and take it back to Zoldek. With this insurgency going on they have transport moving back and forth between the two cities all the time."

"And Pavel, how *is* the body?"

"I've stitched it up and put back the bits they cut off. He'll still look dead, but at least he'll look dignified."

"I don't suppose I want to know what they did to him?" I pondered, my journalistic curiosity almost getting the better of me.

"No, you don't," he asserted, with a firmness that ended the matter.

We both sat there, toying with our coffees. A message came through on his cell. He looked at it.

"Orla, I have to go."

"Well, thank you for all you have done."

My words felt completely inadequate. I wanted to throw my arms around him and, if I was honest, give him my entire body free, gratis, and for nothing.

"No. It's me who should be thanking you. Your broadcasts give us hope. You may not think they make much difference, but believe me, they do! Slowly, often far too slowly, we are taking it all in and we are changing."

He could see that tears were welling up in my eyes.

"I'm glad you are following my prescription," he chuckled, with a broad grin on his handsome face. "Just remember, a good cry is worth any number of tablets."

He leaned forward, squeezed my hand and was gone.

THE SHORT FLIGHT to Zoldek was almost over too quickly. Now, Aslan, my love. Where the hell are you?

CHAPTER 18

Little Gregor slipped across the Chenchian border, exhausted. The events of the last seventy-two hours were a mass of shards inside his aching head. Aching, not because it had sustained a blow, but because of all the things it had had to process. He could still see the faces of the children, frozen in fear, at the moment the attack began and the crudely arranged explosives had been detonated. Almost worse had been Flower, gloating over their last seconds. She must have believed, absolutely believed, that her act would carry her to a better place. He envied her certainty. In the confusion that followed, he thought he had seen Honey rush back to the sports hall.

Vengeance had all but dragged him along one of the corridors to take up a position next to Blade. The firing, back and forth, had been continuous, the smell of burning from the hall foul and asphyxiating. But Blade had not been anxious to fire. Instead he had watched from the darkened room they were in. Gregor remembered seeing a stretcher propped in a corner and feeling nauseous. An hour into the fight, a group of citizens had managed to enter the school not far from them. A violent firefight erupted and it had been then that Vengeance reappeared. Removing his mask and making him and Blade do the same, he'd been told to lie on the stretcher. The minutes that followed were a blur. As far as he could tell, Blade and Vengeance had carried him across the no man's land and out through the press compound.

In the darkness they'd ditched the stretcher, just as a group of distraught mothers approached, and hightailed it to the town. They had only just managed to break into an apartment before the *Specials* were onto them. The lone occupant was knocked unconscious and they'd been about to take up positions when Vengeance told him to check out the stairwell. That's what he had been doing when the apartment was engulfed by a fireball.

He'd hidden inside a trash chute for an hour or more. But no one had even come close. He imagined the soldiers had been looking for three charred bodies and having found them, were anxious to return to the school. For several hours he'd waited in the building, watching, wondering what to do. And then the strangest thing had happened. A huge crowd of men had converged on the school. They'd arrived in cars and trucks, anything that would move, and just abandoned them, covering the final distance on foot. Outside the apartment building he'd found a row of discarded vehicles, some even with their engines still running.

He'd taken the first with a set of keys and a full tank and just driven, expecting to be stopped at every turn. For five hours he'd driven and seen no one. A mile from the border, he'd ditched the car and walked. It was a clear morning and the looming presence of Mount Abochevo was enough to give him his bearings. Even so, he couldn't be sure where the border was, and had just walked and walked, so as to be certain he was inside his own country.

GREGOR HUNCHED HIMSELF into a fetal position and sobbed his heart out. Great, heaving, gasping sobs pumped out of him. His friend was dead. His friend, who had wanted to wreak vengeance on the world; his friend, who had persuaded him to join the Faith Radicals; his friend. … What had it all been about? For him, friendship. As for the rest—the politics, the religion, the passion—he'd gone through the motions, but it had always been about friendship in the end. And now that friendship was dead. No more could he expect to awake each day and experience the certainty of being told what to do and the pleasure in doing it. No more could he be sure what his purpose was.

But as he heaved and convulsed and hugged himself tightly, he could feel no bitterness against his friend's killers. Instead, the eyes of the children bored into him. Dead children and their gravely injured parents staring, pleading with their eyes, but to no avail. The word vengeance had sounded so pure, so proper, so self-explanatory, so morally justified. But now the word sounded like a hollow joke, like a negation of life itself. If everyone in the world thought of nothing more than righting the wrongs that had been done to them, what time would be left for living?

He rocked back and forth until all the angst inside him had bubbled out, leaving a strange serenity. At that moment he knew that what life he had left would be devoted to his fellow men. Not to an idea. Not to a single individual. Not to some great mission, but to the simple human needs of others. Wood gathered. A message delivered. A floor scrubbed. Berries picked. A roof patched. Never again would he follow someone blindly. Never again would he seek to impose his will on others. He thought about his moniker, Death, and managed a smile. How appropriate it had been. In all those years with the Faith Radicals that is what he had been, dead, and he hadn't even realized it. No more. Please God, no more! But it was not to be.

CHAPTER 19

The aging Ilyushin shuddered to a halt in front of the terminal building. I was feeling anxious anyway, wondering how I was going to find Aslan, but the sight of military vehicles pulling up alongside made me break into a cold sweat. An announcement crackled over the intercom, telling us to remain in our seats so that our papers could be inspected. So that someone could be hauled off the plane, more like.

I looked around at my fellow travellers, wondering who might have invoked the authorities' ire. They all sat like me, rigid, wondering the same and hoping that it was anyone but them.

Steps were pushed towards the aircraft door. A young officer holding a clipboard ascended, followed by two soldiers carrying guns. The pen might have been mightier than the sword in the long run, but in the here and now, a good killing instrument remained the most persuasive tool.

We craned our necks forward and watched the civilities between our flight attendant and the soldiers. One of the two with guns swaggered down the gangway towards the back of the plane. He looked predatory, eyeing everyone up with an air of arrogant contempt. It is easy to forget, I suppose, that these are men trained to kill and to think of everyone, other than their own kind, as enemy. His twin stood guard at the front, while the young officer began to work his way down the rows, checking the papers presented to him by nervous passengers.

I could see that he was expressing little pleasantries as he went, and imagined relieved individuals forcing ingratiating smiles. At what point, I wondered, did people lose their fear and instead of re-enforcing authoritarian self-righteousness through their acquiescence, challenge its very right to exist at all? In spite of myself, I felt my stomach muscles tighten as my turn came.

"Miss Kildare," he said, in excellent English, after inspecting my passport, "your permission to enter Chenchia has expired."

"I don't believe that is correct," I answered, in Russian, with what I hoped was the right mix of politeness and assertiveness. "I have two days left."

"Yours was a single entry permit, Miss Kildare. An easy mistake to make."

I stared at him.

"And where does it say so?" I challenged.

"I would like you to come with me, please," he insisted. The transparency of the Chenchian permit system was clearly not a matter he intended to debate.

Around me I could feel the tension turning from fear to excitement. It was someone else.

Exiting an aircraft is rarely dignified at the best of times. I often tried to imagine the last-minute pandemonium before some celebrity emerged through the open door, to wave at an adoring crowd, looking like they had just come from the hairdresser. I was by the window, so the man next to me had to make way. He didn't know whether he should smile at me or ignore me, and came up with a sweaty grimace. I had to retrieve a coat and bag from the over-full storage locker and something fell. The young officer also reached for it and we bumped heads. For a split second, the utter banality of our situation struck us.

IT PROBABLY SHOULDN'T have surprised me, but we didn't stop at the terminal. Instead, we drove at high speed, me in the front of a jeep being driven by the young officer, with the two soldiers sitting behind, and two truckloads of soldiers behind them, straight to the barracks. At least I was not in the hands of the secret police, or not yet, anyway.

The room I was taken to was more like the adjunct to a library than a place of detention. Bookshelves lined the walls and the books resting on them were not for appearance, that was clear. You can always tell a show library from a working one. Show libraries look immaculate and leather-bound. Their object is to impress. Great titles—philosophers, scientists, novelists whose names you know—will all be there. Statements of erudition. The classics that have been read and approved by others. The owners of show libraries do not need to read. That menial chore has been performed by others.

Here, books were everywhere askew. Markers jutted up above the covers, indicating that something important had been found. There was order, certainly, but it was an idiosyncratic order, reflecting a particular person's mind. In amongst the great works were titles that would have meant nothing to anyone save another with the same interests. For a soldier, this one was refreshingly well-read. I was leafing through an illustrated volume on the campaigns of Genghis Khan when the door opened.

"Andrew!" I exclaimed and wondered why I felt less pleased to be seeing my own countryman than the owner of the library. "What are you doing here?"

"That, Orla, is exactly what I would like to ask you."

Somehow, I did not feel that Andrew Meadows was even the slightest bit surprised to see me. He was a nice enough man, not bad looking, either, but you just knew he had an agenda, that every smile, every suggestion, every offer of help was for a purpose. And now here he was, in a Russian army officer's room, inside a country fighting for its independence from that very Russia, who would not allow it because of a crucial oil pipe that had to be there to quench the West's insatiable thirst for energy and satisfy Moscow's yawning need for cash.

"They say my permit's expired," I protested, "but that's nonsense!"

"That doesn't answer my question, Orla."

"You mean, why am I here?"

"Exactly."

"Come on, Andrew. You know why I am here."

"No, I don't. What I do know is that you came here for DEMOS-TV and that we at the embassy had a devil of a job getting you the permits and persuading President Nitup to subject himself to an interview. And right now," he added, looking at his watch "you should be on your way to DC."

"Well, I'm not, am I? I'm here."

"For Christ's sake, Orla. I can see that. Now what on earth are you doing? This is one tricky situation."

"Perhaps, Andrew, we could start our truth-telling by you explaining to me what the hell my government is up to. And let's have no crap about you being here to aid a wayward citizen. Why, precisely, are *you* here?"

I could see that our man from the embassy was weighing up just how much to tell me. If he told me too much, I probably had cause to worry: dead men don't talk, nor dead women. He sat himself down and invited me to do the same. This was going to be a full and frank. The priest was going to tell the acolyte what was behind the altar curtain, or at least enough to suit his purpose.

"Why don't you tell me what *you* think is going on, Orla," he suggested. "That way, no one can accuse me of spilling the beans."

I couldn't help laughing. The man was a pro and as it was my tax dollars paying his salary, I guess that should have made me pleased.

"Well," I said, "it's pretty simple. Seventeen years ago, when the Soviet system started to implode, we thought we would try and wean her oil-rich satellites into our orbit. We encouraged their young citizens to come to our universities. We financed the birth of democratic parties. We supported independence movements. How am I doing so far?"

Andrew Meadows nodded appreciatively, so I continued.

"1989 was a bad year for the Russians. The Berlin Wall fell and they were forced out of Afghanistan. I guess our high-water mark was when the Soviet Empire collapsed in 1991. We probably thought it would be plain sailing after that. A flowering of Western democracy on Russia's southern flank. But it hasn't worked out that way. Instead of democracy, these countries are run by warlords more or less favorably disposed to Moscow, depending on the help they get. And now the worry is the influence of Fundamentalism, which by a curious accident of fate, is spreading—from those countries that supply the West with most of its oil, no less—into Russia's southern republics. Suddenly Washington and Moscow have common cause against the Faith Radicals."

"Did you ever think of joining the service?" he asked. "You seem to have the picture."

"Strangely enough, Andrew, we news people are supposed to have some idea about what's going on in the world!"

"Yes, I suppose so," he acknowledged, grudgingly. Like all priesthoods, his guarded the imagined exclusivity of its wisdom.

"But now to the interesting part," I parried. "Why are you here and why am I?"

He looked at me, but said nothing, so I continued.

"The answer to the second part of that question is easy. I am here because a friend of mine is here. A friend I made when he was learning about the wonders of democracy in my country, which my country wanted him to do. So now it's your turn. Why are you here?"

Andrew Meadows shifted uneasily in his chair. I could tell before he had opened his mouth that I was going to be served a pack of half-truths, and that's if I was lucky.

"This is a dangerous situation, Orla. Your man, Bernie . . . what's his name? . . ."

"Eisner."

". . . yeah. Eisner. He was worried about you going solo in a country you know little about."

"A country I know a whole lot more about than most people in our great nation."

"OK, Orla, but you don't know everything."

"No, I don't. And I'll tell you what I think I don't know. That you and your people are closing down the movements you set up and are helping our new allies to crush all opposition to whatever faction the Russians have decided to back. That's what I think!"

Andrew Meadows had clearly not sold all of himself to the service, because he just sat there looking wretched.

"You have to deal with the world as it is, Orla," was the best he could eventually manage.

"Yes, you do, Andrew. And that world is not built around friendships that are no more than political expedients, or ideals that are merely tools in realpolitik."

"We have our standard of living to protect," he mumbled.

"Sure we do. But our country, of all countries, was not built to defend the status quo. It was built so individuals could pursue life, liberty and human happiness, and not at the expense of everyone else, either."

"Jesus, Orla! What are you wanting me to say here? I'm a diplomat, for heaven's sake!"

"That's a polite word for it," I groaned.

". . .in the service of my country."

Just then the door opened, which was merciful as we were getting nowhere. A tall man, with fine features, and dressed in an officer's uniform, walked in to what was clearly his room. He came over to me and offered his hand.

"Major Leonid Nabokov," he announced, bowing his head slightly. "You are much admired in my country. Your reports are followed. Your last. . . ." he raised his eyebrows, ". . . most distressing. Pavel Trofim told me you were lucky to get out alive."

I stared at him, partly overawed by his manner and partly by what I thought he had just said.

"My last? The killing of the three escaped hostage takers?"

"No. Your one about Alu Dudayev."

"But. . . ," I stammered.

"It was put out by one of the underground channels. Yes, we watch them."

"Michael must have. . . ." And then I stopped myself.

"You know, he was in this room, just a few days ago. A remarkable man. He insisted on going to Seblan. I wish I hadn't helped him, now."

"Can I butt in here," complained Andrew Meadows, whose Russian may not have been as good as I supposed, "but what's all this about?"

"Mr. Meadows, here, has been concerned about you," Major Nabokov explained with a wry smile. "He thinks you should be in America, and so do I."

"It's a conspiracy!" I joked. There was something about the man that I knew I could trust.

"Yes. Life is just that, is it not?" he laughed. "Now, Mr. Meadows and I have some things to discuss. I am going to ask my assistant, Surek Talgayev, to look after you."

"So I am not under arrest?"

"Oh, my heavens no. Pavel Trofim asked me to look after you as soon as you arrived. Inside the terminal you would have had a rather different reception, I think."

As he said this, he looked across at Andrew Meadows and I swear the man almost swallowed his tongue.

SUREK WAS A lovely young woman and I took to her immediately. She had a look of Roaz about her and so Aslan too, I suppose. She told me about meeting Alu Dudayev and how he had known her parents.

"He asked me if I thought my village had a future," she recounted as we drove from the barracks into Zoldek.

"And what did you tell him?"

"I wasn't sure what to tell him. He is. . ." and then she corrected herself, ". . .was a man of honor, but a man of the old ways. I told him that it did have a future, but that it would have to change."

"What was his reaction?"

"He didn't seem surprised. I think he knew change was inevitable. But I think he feared we risked losing something important."

"What?"

"I'm not sure. *Our* honor, perhaps."

As we had driven away from the barracks, she had told me to lie low in the seat. After only a few turns I was told I could sit up.

"Do the secret police often follow you?" I wondered, as we became enveloped within the bustle of the capital.

"We follow each other. The Russian army has always guarded its independence and I'm working for the army. That gives me some protection—and a good salary!"

"How do your friends feel about you working for the Russians?"

"Oh, they don't mind. They would like my job, I think!"

"And what about the Chenchian resistance, how do they feel?"

"What resistance?" she laughed. "The Democrats are all but finished. And as for the Faith Radicals, well after Seblan no one wants to know them."

"So the Russians have won?"

She looked uncomfortable.

"Not exactly," she said.

"Explain," I urged.

"Aslan Dudayev is your friend, yes?"

"He is."

"So how much do you know about my country?" she questioned.

"I know there are three regions," I told her, "That each has been run by one family for generations. That there has been a steady migration from the regions to Zoldek. I know that most of the trouble has been in the capital. That the Democrats, the Faith Radicals and the Chenchian Independence Movement have all been vying for power and fighting the Russian occupation."

"Yes. It has been very bad. Most people want to see an end to it. The Russians, too."

"So what are you trying to tell me? That there has been an accommodation?"

"It had to come. We couldn't go on like that."

"So who have the Russians decided to deal with?" I asked.

"Malik Bassayev," she announced.

Her answer silenced me. I don't know why I hadn't seen the obvious coming. No, that wasn't true. I did know. I had not wished to see it. Ever since Chenchia had become part of my life and, with it, the rivalry between Malik and Aslan, I had assumed that Aslan would come out on top. He was mine, he was America's, he was so obviously the right person to lead his country. And I had been totally wrong.

"Do you know where Aslan Dudayev is?" I asked, half-fearing the answer.

"There are rumors."

"What rumors?"

"That he is dead. That he has fled the country. That he has been captured. You are not the only person who wants him. The Russian secret police want him. The Americans want him. The Russian army want him. Malik's men want him."

"What about the Vorsky region?"

"It is holding out, but the Sharosky region has pledged its allegiance to Malik and with Alu Dudayev gone and Aslan no one knows where, the feeling in Vorsky is that they too should go with Malik. After all, he is married to Alu Dudayev's daughter."

"Akhmad Bassayev, Malik's father. What about him?"

"He has slipped into unconsciousness, we are being told. His son is now in total charge."

"You know I am almost certain," I told her, "that it was not Sergei Kadyrov at the siege in Seblan."

Surek shrugged.

"He is no longer in the Sharosky region, that is all we know. Yana, his first wife, is certain he is dead. It is she who has agreed to pledge the region's allegiance to Malik Bassayev. But that *was* only after we had learned from your broadcast that Alu Dudayev was dead."

"So it's just happened."

"Informally. The formal pledge has yet to take place."

"Couldn't she have waited for Aslan?"

"I don't wish to hurt your feelings, but many feel that Aslan Dudayev was . . . well . . . too Western. Now even your Americans do not want him. They have been working with our secret police to . . . how shall I put it . . . close down their operations here in Chenchia."

"You are very well informed."

"The army is very well informed. Major Nabokov wanted me to tell you these things."

"Why?"

"His father respected the Dudayev family and he does too."

"So this is a personal matter for him?"

"Yes, just personal. He believes that if Aslan Dudayev is alive, it would be best if he left for America with you."

I started to feel sick and ashamed. Sick because my life was being invaded by a possibility I had often fantasized about, but

never seriously entertained. Ashamed, because I worried that neither I nor my country were up to the challenge. Aslan Dudayev,
warlord, was one thing; Aslan Dudayev, American immigrant,
quite another.

"What would you like to do?" Surek asked. "You can stay in my
apartment. It is small and three of us share it. But you are welcome.
There is a sofa. Perhaps you can find him before anyone else does."

"Thank you. But there are two people I must locate first. Can you
help me?"

"I'll try. Who are they?"

"Khalim, an old friend of Aslan's."

"That'll be Khalim Zakayev. They were at school together."

"Yes."

"And the other person?"

I fished through my notes.

"Have you heard of somewhere called the *ZeZe* Club?"

Surek giggled.

"It's where I might have gone if I hadn't got a job with the Russians!"

"There's a girl called Amanta there I'd like to speak to."

"*Orla, wake up!*"

I'd fallen asleep on Surek's bed.

"What time is it?"

"Past midnight."

"God! What have I missed?"

"Nothing. We have been creeping around trying not to wake
you."

"Your friends?"

"They're out. But we need to hurry. The girl, Amanta, she should
be at the club now."

"You've been there?"

"Earlier, while you were sleeping."

"Khalim? Have you found Khalim?"

"No. But I've sent out a message."

"Hey, my suitcase!" I whooped, seeing it in the corner.

"Major Nabokov had it collected from the plane. I brought it over."

I showered and put on the little black dress I'd purchased in Moscow with Bernie's money. Even at night, Zoldek seemed a dismal place, although the darkness did hide some of its scars. The *ZeZe* Club was in a deserted, nondescript street and only a blue neon sign depicting a champagne glass next to the letters *ZeZe* hinted at the possibility of human life, even if only low life.

"They'll think we're hookers," Surek whispered as we slipped inside.

She said something to a King Kong behind the desk, who nodded and had another gorilla take us to a table. Being known as the assistant to the Russian garrison commander might have carried risks, but it also had advantages. Surek was clearly the sort of person who knew how to make the best of the bargain.

"Amanta," she said, nodding in the direction of a small stage where a girl was wrestling with a python.

"I hope I don't have to talk to that thing as well!"

"Oh, I suspect it's tame compared to most of the other snakes in here. I think we are about to be offered some sake."

A table of Japanese businessmen were leering in our direction and summoning a waiter.

"Are there many of *them* in Zoldek?" I asked, not thinking of the Chenchian capital as a place of cultural diversity.

"A Japanese company is building a refinery, in return for oil."

As she predicted, a waiter came over and announced that the 'gentlemen' wanted to buy us drinks. Surek told him to tell them we were secret police and as soon as our message was delivered, we noticed a distinct drop in their ardor.

"I must remember that line," I told her. "It seems to be pretty effective."

"Just don't overuse it," she cautioned. "The Russian secret police run most of the vice rings in Zoldek these days."

We watched the python slither its way round every part of Amanta's lithe body, to the delight of the club's clientele. This was followed by a boy-girl act that wasn't a patch on Liviana and Sebastian, although their simulated fornication went down well with the crowd. Then, out of the darkness, Amanta, minus python, appeared and sat at our table.

"You must be Orla," she said, leaning over and shaking my hand and then Surek's. "Liviana told me you might be visiting."

"You know her and Sebastian?" I couldn't quite get him out of my mind.

"Of course," she laughed. "This is her club."

"She owns it?" I said, genuinely surprised.

"Part-owns it. She always has well-connected partners. Now how can I help you? I have to spank a naughty schoolboy in a few minutes."

"Seriously?"

"Our audience has simple tastes!"

"I bet!" I acknowledged, looking across at the Japanese party who were going wild with excitement and had managed to persuade a couple of 'hostesses' to join them. "I'm looking for a friend of mine, Aslan Dudayev."

"You and everyone else in Zoldek."

I obviously looked surprised.

"How much does she know?" Amanta asked, turning to Surek.

Surek shrugged. "More than most."

Amanta turned back to me.

"So you know that your country's spooks are now working with the Russian secret police?"

"I was beginning to suspect it."

"Well, believe it. It's been going on for months now. The Democratic Movement, which your country set up, has been wiped out. The Chenchian Independence Movement, partly financed by you, has virtually disappeared. Since Seblan, the Faith Radicals, too, are a spent force, for now anyway. And after tomorrow, all the regions will almost certainly be united under the leadership of Malik Bassayev, who has Moscow's backing."

"After tomorrow?"

"You know about the funeral?"

I looked at Surek.

"No. What funeral?"

"Alu Dudayev's body is being flown in from Seblan," Surek explained. "He is due to be buried here in Zoldek tomorrow afternoon, in the main cemetery. The authorities have given permission for a burial with full honors."

"But why in Zoldek?" I asked. "Surely he would want to be buried in Vorsky?"

"She does know something about our country!" Amanta quipped to Surek. "Perhaps she can also work out why the authorities are so keen."

It was suddenly all too clear to me.

"They are trying to trap Aslan."

Amanta nodded.

"If he shows up, he is a dead man. The Russian secret service will deal with him. If he does not show up at his father's funeral, the Vorsky people will turn to his sister's husband, Malik Bassayev. Either way, he is finished here."

"And my people?" I asked despondently. "What part are my people playing in all of this?"

"I think your friend is an embarrassment to them," Surek speculated. "I believe they would have taken him out, I mean to America, if he'd been willing to go."

I sat there in that place of mindless pleasure like a piece in check on a chessboard, but without a mate. All I knew was that I had to help Aslan, somehow, even though I could envision no future for him that made the slightest sense.

"Look, Orla. I must get back to work," Amanta apologized, reaching across for my hand. "I'm sorry I could not be more help."

"Do *you* know where he is?" I asked, all too pitifully.

"*Moya dorogaya*, I don't know if he's alive or dead. All I do know is that if I were him I'd be in the Vorsky mountains, where I grew up. Not here."

I was staring at nothing, feeling dead, aware of what was going on around me but disconnected from it, like a junkie, when I noticed Surek's bag moving on the table. At first I thought I must be hallucinating. Then she noticed it too. It was her cell.

"A text message," she said. "Does *the place with the heron* mean anything to you?"

"How long will it take us to get to Vorsky?" I asked, suddenly feeling alive.

"That depends which part."

"There's a village, a mile or so west of where the Klist and Mhemet rivers join."

"I know it," Surek confirmed.

"How long will it take us to get there?"

"About two hours, if we don't get stopped."

"Can you take me?" I asked.

"You mean now?"

I nodded.

Surek looked at her watch and shrugged.

"OK!"

"*I APPRECIATE YOU* doing this," I told her, as we sped out of Zoldek on a deserted road.

"Major Nabokov said I was to look after you," she joked. "I'll put in for overtime!"

"Do you think we'll get stopped?" I wondered.

"The secret police are much less efficient than they would like us to think. At this hour, they'll be silking it up with their lady friends— or boyfriends. The army won't be any bother. I have a pass. My parents still live in Vorsky."

As we cleared the city limits, I spotted the tail lights of a car pulling up onto the verge.

"Ahead, on the left," I said. "Is that them?"

Two young women were caught in its headlights as we passed.

"Yeah," Surek confirmed. "But they won't be interested in us. They're probably just making sure the night's takings don't walk out of town."

"I don't fancy those girls' chances!"

"No, probably not. I guess we *have* lost something along with the old ways, but we've gained things too."

"What? The opportunity to get paid for sex?" I questioned.

Surek let out an engaging giggle, that made me feel prudish.

"Some of the old women in my village say they would be millionaires if they'd been paid every time they'd had to endure their men!"

"Hah!"

"I prefer working for the major myself, mind you," she admitted.

"No strings?"

"No. No strings. He has a charming wife—unfortunately!"

I realized I was listening to a thoroughly modern woman; independent, self-confident, worldly. How different she would have seemed if her village had been the only life she knew. I suspect we become nostalgic for the past when we have forgotten its drawbacks or have never known them. It is the certainty of the past people crave, I think, against the uncertainty of the present. It has been locked away, it has happened, it is known. For me, though, it is uncertainty that makes life worth living.

We could have driven without lights, if we'd had to. The valley was drenched in moonbeams. The pipe and the road dissected the landscape ahead of us, as far as the proverbial eye could see, a technological rearrangement of a centuries-old pattern invisible to the naked eye, that was only grudgingly coming to terms with its new, twin arteries, one of which accelerated the movement of people away from the regions into the capital and the other that placed an importance on the valley which served only to dislocate it from its time and place.

It was after three when Surek slowed and told me we had arrived. But I did not recognize anything. The village seemed more spread out, less coherent, than I had remembered.

"We came in from the other direction, on the old road," I told her. "We were nearer the river."

"Well, that's what we will do," Surek suggested. And after we had motored past the houses, she turned off the new road onto the old and started coming back.

"Do you recognize anything yet?" she asked.

"I think so. We were on horseback. But really, you can stop here. I just need to find the river.

"Do you want me to come with you?" she wondered.

"No," I told her. "It's better you stay here."

AT FIRST I stumbled uncertainly forward in the direction of where I imagined the river to be. Things seemed familiar, but I couldn't be sure until I came head-to-head with the donkey. Its belligerent manner was unmistakable and I soon found myself at the water's edge.

I was feeling nervous, so much had happened since the last time. Would Aslan be there? His text message had come in over two hours ago. Of course he would have had to get from wherever he was. Would two hours have been enough? And what would we say to each other? Orla's pool had taken on an almost mythical majesty in my mind. Seeing it again was bound to be disappointing. Then, we had shared a night that seemed to stretch to infinity, timeless, devoid of any claim but our claim on each other. Even the appearance of Ula and Michael had been no more than an interlude of blissful comedy set within a bigger moment that had belonged to only us.

And now I felt like a cheating wife returning to her husband. Leonid Nabokov's words, *he should go back with you to America*, and my reaction, hung like a shroud over our relationship. Relationship! What relationship? We had none. We had been two student lovers, very much in love, as much with the idea of each other as with our newly-forming selves. And yet that night had been real, hadn't it? Yes, it had been real alright! But perhaps its sweetness hung from the simple fact of having been a precious echo from a past neither of us could reclaim.

I reached the pool we had swum in, but there was no heron. I stood, watching the moonlight bounce off the water as it had done before. The swish of the current through the low-lying willow branches almost took me back, but a snapping twig pulled me up with a start.

"Aslan?" I called out.

A person approached from the bushes and I felt afraid, because even though its face was still in shadow, I knew it was not him. The movement, the shape, the thing unique to each of us just wasn't there.

"Who's that?" I called out again.

"It's Khalim, Miss Orla."

"Khalim! Where's Aslan?"

I realized immediately how ungracious I must have sounded. He had probably travelled many miles to reach me, at great risk.

"He is alright. He sent me."

Somehow, *he sent me*, made it all better. There would be no embarrassing moment. Like a teen who had gone further than she intended and was petrified by what might happen next, I felt elated and spared because *he* had sent a message!

"Khalim, it's so good to see you. What is going on?"

"We have an expression, Miss Orla. The flood is rearranging the stones. Yesterday the riverbed looked one way. Tomorrow it will look another. It is just the way it is."

"But Khalim, you of all people know that Aslan is a better leader than Malik Bassayev."

"A better man, certainly. A more honorable man, without a doubt. But a better leader for these troubled times? I'm not so sure."

"But *you* can't desert him!" I protested and as I heard my words I wished I hadn't uttered them.

"You must know I won't," he said with a dignity that made me feel so very small. "But ever since his father sent him to America his star has moved to a different part of the sky. I think even Alu Dudayev realized that. It might have been different. It just wasn't."

"But what is he going to do?"

"First, he must bury his father. And then he must heal the wounds of his country in the traditional way."

"What traditional way?"

"He wants you to leave, Miss Orla. He says there is nothing more that you can do."

"But Khalim! There *must* be something!"

"Listen, Miss Orla, you are a fine person. But you are American. Dreams do not always come true, especially in my country."

"No, Khalim, you are right. And dreams do not always come true in my country either. We just pretend they do."

"Then you understand that belief is sometimes more important than the truth."

"That is an old-fashioned idea, Khalim."

"Not everything that is old is wrong, Miss Orla. Now I must go. There are even people in Vorsky who cannot be trusted with Aslan's life. The flood is rearranging the stones."

"He is lucky to have you as a friend," I said.

"I think that is a curse we both share!"

He hugged me, kissed me on both cheeks and was gone.

I FOUND SUREK asleep in the car. It wasn't quite four in the morning yet and if we got a move on, I reckoned we'd be back in Zoldek before six. There *was* one last thing I could do for Aslan and his father. To achieve it, I had to see Leonid Nabokov as soon as possible and persuade him that Alu Dudayev should be buried in Vorsky, amongst his own people.

CHAPTER 20

We were back in the apartment just after six. An army patrol had stopped us outside the city, but as soon as they realized whose car it was, they let us through. Surek and I felt dog-tired and were determined to get some sleep. I managed an hour on the sofa before one of her flatmates came in to make breakfast.

"You're always sleeping," she said, looking half-asleep herself. "My name's Klara. Can I make you some coffee?"

"Thank you. My name's Orla, by the way."

"I know. I've watched your broadcasts."

"Oh! I'm surprised they don't block them," I told her, trying to look less wretched than I felt.

"Not everyone in Moscow is against them. Not blocking is Russia's version of democracy, I think. When did you guys get to bed?"

"About an hour ago."

"Wow!"

Just then a second girl, still wearing a nightdress, crept in, rubbing her eyes.

"This is Renata," Klara introduced, handing me a mug of coffee.

Renata grunted and pulled a carton of milk from the fridge, a bowl from the cupboard and a packet of cereal off the shelf. In one of the villages, such a scene would have been impossible, I thought. These girls would have been living at home with their mothers. By now they would have drawn the water, tended the fire, milked the goat and baked bread. It was not hard to see why the road to Zoldek offered a brighter future to some and a bleaker one to others.

"Do you get paid a lot?" Renata asked, as she prodded her bowl with a spoon in a distracted sort of way.

Her question shocked me. I preferred to be thought of as a knight in armor fighting for virtue, rather than a mere salaryman.

"Yes, quite a lot. But it never seems enough!"

"Tell me about it!" Klara complained.

"So what work do you both do?" I asked.

"Renata works for a car dealer and she's going out with one of the salesmen."

"Klara!" protested Renata, still unsure whether to swallow her cereal or prod it some more.

"Well, you asked Orla about her salary."

Renata shrugged. She was in no mood for a fight.

"And what's your job, Klara?" I pressed.

"I work for GAZ, they look after the pipe. Engineers mostly, interesting people."

"Boring people," muttered Renata.

"Ah! I see you've all met," observed Surek, who walked in fully dressed and looking as fresh as a newly-picked peach. "Do you want the bathroom, Orla? It's free. If you're going to persuade Major Nabokov to alter the funeral, you'd better see him right away. He's always in his office by eight."

"Is that the old warlord they're burying today?" burbled Renata, showing an unexpected flicker of life. "They say there's going to be a shoot-out!"

"Renata!" protested Surek.

I looked across and shook my head. The fewer people who knew about my connection the better.

"So!" mouthed Renata. "That *is* what they say."

"Yeah," chipped in Klara. "Between the dead man's son and Malik Bassayev. I'm for Malik. My family's from Urus."

"I'm for the other one," Renata announced.

"But you're from Sharosky," Klara pointed out.

"So!" Renata said again. "They say he's dishy."

God! I thought. What has the modern world bequeathed to these people. The future of their troubled nation was being decided and they were expecting a contest between Rocky Balboa and Mason "The Line" Dixon.

"I expect you're for him too, Su," speculated Klara, "being as he comes from your region?"

Surek shook her head.

"Airheads!" she muttered. "Now come on Orla, if you want to use that bathroom you'd better grab it before one of these political scientists here beats you to it. We need to get to the barracks."

IT WAS HALF eight when we arrived. Surek left me in an ante-room while she went off to get her Major started for the day. I wasn't sure how much she would tell him about our night's adventure, probably most of it. Leonid Nabokov was the sort of man one confided in and who expected nothing less.

I was beginning to feel like Alice in Wonderland once more. The world was inside out, upside down and completely unreal. I wasn't sure what my point was any more. To report? No, I wasn't there to report. I was there to help a friend. But my friend didn't want to be helped. He knew, as well as I, that his trajectory was quite different to mine, and just because our paths had joined for a brief, wonderful period, did not mean that they should or would join again. Even my coming here was beginning to feel like a mistake. So I had exposed Russian barbarity and attempted to put President Nitup on the spot. I had exposed Chenchian barbarity, or more precisely the barbarity of its Faith Radicals. I had laid bare the grief of Seblan, the confusion surrounding the siege, and its murderous aftermath. Most important of all, I had earned Bernie a ton of money and boosted the station's ratings. Most important of all! Was that not really the bottom line?

And the real story of what had been going on in Chenchia, what about that? What about it, indeed! Did anyone actually care? Did I know what the real story was? Did anyone? Was it possible to simply report without implying this or that, without suggesting a story that should have a beginning, a middle, and an end? The truth was that life was a series of events that became a story. Yes, individual men and women had goals, objectives, and outcomes they craved, but the story was made up afterwards to fit the facts—at least to fit whatever facts were actually known.

"Orla, good morning. Come on in. Do I gather you have not had much sleep?"

Leonid Nabokov looked more like a professor than a soldier, his height tempered by a stoop, as if he was trying to keep on the same plane as the little people, by bending down, ever so slightly, towards them.

"How much have you heard?" I asked.

"Enough!" he laughed. "Now can I ask Surek to get us some refreshments? I don't believe you've eaten yet this morning."

I told him I would like that very much and followed him into his office.

"You like books?" I said, admiring again his collection.

"I am writing a short history of this region. You know that in the 14th century, under Genghis Khan's son, Ögedei, it was part of the Mongol Empire. Its people have been at war, off and on, ever since."

"I suspect most peoples have been at war, off and on, over the course of their history," I suggested.

"Sadly true, but being caught between two great powers is a particular curse for any people. Now I understand you want me to change a state funeral..." and he looked at his watch, ". . . .at six hours' notice!"

"Is it possible?"

"I wanted Alu Dudayev to be buried in Vorsky myself. It was only our secret police who insisted it take place in Zoldek. And in the end, they usually have the last word as they report directly to the Kremlin."

"So that his son would be more vulnerable," I stated dryly.

"I think your Andrew Meadows may have been helpful in this."

"Andrew?"

"I believe the tarantula and the scorpion want to dance to the same tune, for once."

"That sounds like a dangerous dance," I grimaced.

"Yes. Not one to get involved in."

"You mean me?"

"I mean anyone."

"So has it been changed?"

"I'm waiting on a call. But I do have one trump card. We have the body!"

Surek brought in fruit juice and some cakes and I marveled again at her freshness. Sometimes I did want to be twenty again—but only sometimes.

"Are you sure you want to put yourself through this, Orla?" Leonid asked. "I could have you flown out of here in a couple of hours."

"I can't see how I can do anything else," I confessed. "Do you know what will happen?"

"I know what is supposed to happen."

I looked at him, wanting more.

"What is supposed to happen," he continued, "is that there needs to be only one warlord here in Chenchia and the Russians have already decided who that should be."

"But does it have to end in death, for the one who it will not be?"

"If we are to have stability here, one family must take control of the whole country. The Russians understand that now. Before, they thought they could crush all opposition and install a leader, but in that, they have failed. It has become too costly for them."

"If the people of Vorsky stood behind Aslan, would they accept him?"

"Only if the other regions fell in behind him as well. And," he emphasized, "only if they did not think he was going to be an American stooge."

"From what I gather, we have washed our hands of the region. So they should not fear that, surely?"

"But there is always the future," he cautioned.

"But is it possible? *Could* they accept him?"

"It's possible, I suppose."

His telephone rang and I watched him listen, say *yes* several times, and then replace the handset.

"Well, it's agreed. Vorsky. Now, I suggest Surek takes you back for some sleep. The coffin will leave here at one o'clock under a military escort. The burial will take place under the shadow of Mount Abochevo, at four. The people of Vorsky will take the coffin, on horseback, for the last hour up into the foothills. I have been told you can go with them, but there will be no Russians. You will be on your own."

"Not entirely," said Surek who had come into the room to collect the tray. "I will be there, and could accompany you, if you wish."

"Of course," admitted Leonid Nabokov, having forgotten for a moment, I think, that his assistant was a Chenchian from Vorsky.

"Yes, I would like that," I told her.

"Now, Orla," the professorial soldier said, getting to his feet, "it has been a pleasure meeting you, a great pleasure. There is a military flight leaving Zoldek for Moscow at midnight tonight. I have arranged for you to be on it. I am sure your Andrew Meadows will get you onto a flight to Washington tomorrow. I have alerted him. He seems very anxious to have you leave!"

I LAY ON THE SOFA. I was tired but couldn't sleep. I got up and spread out my rough clothes instead. Riding again. It was as well Michael would not be with me, although I would've liked his company. I lay on the sofa again and closed my eyes. My head was spinning. I remember, in history class, wondering how Anne Boleyn, Henry VIII of England's second wife, had prepared for her execution. By all accounts she had died with courage, protesting her innocence of the adultery she had been accused of. Hers had been a political murder, sanctioned by a man who was to lay the foundations for England's Church and greatness. She'd been about my age, somewhere between 29 and 35, and her daughter, Elizabeth, would become her country's greatest queen. And how would I have reported that?

King rids court of plotting libertine. Queen sacrificed to court intrigue. Mad dictator disgusts world! Certainly the king's jollity after the execution surprised several contemporaries, but back then, there wasn't a 'world' to disgust. Back then, ritualized murder was an accepted part of the political lexicon. And why shouldn't it be so today? Only our democratic sensibilities balk at such a practice, even though it was the democratic impulse that ran wild across Europe in the twentieth century, killing countless millions.

I guess how I would have reported the death of my heroine—as Anne had been back then: I had imagined myself in her lovely jeweled clothes influencing the course of history—would have depended on which side of the fence 'Bernie' had been sitting. There's always a Bernie. "Reports don't just come out of thin air, Orla, they cost, and have to be paid for," was one of my Bernie's little gems and I guess he is right at that. Would Aslan attend the funeral? Well, he had to, surely? Would there, as Renata had hoped, be a shoot-out between him and Malik? It was possible, I suppose, but at the funeral? One way or another, the leadership had to be resolved, I could see that now. Part of me was anxious for Aslan. Part of me just wanted to know the outcome. And if I was honest, part of me was convinced Aslan could still come out on top.

THE MILITARY ESCORT was limited: a jeep, followed by a truck with the coffin inside, followed by another truck with soldiers. From the outside it looked much like any of the patrols that plied Chenchia's new highway. The weather had turned bad, and spots of rain were already falling when we left. For some reason, I expected a stream of cars to be following, but ours was the only one. Shoot-out or not, the Renatas of the world had decided to stay away.

I hardly recognized Surek Talgayev. Gone was the modern city girl with an eight-to-five job. In her place was a girl from the Vorsky region in traditional clothes: a wool vest, baggy trousers and leather boots. In the back seat was a large, warm-looking jacket, a wool scarf and one of those dark brown, astrakhan hats, made from the curly fleece of a young karakul lamb. Underneath all of that, I could clearly make out the end of a Kalashnikov.

"I like the hat," I said, trying to ignore the gun.

"I brought two. It's liable to get cold."

I thanked her, and we said little more to each other for the best part of two hours. She seemed unusually silent.

By the time we reached the confluence of the Klist and Mhemet rivers the rain was falling hard. I started to notice groups of horsemen trotting along the old road from Urus and others descending from the Sharosky hills.

"It's going to be big," Surek said. "Alu Dudayev was much respected."

When the trucks eventually came to a halt next to the trail that led up into the Vorsky mountains, we were surrounded by several hundred horsemen and the Russian soldiers looked nervous.

"Stay in the car," Surek instructed. "I must find my father. He will have our horses."

I watched as the soldiers first climbed out of their truck and then climbed back in. One look at the sea of angry faces was enough to convince them they were not needed. Four or five Chenchians dismounted and started to unload the coffin. Others brought up two horses yoked together with a sling between them. When the coffin was clear of the truck it was raised up and a barrage of shots was let loose into the air. The horses strutted and pranced excitedly, but none ignored their training and tried to break free.

The coffin was then lowered into the sling and strapped. There were more shots, fired this time I felt as a deliberate warning to the Russian soldiers. I watched the vehicles pull away, turn, and start their journey back towards the barracks at Zoldek. For several minutes my view was restricted to the flanks and legs of horses, foaming with sweat and dripping rainwater, as they passed the car, brushing up against it at times, in pursuit of the cortège. Major Nabokov's words *You will be on your own* came back to me.

The rain was now so heavy that I could see very little. I was beginning to think that Surek had left me, when a rider leading an empty horse stopped a few yards from the car. I picked up the second hat from the back seat, put it and my coat on and stepped outside. The rain hit my face causing my eyes to shut. I pulled the top of my jacket tight, but still felt rainwater seeping down my neck. I walked forward, slipped on the mud, but managed not to fall. Grasping the reins and saddle of the empty horse, I pushed my left foot into the stirrup. The animal moved, I hopped once, twice and then hauled myself onto its back. They say that people weigh each other up in the first few seconds. I am sure this is the case with horses and those who ride them. For a moment or two the beast tested me, this way and that, but I gathered tight the reins, pressed my knees into its sides and turned it into the hill.

"Alright?" Surek shouted.

"Yes. Alright," I shouted back. "Where's your father?"

"With the men," she answered, and turned away.

As we climbed, behind several hundred horses strung out in front of us, I understood what it must have been like, once, going into battle.

THE CAVALCADE KEPT up a brisk pace. For much of the way the trail was only wide enough for two abreast. I guessed a mile or more must have separated the front from the back by the time we broke through the narrow lower gorges and ascended the foothills. The rain had eased somewhat and it was possible to see ahead. Groups were now joining us from either side. These would be people from Vorsky itself. There were some things I thought I recognized. We must have travelled this way when I first came with Aslan, to see for myself what the Russians had done to his father's village, Argun. But on that day it had been dry, bone dry with dust devils wisping up here and there, like flighty sentinels.

It hardly seemed possible that only fourteen days separated then and now. I felt I had seen so much and understood so little. It had been like opening one of those Russian dolls. Whenever you thought you had unearthed a truth, you found that you had only revealed another question. It was Winston Churchill, I think, who said Russia was a riddle, wrapped in a mystery, inside an enigma.

We were now on a plateau. Somewhere above us, in the clouds, was Mount Abochevo. There must have been at least two thousand horses all jostling for position. The pair carrying the dead warlord stood alone, in the middle. As I approached, it became clear that we were grouping into regions. The largest contingent, from Vorsky, took up position under the mountain. To the east, the riders from Sharosky began to assemble, with the riders from Urus facing them on the west.

I recognized Yana, Sergei Kadyrov's first wife. She clearly had taken charge of the region since her husband's disappearance. Malik Bassayev, on a pitch black horse, stood out in front of the riders from

Urus. As I joined those from Vorsky, I tried to make out who was at the front of our group, but being at the back I could only see heads, not faces.

Close to where the two horses were standing a large hole had been dug. As the rain eased, it was possible to see straight down into the valley below. I could just make out the river. Fortuitously, I suppose, a slight rise in the ground obscured the pipe and new highway. From this height, it was possible to see Chenchia as it had always been.

I was so busy trying to make out what was going on in front, that I did not notice the two horses come from behind. Like the parting of the Red Sea, the Vorsky riders suddenly made way and a second coffin was carried between them to the front. There it stood for a moment, and a groan came from the mouths of the Vorsky people. I was confused and looked around for Surek, but she had moved away from me.

I then saw Roaz Bassayev leave the Urus contingent and ride across the open space towards the two horses that had taken up their position in front of us, with the second coffin. The second coffin was led forward to join the first, leaving Roaz alone at the front. A loud cheer came from the Vorsky riders, and I realized, at that moment, that the second coffin must contain her brother, Aslan. When I recognized the person leading the horses as Khalim, I was certain.

Now, it was father and son in the opening, on the plateau beneath the mountain. I wanted to shout out, to say something, to demand *when* Aslan and Malik had competed for the honor of leading the Chenchian people. Surely that is what honor required? But my mouth stayed shut. I could not move and besides, these were not my people. My only connection was that I had loved one of them—and was I alone in that? I hardly thought so.

CHAPTER 21

$\mathcal{M}$alik Bassayev studied the assembled horsemen from the three regions. He left the Urus side and walked his mount to the center, beyond the four coffin-bearing horses. With his back to the valley and face towards the mountain and towards what were now his people, the people of Chenchia, he raised his arm in a clenched fist. A roar came from the riders, led by Yana for the Sharosky people and by his wife Roaz for the Vorsky and Urus peoples. The pieces of the jigsaw had finally fallen into place.

In his ears, the roar sounded like a baptismal wave. He tilted his head back and jabbed his fist again towards the sky. A second roar, even louder than the first filled the air, like a purging of demons, as if he and his people were letting go of the ghastliness that had entrapped their lives and were reaching for a new purity of purpose, a new beginning.

He nodded and the two coffins were lowered into the ground. The earth, such as it was, and the stones were pushed back and riders came from each of the regions pulling bundles of wood soaked in spirit. These were piled high above the grave and set alight. It was now getting dark, and the initial burst of flame lit up the riders and drew them in upon itself under a radiant veil of intimacy. Malik, riding slowly around the semicircle, his black horse glistening with moisture and light, was greeted with volleys of shots from all those he passed. At the end of his triumphal he moved back towards the pyre and was joined by Roaz and Yana. Yana handed him a silver flask. He drank from it and passed it to Roaz. She lifted her head and took a long draught then returned it to Yana who completed the bond.

That was the signal of unity they had all been waiting for. The riders converged and mingled around the flames, firing shots into the black sky and handing each other leather pouches filled with water from the Mhemet River. Malik rode amongst them, not a flicker of a smile on his face, which concerned them not at all. For he was now their warlord.

CHAPTER 22

I watched Malik's coronation with mounting anger. I needed to know what had happened and started to edge my horse around the back in search of Surek. I eventually found her with the other women, standing in a group on higher ground, some distance from the men. She saw me coming and advanced to meet me.

"Where is Aslan?" I demanded to know.

"He died last night," she announced without emotion.

"When did you know?" I asked accusingly.

"Just before we came here."

"So all that time, while we were driving, you knew?"

She said nothing.

"How did he die?"

"A Faith Radical, Gregor Yepishin, found his hiding place and shot him."

"While I was talking to Khalim?"

Again, she said nothing.

"So there were no witnesses? How convenient!"

"Do you want me to take you back?" she asked. "The men will be celebrating for a long time now. We women are not welcome."

"Tell me about this Faith Radical."

"He was well known. Some even say he was at the Seblan siege and got away."

"Don't be ridiculous!" I protested. "I was there."

"But you wouldn't have known if someone had escaped, now would you?" she insisted.

"Besides," I said, ignoring the fact that she might have been right, "why would he have wanted to kill Aslan?"

"They killed each other. Two men on the run, nervous. It is easy to understand."

"How do we know they killed each other?"

"Khalim found them when he got back from seeing you. They were both just lying there, dead."

"I don't believe it!"

"It wasn't your fault," she said, trying to reassure me. "It was an accident."

"I need to hear this from Khalim. It is just too convenient."

She shrugged and I left to find him.

The celebrations were now in full swing. How I was going to find one man in amongst two thousand, I didn't know. Most had now dismounted and were sitting, smoking and laughing. I rode between them, collecting surprised looks as I went. There was no hostility, just the sort of looks you get when you have walked into the wrong room by mistake. They probably knew who I was. The only Western face. The American friend of Aslan Dudayev. The friend of one of the men underneath the fire. The friend of both, for that matter.

My horse almost backed onto a group of four. They shouted out in mock horror.

"Khalim Zakayev?" I shouted back. "I'm looking for him."

They gestured off to my right, so I tried that direction. Every twenty yards or so I asked again. "Khalim Zakayev?" Mostly I got shaken heads, but there were enough loose gestures indicating some vague knowledge of his whereabouts to keep me going. I was on the point of giving up when I came upon him, in a group, passing round a pipe and joking. I just remained there on my horse, watching. One by one the people next to him noticed and stopped talking. Only when the last had clammed shut did Khalim himself look up.

"Miss Orla!" he grinned.

He had been inhaling something, that was clear, and not just for the last half-hour.

"Tell me Khalim? I need to know."

I stared at him with great anger, I don't know why great anger, as he had known Aslan for longer than I, but somehow I blamed him. Or perhaps I was just blaming myself.

He held out his pipe.

"Here, Miss Orla!"

I was on the point of riding my horse straight into him when I felt a hand on my shoulder. It was Roaz.

"Orla," she said firmly. "Come with me. We must talk."

I followed Roaz's horse through the melee. We passed Malik at some distance, but if he noticed me, he chose not to show it. He had a hard face and I wondered how many bargains he'd struck with the devil in order to secure his crown. Gradually, the groups of seated men thinned and we started to climb a knoll. At the top, she stopped and turned and we surveyed the scene below. The fire had died back and a moon was now coming and going, like a child's game of hide-and-seek, from behind thinning rain clouds that were racing away because they had lost their moisture.

"It's good, isn't it?" she said quietly, with evident satisfaction.

"What's good about it?" I cursed. "Your brother and father are dead and I wouldn't be surprised if it was your own husband who killed one of them."

She didn't answer immediately. But when she did, her voice had a sharp edge to it.

"He was killed by Gregor Yepishin. That is all we need to know."

It was now my turn to remain silent.

"I just don't know how you can live with all this," I said eventually.

She turned to me.

"Orla. What I know about you, I like. And I know my brother held you close to his heart. But there are some things you must understand. This is our country. This is where we live. We do not have the luxury you have of being able to move around the world, passing judgment, and then returning to settled ways. Our ways are not settled. They are evolving. And we have to live with a clumsy neighbor who can cause us great injury at any time.

"When my parents sent their son to America, it looked as though Russia was in retreat and a new way might be open to us. But that was not to be. My father would have understood what happened here today and you should too. My husband is not a bad man. In fact, I have come to think that he may be a great man. He is a man of his time and of his people. Go home, Orla. One day, I hope you will realize what sacrifices have been made."

"It just doesn't seem right," I said feebly.

"Only to you, Orla. Now let me send Surek. You must get off the hill."

Roaz turned to leave and I suddenly remembered.

"Wait!" I called out.

She pulled her animal back towards me.

"What is it?" she asked.

"Here," I said. "Your father wanted me to give you these."

She took the string of beads I handed her and studied them with great affection, rubbing the little stone spheres gently between her fingers. Roaz was too strong a woman to let emotion get the better of her. I knew she understood that she had been given her father's blessing.

You are the leader of our people now, was the message his simple gift conveyed.

As WE MADE our way down, Surek in front, her mother behind, I felt a mixture of light-headedness, tinged with grief. It was as if a weight had been lifted from my shoulders. I hadn't understood everything Roaz said, but somehow, she had taken the burden from me, made me see more clearly that I had only been a guest in their world, and that their problems were not mine to solve. As for Aslan, well that was bitter-sweet. Could I have asked for more? We had shared great riches, but like a miser I had wanted to hoard them. It was hard to accept the ephemeral nature of life. When one is told that such-and-such a desert was once a rainforest, or that a high plateau covered in scrub once supported fishes beneath a sea, it is disconcerting. But perhaps it shouldn't be. Perhaps we should be more alive to the moment because, in the end, the moment is all we have. There is a continuity, made up of these moments, but none of us are the great conductors we think we are. The symphony is being written around us, and we each compose merely a note.

After arriving at the car, Surek's mother took our horses and the two said their farewells. How far apart their lives now were.

CHAPTER 23

I had been working in DC for three months when the note from Andrew Meadows arrived. Dirk was putting up with me. I say 'putting up with' because I was poor company. We were approaching an election and Bernie wanted me around. At least that's what he said. He'd even lifted my salary and had me co-hosting DEMOS-TV's news program on the unfolding political battle. I think he knew my time in Chenchia had been bruising. But I'd done well for him and he wasn't ready to let go. Dirk had less reason to indulge my poisonous mood and there were even times when his patience annoyed me.

I tried to push what had happened out of my mind, but such an intense experience in so short a time leaves a deep cut. If I was honest, I think the thing that upset me most was my own reaction. The suggestion that I might take Aslan back to America with me had run right against my instincts. And yet there I was, outraged at what had taken place. These two things now grated inside me, like sandpaper, paring down my sense of moral worth.

The handwritten note simply said—*Orla, we do try to look after our own, contrary to what you might think. Andrew.* I'd opened it in a rush, leaving my apartment, late as usual, for an interview with a Senator about to dish the dirt on one of his colleagues. I didn't know what to make of the letter. A pang of guilt, perhaps? The prelude to him asking for a date? At least someone besides me had been thinking about what had happened. It almost made me want to see this 'diplomat', if only to indulge in some mutual self-flagellation.

That evening, Dirk came round for dinner. I felt the least I could do was cook him something nice, as a meal was about all I had felt inclined to offer since coming back. I wondered if I would ever get Orla's pool out of my mind. On the way in he noticed a calling card on the floor, one of those small cards people carry in their wallets in case they have to show someone who they are: plumber, lawyer, graphic artist. It is all part of that game we call networking. I have a dish next to my door for these things, and he dropped it in.

Dinner was not a great success. We got into an argument about the power of business to influence the legislature, which was silly, because Dirk knows more about this than most people. He said it was a lot harder than one might imagine and that the religious groups had more clout now because they could deliver votes. I'm sure I would have picked a fight about almost anything, just to forestall the dreadful prospect of intimacy. Part of me wanted to let go, but not yet.

Three days later I needed an electrician, and was sifting through the dish with the calling cards. Tradesmen often pushed their particulars into my mailbox and I just add them to the dish. When the dish gets too full, I have a cull, which is quite therapeutic. Out, out, out, interesting: I'll keep you, out, . . . Searching for a card that had the word *electrician* on it I came across one that looked strange to me:

ALLAN STRONG
LECTURER
JOAN B. KROC SCHOOL OF PEACE STUDIES
UNIVERSITY OF SAN DIEGO
5998 ALCALÁ PARK, SAN DIEGO, CA 92110

I doubted anyone would have put it in my mailbox and couldn't remember having been given it. So I set the card to one side and continued to look for an electrician. Not finding what I needed, I had to resort to the phone book.

A WEEK OR so after this, Bernie sent me to Southern California. There was to be a big demonstration by illegal Mexican laborers. It would swing votes and he wanted me to cover it. On the way out of the apartment, I slipped the USD card into my bag. There was something about it that had arrested my attention.

I think it was on the flight west when I started to speculate. Could the card have fallen out of Andrew's letter? Allan Strong? The only Strong I knew was Denis. The thought of Denis and Andrew made me think of Aslan, although I hardly needed an excuse. Allan—Aslan? The complimentary wine was playing tricks with me. But the notion just grew. Could Allan Strong possibly be Aslan Dudayev? If the card had fallen from Andrew's letter, what other explanation could there be?

AFTER REPORTING ON the demonstration for my channel, I drove to the University of San Diego. I had to see for myself who Allan Strong was. I parked the car and was just about to cross the quadrangle when I saw him. A little softer than before, but still fine looking, he was walking briskly, books under one arm, with an attractive young woman by his side. He didn't notice me. I smiled and the heavy baggage I had been carrying suddenly fell away. At last I was free and so, I hoped with all my heart, was he.